INCREDIBLE, LEGENDARY, OBVIOUS

 OREST STELMACH

PENWOOD

For Ukraine

ONE

THE DEMONSTRATION of extraordinary skills beyond the capability of a human being began an hour before dusk near the base of a cliff.

Adam held the wheelchair steady as his Uncle Victor sat facing Nazarov along the crushed stone parking area. Nazarov worked for a Russian oligarch by the name of Sternfeld who'd made his money in pearls and precious stones. The latter had escaped New York and London before sanctions kicked in. Now Dubai was his oyster.

"Your phone, please," Victor said, in Russian.

"You can't be serious," Nazarov said.

"No pictures allowed. I'll return it to you as soon as the courier has completed the demonstration. In the meantime, it'll rest in the holder attached to my chair. No one will touch it. You'll be able to see it at all times."

Nazarov objected but eventually handed Victor his phone. Victor secured it as promised. Then he placed four fingers in his mouth and whistled.

A man in his early thirties came racing from around the

bend of the cliff face. He was the same height as Adam, a touch over six feet tall, but that's where the similarities ended. He had wavy blonde hair and the sculpted physique of a highly trained athlete, as opposed to Adam, who wore his brown hair cropped short and looked as though he often forgot to eat.

The man wore a protective helmet and a harness. A collection of carabiners, quick draws and a chalk bag dangled from his belt. He scanned the rock formation from left to right and then ascended up the initial boulder. He used blocks in the cliff's face to vault himself upward while clipping his rope to existing bolt anchors along the way. When he reached the first of four rooftops, he didn't pause to rest. Instead, he accelerated during each of his three successive climbs. Once at the top, he repelled to the ground in four breathtaking bursts off the cliff wall.

Nazarov watched the climb without saying a word. When it was finished, he walked over to Victor and held out his hand.

"May I have my phone, please? Great athlete? Obviously. Good climber? Sure. Beyond the capability of a human being? You can't be serious. Though in a way, I congratulate you, Victor. Really, I do. You've taken a mere mortal and made people think he's some kind of superhero. No one sprays black mist like you do."

"I disagree," Victor said. "You're not seeing the entire picture. In fact, you're seeing precisely half of it. If you were to take the opposite perspective for a moment, all would be clear to you."

"What opposite perspective? What are you talking about?"

"Turn around," Victor said, "and look behind you."

Footsteps sounded in the brush along the descent on the opposite side of the parking lot.

Nazarov wheeled.

Leaves crunched. Branches cracked. The sounds suggested a man or group of men were approaching quickly.

2

Nazarov stepped back.

"Don't run," Victor said. "Whatever you do, don't run. That would be a mistake."

TWO

AN HOUR EARLIER, local police stopped Adam and Victor at a roadblock in front of the entrance to the popular climbing area to confirm their identities before allowing their car to pass.

Adam wasn't sure what impressed him more – that Nazarov had succeeded in convincing Victor to let him meet the courier in person, or that the Russian had somehow managed to cajole the local police into closing all the access roads to the mountain. No client had ever met the courier. And the mountain in question wasn't east of Moscow. It was north of New York City. They were at the Trapps in the Catskills, but still Nazarov had managed to exert his influence.

All this meant the job had to be money, Adam thought. His investment portfolio had grown steadily over the years. His cut from this job might be the payday that would allow him to buy the sublime thing he wanted above all else.

To hell and back for a luxury apartment in Florence.

After they arrived at the base of the mountain, Adam wheeled Victor in his chair toward the trio of black Range Rovers that awaited them. Eleven SUV doors opened almost simultaneously. Men in dark suits stepped out. Half of them emerged carrying briefcases. One of the men opened the twelfth door, and Nazarov appeared. His suit looked Italian, but the fit wasn't quite right – it was a bit too snug. Nazarov pulled on his cuffs, straightened his pant legs and fidgeted in place.

The men with attaches formed a circle around their boss. They cast their eyes onto the horizon and raised their briefcases to their chests as though prepared to deflect speeding bullets.

"So many Notary Publics for a handshake deal," Victor said.

"A man needs to take precautions these days. Where is your protection?" Nazarov appraised Adam with a mixture of amusement and disbelief.

"No, no," Victor said. "This is my nephew. He is my caretaker. I take twelve different pills a day. He makes sure I take the right ones at the right time. Life is, after all, all about timing."

"And you're not worried?" Nazarov said. "You've been in America for what ... forty years? You must have made enemies."

"Obsessing about assassination is like fathering a child at my age. Both speak of issues with mortality. And for the record, you've been misinformed. I'm not Russian. I'm Ukrainian."

Nazarov frowned. "All these years ... how could I not have known?"

"Because it was never in my interest to publicize it. But don't worry. I'm an American now. Which means I'm a businessman – and most definitely not political."

Nazarov studied Victor for an extra beat, then gazed at the cliff face.

"Speaking of business," he said, "your courier is quite the legend. There are all sorts of stories about him out there. But the one you hear the most is the one from Buryatia in Eastern Siberia. A transport plane went down about ten years ago. A bunch of locals – Evenki reindeer herders– swore they saw a young man run straight up a cliff and carry eight people off the plane before it exploded. No climbing equipment. Just went vertical, like a koala up a tree."

"I've heard this story," Victor said.

"Good," Nazarov said. "Because I want to see the courier do something similar tonight, and then I want to talk to him personally, before I agree to this outrageous fee you're demanding."

"Then you should prepare to be disappointed," Victor said. "You talk to me and no one else. And as for the story, like so many legends, it's the product of idle time and fertile imagination. Yes, the courier was there in Buryatia that day. And he did climb the mountain and rescue some passengers. But what the witnesses failed to tell everyone is why he was there in the first place. He's an avid sportsman. And he was there to climb the mountain with all the necessary gear. That's how he was able to get to the plane. Everything else is fiction."

"I'm confused," Nazarov said. "That means he's an ordinary man. But you promised me a demonstration of extraordinary skills beyond the capabilities of a human being."

"And that I shall deliver," Victor said.

Nazarov shook his head. "I don't see how that's possible."

"The demonstration is for your eyes only, I'm afraid."

Nazarov frowned.

"Your bodyguards must leave," Victor said. "The courier's anonymity is an essential part of his success. A man transporting a priceless object can't be robbed if he can't be identified."

"One of my men has to stay with me," Nazarov said.

"No one will harm you here. Look at the purple hews in the American sky above. Not a single Turkish combat drone among them. And West Point is ninety-three kilometers away. Even their finest sniper would have difficulty at that range."

"I don't appreciate your joking during a time of war," Nazarov said. "You do understand that, don't you? This is a time of war. My man stays or the deal is off."

"So be it," Victor said. "I wish you safe travels."

Victor glanced at Adam, who promptly turned the chair back towards the car.

"Wait," Nazarov said.

He walked over to his crew and spoke briefly to the man who'd opened his door. Afterwards, the latter glanced at his colleagues and made a circular motion over his head. They climbed back into their vehicles and took off, leaving clouds of dust behind them.

Then the man climbed the cliff face, footsteps approached from beyond the parking area, and Nazarov froze in place per Victor's instructions.

THREE

THE FOOTSTEPS STOPPED ABRUPTLY. The mountain turned silent except for the squawk of crows.

Adam watched Nazarov, prepared to shield his uncle if the man made a threatening move.

"Don't run," Victor said, "because if you do you'll never understand what you've just witnessed, and if this package is as important as you say it is, you may regret it for the rest of your life."

Victor put four fingers in his mouth and whistled again.

The climber's twin emerged from where the footsteps had sounded. He was dressed in the exact same clothes and carried the same equipment, right down to the colors of his carabiners and quick draws. The second climber was, for all intents and purposes, his brother's clone.

He jogged over to the cliff and began climbing. His brother – the original climber – joined him. They ascended the face simultaneously in synchronized fashion, one vaulting higher than the other only when a particular hold required an upward surge. Otherwise, they rose in tandem up the rock formation in a mesmerizing display of coordinated athleticism.

Nazarov tried to remain as inscrutable as before but his eyes deceived him. They'd come alive the moment the two climbers had sprung onto the face of the cliff. He turned to Victor after the twins descended and disappeared down the hill beyond the parking area.

"I'll be damned," he said.

"One man with skills – no matter how extraordinary – is still just a man," Victor said. "He cannot possess capabilities beyond those of a human being."

"But the courier is actually *two* men," Nazarov said. "A pair of identical twins saved those passengers in Buryatia. And if you have two men with extraordinary skills, and the rest of the world thinks they belong to one man, then that man might look as though he possesses capabilities beyond those of a single human being."

Victor regarded Nazarov with satisfaction, then looked up at the sky. "It really is going to be a lovely fall night, don't you think?"

Nazarov collected his smartphone and sent a text message. Less than thirty seconds later, the Range Rovers came screaming back.

"I agree to your fee," Nazarov said.

He extended his hand.

Victor shook it.

"There's no time to waste," Nazarov said. "We move tomorrow. I'll call you at daybreak with final arrangements."

After he left with his entourage, Adam helped Victor into the rear passenger seat of the vintage Lincoln Town Car, stored the wheelchair in the trunk, and took his place behind the wheel. He started the long drive back to Manhattan's Lower East Side.

"How do you think the twins did?" Victor said.

He asked the question in English, his preferred language

when he spoke with Adam even though they were both fluent in Ukrainian and Russian. He had no American friends and insisted on practicing with someone on a daily basis.

The twins had been part of Victor's crew their entire adult lives. But they hadn't rescued those passengers in Buryatia, nor were they commanding the fee that Nazarov was going to pay.

"They looked like they scaled that wall a hundred times yesterday," Adam said. "Does it bother you we deceived the client?"

"The client wanted to meet the courier in person and see him in action," Victor said. "And he did. It just so happens that the courier was helping me with my wheelchair. If the client inferred otherwise, that's his doing."

"Did he seem a little off to you?" Adam said.

"As opposed to whom?" Victor said. "All the proper citizens we do business with?"

"He looked uncomfortable in his clothes."

"He works for an oligarch whose world is collapsing because of Western sanctions, which means his world is collapsing, too."

"What's the job?" Adam said.

"An extraction. The oligarch's chalet in the Alps has been seized by the Swiss authorities. There's a package in a hidden safe. It measures six inches by six inches, two inches deep. It's non-toxic, non-biological and airport X-ray won't be a problem. He needs it yesterday. Needless to say, under no circumstances are you to open it."

"Really, Victor? If someone I didn't know said that, I'd talk about how important my reputation is to me. If someone I knew said that, I might be insulted. But given it's you, it makes me think you actually want me to open the package for some reason."

"You're thinking too much," Victor said.

"I've never heard you say that before. How much?"

"Five hundred thousand."

Adam lost his breath. His cut was fifty-percent. That was the good news. The bad news was that the fee was a function of hazard and uncertainty.

"Delivery?" Adam said.

Victor didn't answer immediately.

"Victor?"

"In Warsaw. The twins will meet you there."

Adam usually imagined a map of the world when Victor told him where he was going, and thought about the countries that surrounded his destination. In this case, however, he had no interest in contemplating the relevant geography.

"I don't work east of Poland, Victor," Adam said.

"Yes, yes," Victor said. "You don't work east of Poland. And you don't do dictatorships or countries that don't have a McDonalds. Poland is not east of Poland."

Adam had never taken a job in a country adjacent to one at war. The thought of doing so left him uneasy. The most carefully crafted plans sometimes went awry. A package coveted by more than one party sometimes crossed borders unexpectedly. Based on his arrangement with Victor, Adam could still walk away from the job. But the thought of letting down Victor was unbearable. He wasn't really Adam's uncle – they weren't blood relatives. But Adam owed him his life as he knew it. Plus, there was no denying how much he wanted the money.

"Who's going to manage your prescriptions when I'm gone?" Adam said.

"Nina will come over twice a day," Victor said.

"Your daughter has trouble multi-tasking. I found half of one of your blood pressure pills on the kitchen counter last time she took over for me. That means you didn't get the proper dosage one of those days."

Adam glanced in the rearview mirror. Victor was looking

right at him. Gone was the thoughtful expression he usually wore when he was trying to sell Adam on something. In its place, Adam spied a different look. It spoke of conviction and urgency.

"Fate favors the bold," Victor said. "This is the job we've been waiting for. It's five times the usual fee. I want my grandchild to go to a good American university. I want to leave him a proper inheritance. If I didn't know you can do this, I wouldn't have put you out there. You have a gift. You can make anyone your willing accomplice. To hell and back for an apartment in Florence. If not now, when?"

Adam returned his focus to the road, or at least tried to do so. He thought about Nazarov again and couldn't shake the notion that the man had been hiding something.

"The client," Adam said. "He really doesn't know about me?"

"No one knows about you."

"You know everything there is to know about me, Victor."

Victor paused. When Adam glanced in the rearview mirror, Victor looked more like his usual reflective self.

"Do I?" he said.

They drove in silence the rest of the way home.

FOUR

ANASTASIA IVANOVA WATCHED from the doorway as three of her subordinates walked into the administrative building in downtown Kherson, Ukraine, and wrapped a plastic bag around the Deputy Mayor's head. They moved so quickly the Deputy Mayor didn't realize what was happening until panic set in. Two men held him in place while her protégé, Nikolai Zimin, tightened the bag around his neck. The Deputy Mayor struggled to breathe, alternately stretching and collapsing the bag with his breaths.

Tasia saw the horror in the Deputy Mayor's outstretched eyes, his lips splayed against the bag, the plastic rendering them twice their actual size. She watched and waited until the bag stopped filling and contracting to its extremes.

"Enough," she said, in Russian.

Nikolai removed the bag from the man's head. The Deputy Mayor gasped for air. Only then did Tasia realize he didn't have a wrinkle on his face or a gray hair on his head. He was so young for a politician. Tasia had just turned forty a month ago – the Deputy Mayor looked much younger and he was helping govern a pivotal coastal town with more than a quarter million people.

This was consistent with the statistics. The average age of the public servants who ran Ukraine was forty-four. In Russia, the average was sixty-five.

If the future belonged to the young, how could this possibly turn out well for Russia?

Tasia gave the Deputy Mayor some time to compose himself.

"You're coming with us, Mister Deputy Mayor," she said. "The question is, are you leaving this building with your beautiful head of hair showing, or with a bag over your head? I vote for the first option. Because you're a pretty handsome guy and probably a really nice guy, and I'm sure all the ladies in the office would be very upset if you picked the second option. And we're not here to upset anyone. We're just here to invite you to a meeting."

"If that was the case," the Deputy Mayor said, "you could have just invited me."

"Would you have come?"

The Deputy Mayor thought about what to say next. "I have a wife and two children. I don't want any trouble."

"Wise choice," Tasia said. "Because that's the thing about plastic bags. They're not helpful to the environment or proper breathing." She glanced at Nikolai. "Take his phone. Then find a bottle of water for the Deputy Mayor on the way out. We reward cooperation, don't we?"

"Yes, Lieutenant," he said.

Tasia's Russian-made Lada-Niva Legend SUV was parked in front of the partially bombed-out administrative building. Nikolai drove. The Deputy Mayor sat between Tasia and one of her other boys in the back seat. That made him the lucky one, she thought. He didn't have to suffer a window seat with a perfect view of urban annihilation.

Bent steel, sheets of torn wall-board and shards of glass littered the block across the street. Burnt-out cars and decapitated street lamps formed grim obstacles. At every turn, at least one apartment building, store, or other civilian haven had been purposefully blown to smithereens - anything to induce terror and break the will of the people. Stray dogs appeared in alleys all too frequently, many of them limping around without a paw or a leg, all of them searching for food. After a month in Kherson, Tasia had trained herself to look past the dogs instead of allowing her eyes to linger on them. She did it out of self-preservation. Their images hounded her day and night.

With all this devastation, one would have expected the locals to be hiding in their basements, but such was not the case. The Boss had grossly misunderstood and underestimated the Ukrainian people. There they were protesting at the city square, waving their blue and yellow flags, pumping their fists at a pair of tanks and a row of soldiers who wanted nothing to do with them. The Ukrainians chanted "Go Home," their voices competing with an outdoor stereo system that was blaring their unofficial theme song – *We're Not Gonna Take It* – by the American heavy metal band, Twisted Sister.

It was a good choice, Tasia thought. Everything about this thing the Boss called a *special military operation* was completely twisted.

The drive to Tasia's office took twenty minutes. The Fifth Service of the Russian Federal Security Service – the FSB – had set up a filtration camp on the outskirts of Kherson, near access roads leading to Donbas and Russia.

Once they arrived, Nikolai escorted the Deputy Mayor to an interrogation room with a table and three chairs. Tasia sat beside Nikolai, whom she'd placed in charge of the interrogation. In her experience, trust fostered loyalty.

"We're here from Moscow to help you," Nikolai said. "There's three parts to our mission and we're going to start with the most important one. Where are the Nazis?"

The Deputy Mayor frowned.

"We're here for the Nazis," Nikolai said. "Who are they and where can we find them?"

The Deputy Mayor stared at him with a blank face. "I have no idea what you're talking about."

"We've come to liberate your country and get rid of all the Nazis," Nikolai said. "We're going to find them one way or another. It would be easier for you and your people if you helped us."

"I don't want any trouble," the Deputy Mayor said. "I'm being totally honest with you. I really have no idea what you're talking about."

"What about the Azov battalion?" Nikolai said.

"They're to the northeast in Donbas," the Deputy Mayor said. "They've been fighting there for like a decade. I'm sure there's some right-wing types left in that unit. But since it got folded into the Ukrainian National Guard it's down to about nine hundred soldiers. Let me put it to you this way. I've lived in Kherson for thirty-five years. I've never met a member of the Azov battalion. And not just that. I've never met a single Nazi in my entire life, and I don't know anyone who has."

Nikolai frowned. Every hero needed a villain, Tasia thought, and young Nikolai so desperately wanted to be a Russian hero.

"What about the persecution of the Russian speakers?" Nikolai said.

"There is no persecution," the Deputy Mayor said. "I speak Russian. I don't speak Ukrainian. Ninety-five percent of the city speaks Russian even though we're all Ukrainian. We're not complaining. No one's bothering us. We're fine."

Nikolai cast a bewildered look at Tasia.

"What about our veterans from World War II?" he said. "We heard they were beaten-up badly during the Victory Day Parade last year."

"That's ridiculous," the Deputy Mayor said. "They're revered. There aren't many of them left but they're part of the Parade. There's a special bus for them. I have a video – on my phone – if you'd like to see it."

Nikolai appeared flustered. He hesitated, not knowing what to say or do next.

Tasia understood his reaction. Nikolai wanted to challenge the subject, apply force to make him reveal the truth. But Nikolai's gut was telling him the Deputy Mayor wasn't lying. The man was so obviously speaking the truth.

She sensed Nikolai needed a face-saving exit from a fruitless interrogation.

"If we examine your phone," Tasia said, "are we going to find anti-Russian propaganda on it?"

"Why would you?" the Deputy Mayor said. "You invaded us. We didn't have a problem with you." He swallowed as though he'd spoken rudely. "I mean, I don't have a problem with you."

Tasia and Nikolai stepped out of the room and searched the Deputy Mayor's phone. They read e-mails, studied pictures, and found nothing suspicious.

"Do you believe him?" Tasia said.

"He's a politician. Politicians lie for a living. But, yeah, I believe him. He's scared. He's a family man. Which begs the question ..."

"Yes?" Tasia knew the question but wanted her subordinate to be the one to ask it out loud.

"If he's telling the truth," Nikolai said, "what the hell are we doing here?"

Exactly, Tasia thought.

"What should we do with him?" Nikolai added.

"He's not going anywhere," Tasia said. The words rolled off her tongue so quickly they almost collided. She couldn't wait to set the poor man free. "He's cooperating. We know where to find him. Let's give him his phone back and let him go."

Nikolai thought about her suggestion for a moment and nodded.

A voice sounded from behind. "Wait."

Tasia turned.

A man shut the door to the observation room that overlooked the interrogation via a two-way mirror. He was tall and lean with a carefully groomed moustache on a cheeky Russian face. Sergei Turkin's celestial blue eyes were as legendary as his *nom de guerre* – Sergei Strelkov. The latter was the Russian word for *rifleman* or *shooter*.

"Colonel," Tasia said. "What an unexpected surprise."

"I was pleased to see you've been assigned here, Lieutenant," Strelkov said. He spoke with an unusually gentle voice and annunciated his words with such precision that his every proclamation came across as the word of God. "I've taken over command of the Fifth Service in Ukraine."

"That's wonderful news," Tasia said.

At least half of her compliment was sincere, she thought. He was a fanatic known for excessive cruelty to those he perceived to be Russia's enemies, but he also had a reputation among the women of the FSB as a total gentleman.

Strelkov glanced at Nikolai. Tasia introduced him.

"Excellent job in there," Strelkov said. "You kept your cool even when you didn't hear what you wanted to hear. That showed me something."

Nikolai blushed.

Strelkov patted him on the shoulder and turned to Tasia. "But what do you say we step back in there for a moment? There's one more question I'd like to ask the Deputy Mayor personally. I think you'll both find the exercise very instructive."

Ever the gentleman, he let Tasia go first.

She led the way back to the interrogation room, her heart filled with dread.

FIVE

STRELKOV'S MORNING started out poorly for an all-too familiar reason – because of matters dearest to his heart that were beyond his control. In this case, his mother-in-law had developed a toothache overnight that was absolutely killing her. She lived with Strelkov's wife and three children in a three-bedroom apartment in Moscow. When his wife called the dentist, he refused to see her mother until after 5:00 p.m. His assistant told her that the dentist's schedule was slammed.

If Strelkov had been in Moscow, he would have driven to the man's office and reminded him that the word *slammed* had an alternative meaning, one that conjured images of said dentist trying to remove his head from the other side of his office wall. But he wasn't in Moscow. Hence, he had to leave a pointed message with the assistant and pace around his office for an hour until the dentist finally called him back. When Strelkov finished introducing himself properly, the dentist agreed to see his mother-in-law as soon as she arrived in his office, stuttering and slobbering his way through an apology.

The end result was that now Strelkov had a toothache, too.

It was a sympathy illness. He was prone to them where his family was concerned.

After solving his wife's crisis, he watched the unit he'd inherited interview the Deputy Mayor of Kherson. He wasn't surprised to see Ivanova and Zimin go soft on the man. They'd never worked behind enemy lines before, and probably didn't understand the nature of this war and Russia's true objectives. They needed to be schooled immediately.

He asked them to return to the interrogation room for a few follow-up questions. Once inside, Strelkov approached the Deputy Mayor as though they were fellow delegates at the United Nations. Strelkov smiled, introduced himself, and shook the man's hand. It was limp and sweaty, evidence the so-called Ukrainian had no backbone.

"I just got here yesterday," Strelkov said. "I need to get the lay of the land. Can I call on you if I need some advice? With restaurants, drinking establishments and laundry and things? You locals, you always know the best places, the secret handshakes."

"Sure," the Deputy Mayor said, looking bewildered.

"I appreciate you. Come, come," Strelkov said. "I'll walk you out and one of my colleagues will give you a lift back to your office."

The Deputy Mayor rose and circled around the desk. Strelkov stood between him and the exit. He could smell the fear oozing out of the man's pores. This is what happened, Strelkov thought, when you took a living thing that was genetically predisposed to harvesting crops and placed it in the company of those whom God had created to rule the world – *Russians*.

"You know," Strelkov said, "I was in charge of the day-to-day operations that returned Crimea to the Russian Federation."

The Deputy Mayor simply stood there, pale and petrified. Still, he mustered sufficient courage to look Strelkov in the eyes.

"Oh," he said.

"All those reports in the press about Crimeans demanding to be liberated from their Ukrainian oppressors?" Strelkov said. "The overwhelming support from the *Verkhovna Rada* – the Supreme Council of Crimea? That was all made-up. Complete and total nonsense. When I first asked the Councilmen to sign their decree of support, they told me to go to hell. You know how I got them to change their minds?"

The Deputy Mayor didn't react, but when Strelkov continued smiling and waiting for a reply, he finally shook his head.

"There was a Ukrainian activist," Strelkov said. "A nineteen-year-old student. He covered the Russian flag I'd hung outside our headquarters with a blue and yellow one. So, I had him arrested and brought to the next meeting with the Council. And less than five minutes from the moment that meeting started, all the Councilmen signed the decree asking for Russian support. You want to know why?"

The Deputy Mayor appeared too frightened to answer.

Strelkov smiled. "No, seriously. It's a fascinating historical tidbit I've only shared with a chosen few. Do you want to know why?"

The Deputy Mayor almost choked on his own saliva. "Sure," he said.

"Thank you." Strelkov smiled with appreciation. "They signed the decree because this is what I did to that activist."

Metal snapped against metal. A knife gleamed in Strelkov's right hand.

He thrust it into the middle of the Deputy Mayor's abdomen. He sliced left, twisted the blade one-hundred and eighty degrees, and cut hard to the right. When the blade reached the oblique muscle, Strelkov yanked it out and simultaneously released his grip on the handle. As the knife went flying behind him, Strelkov thrust his hand into the Deputy Mayor's abdomen and pulled out his intestines before the blade hit the floor.

The Deputy Mayor screamed.

His intestines unwound to his feet like a misplaced tail of flesh and blood.

Strelkov pulled a sidearm from beneath his jacket and flipped his grip so that the butt end faced the Deputy Mayor.

"You may not have a problem with us, Mister Deputy Mayor," Strelkov said, "but you are correct. We definitely have a problem with you. And the problem is simple. You exist."

Strelkov's voice never wavered, nor did it sound less polished or composed than it had earlier. He crushed the Deputy Mayor's skull with his gun, spilling the man's brains all over the vinyl floor. At one point while he was pulling his hand back to strike again, Strelkov glanced over his shoulder. Ivanova looked horrified. Zimin – not so much. His lips remained parted but a glint shown in his eyes.

When Strelkov was satisfied that he'd sufficiently shocked them, he stopped and retrieved his knife. Blood, bone and brain matter covered his clothes, hands, and face. He was breathing heavily.

"There are three hundred and sixty mayors in this alleged country," Strelkov said. "Assuming each town has at least one deputy mayor, that's at least seven-hundred twenty town leaders. Make his body disappear. If enough of them vanish, the others will get the message. Russia is here and we're not leaving."

Strelkov headed toward the slop sink near the men's toilet to wash his weapons.

Good news, he thought.

His toothache was gone.

SIX

ADAM PULLED over to the side of the road on his rented mountain bike one mile south of the center of the Swiss village of Zermatt. He drank from his water bottle, removed his binoculars from his backpack, and scanned the horizon. Chalets sat nestled along the lower levels of the Alps surrounding the village. The expansive windows beneath their overhangs glistened in the sun. The near-perfect pyramid of Matterhorn towered to the south at the Italian border.

Sternfeld's house appeared above a cluster of pines on a ridge forty feet higher than the other private residences. The forty feet consisted of a vertical cliff that Adam would climb free solo style this evening – without ropes or harnesses – preferably in five seconds or less. Speed was of the essence because he'd be climbing within full view of the people in the village below. He needed to vanish onto Sternfeld's property before a witness could look twice and confirm what he'd thought he'd seen.

The only other entrance to the chalet was the one Adam preferred whenever possible – the front door. According to Nazarov, that was a non-starter. The State Secretariat for

Economic Affairs of Switzerland had seized the property. Meanwhile, activists in France were breaking into such homes, changing the locks, and inviting Ukrainian refuges to live there rent free. The Swiss didn't enjoy attention, especially the embarrassing kind. As a result, they were taking extra precautions.

Nazarov had sounded well-informed, but Adam preferred to rely on his own due diligence. He double-backed to the access road to Sternfeld's house. Two concrete barriers blocked the entrance. A county ordinance warned vehicles and pedestrians that the road was closed, and that violators would be subject to fines and arrest. Adam stopped, removed his camera from his backpack and hung it around his neck. Then he circled around the barriers, switched into a lower gear, and powered up the mountain to the chalet's entrance.

A ten-foot-high wrought-iron fence surrounded the property. Signs on the matching gate warned that this was private property and that visitors should keep out. Two security cameras caught Adam's eye. One was painted black to match the gate and inconspicuously attached to a light pole. The other was government-issued gray and chained to the fence. The red dot in the latter suggested it wasn't motion-activated but rather filming at all times.

The chalet faced the road from beyond the driveway, a larch wood structure made from local conifers to withstand the intense heat from the Alpine sun. Its oversized roof sloped gently downward. A white BMW crossover vehicle with reflective orange stripes sat parked near the house. It featured blue emergency lights atop its roof, and the words *Military Polizei* painted on its doors. That was consistent with Nazarov's intelligence. Military police officers on loan from the Federal Department of Civil Protection were guarding the property – the local county police didn't have the manpower to help.

Adam knew he had seconds until he was accosted. He looked through the viewfinder of his zoom lens and scanned the windows in the front of the house. Shades were drawn on all three levels. The house appeared closed for the season. That made perfect sense. The Secretariat had seized the property but Sternfeld still owned it. Legally, the police couldn't go inside the house. No one could.

"You," someone said in Standard Swiss German. "Stay right there."

A military policeman in a camouflage-patterned uniform bounded toward Adam from beyond his vehicle. He wore a sidearm on his right hip. His boots seemed heavy. As he approached, he reached for the radio transmitter attached to his left shoulder and spoke into it.

One car, two policemen, Adam thought.

Adam smiled and waved. "Is this the oligarch's house?"

Up close, the policeman looked pre-maturely old and angry. The skin on his face was smooth but its creases spoke of stress. His name appeared on a cloth tag sewn into the flap over his shirt pocket – Terzic. Adam recalled a job that involved a Middle Eastern hotel magnate who shared the same name. It was Arabic in origin.

"The street is closed," Terzic said. "It's not possible you didn't see the sign. That means you thought you'd come here, do what you want to do, and lie your way out of this."

"I just wanted to see the oligarch's house," Adam said. "I'm sorry. I'll leave right now."

"No, you will not," Terzic said. He muttered something under his breath in one of the three dialects of Swiss Alemannic German. The Swiss spoke it primarily in casual situations.

Adam didn't understand a word of it.

"Show me your passport," Terzic said, switching to Standard Swiss. "Now."

Adam's toolbox included seven passports under false names that Victor had procured for him. Unless a job dictated otherwise, he always used the German one. It was ranked second in the world – exceeded only by Japan and Singapore – with a global passport power rank of one hundred ninety, the latter representing the number of places one could travel without a special visa. The power rank also implied a certain global prestige and trustworthiness. At least that's what Adam had always assumed.

"Werner Ziegler," Terzic said, reading Adam's passport. "From Munich. What is your profession, Mister Ziegler?"

"I'm a caretaker," Adam said. "For the elderly."

"And what were you planning to do with the picture you just took? Sell it to the highest bidder? Post it on your blog on the internet?"

"I didn't take a picture," Adam said.

"The Swiss Military Police does not want its business made public. You will surrender the memory card in your camera to me right now, or you will be arrested and placed in jail immediately."

"But I didn't take a picture," Adam said. "I can scroll through the memory card and show you."

"Which will it be, Mister Ziegler?" Terzic said. "Your memory card or your freedom? Everyone is accountable for their actions. Even Germans. Can't pivot from Russian gas for fear the stove goes off while you're cooking your precious Weiner schnitzel. Won't deliver weapons to prevent a genocide for fear it might piss off your new Fuhrer. When it comes to the safety of Europe, you're as pathetic as we are. Give me the memory card. Now."

Adam removed his memory card from his camera and handed it to the policeman. It contained a few irrelevant shots of Zermatt – nothing else.

"If you come back here ..." Terzic said, "if I see you here again ... you'll go straight to jail. I'll personally see to it that your trip is unpleasant. And you won't be able to do anything about it. That I promise."

"Don't worry," Adam said, smiling. "You won't see me again. That I promise. *Assalamu alaikum.*"

Terzic glanced at him with surprise. He answered the Muslim greeting with a reluctant measure of appreciation mixed with disdain.

"*Alaikum salaam,*" he said.

Adam rode his bike back to the Grand Hotel Zermatterhoff knowing he'd be inside the chalet in less than eight hours, and Terzic wouldn't be able to do anything about it.

He'd have to reconsider his choice of passports going forward, though. Apparently being German wasn't as helpful today as it had been a month ago.

SEVEN

ADAM ALWAYS STAYED at the finest hotels wherever he traveled on the job. He preferred to hide in plain sight by blending in with an affluent crowd rather than skulk around the fringes of foreign cities. Also, the more discriminating the establishment, the more it invested in guest security, and the finer its breakfast buffet. The latter was Adam's standard reward for a job well done the previous evening.

Once he was back in his room in the Zermatterhof, Adam performed a half-hour exercise routine that consisted of push-ups, abdominal exercises and stretching. He took a hot shower and collapsed onto his king-sized bed for a nap. His exhaustion from the time change and travel was exceeded only by the joy of wrapping crisp Frette sheets around his body. A lingering sense of nervous anticipation prevented him from falling asleep immediately, but the delay lasted no more than a few minutes.

He ate his first meal in twenty-four hours in his room after he woke up. The risotto was made with saffron from the Swiss county of Ticino near the Italian border. A special local sausage that contained pork, spices and red wine accompanied his entree. He drank bottled water with his meal and coffee for dessert. Afterwards, he studied the architectural drawings of the chalet that Nazarov had provided Victor. Adam had memorized them within the last twelve hours, during the eight-hour plane ride from JFK to Zurich, and the two and a half-hour train ride to Zermatt. But until he finished a job, he always worried that he might forget a critical detail, so he continued studying them out of sheer paranoia.

At sunset, Adam packed the necessary gear into his low-profile nylon backpack. He put on a compressed athletic jersey, a light windbreaker, jeans and a pair of trail-running shoes. He left the hotel with his camera dangling from around his neck for all the doormen to see. One of them offered some tips on spots from which he might capture the village of Zermatt in all its night-time glory.

All places of interest in Zermatt existed within a thirty-minute walk of each other. Tourists and locals mixed in the streets but the roads were far from packed during the off-season. Adam drove his bike to the place where he'd stopped that morning. He waited for a few pedestrians to scatter, then slipped into the forest to his right. Once he was out of sight, he removed a cable from his knapsack and locked his bike to a tree. Then he stripped to his underpants, changed into a hooded spandex bodysuit and swapped the trail runners for a pair of climbing shoes. He also put on his rock climbing gloves, though he didn't expect to need them until he arrived at the chalet. He packed his clothes in an extra nylon bag and secured it to his bicycle. After returning the knapsack to his back, Adam took off.

He darted through the conifers at a quick but comfortable pace, bouncing off his toes the entire way to minimize the noise from his feet. The canopies of branches obscured his destination until sudden gaps revealed the mountain and allowed him to adjust his course. When the cliff appeared to be two hundred feet away, he stopped, pulled out his binoculars and studied its face.

Adam proceeded to visualize his path up the cliff and commit each step to memory. He couldn't help but think of Eva as he did so. The cliff looked so much like the one they'd negotiated in Siberia their last day together before she fell into Lake Baikal and vanished forever. Ten years had passed since then but not a day went by that he didn't think of her at least once.

When he was finished with his preparations, Adam measured three strides from the base of the cliff and leaped forward. His right foot landed square on the first foothold. By the time his left foot connected with the second one, his eyes had found the third, fourth and fifth. He sprinted to the roof of the cliff as though it were a flat trail in less than five seconds. He glanced over his shoulder – the village shone amidst the lights more than a quarter mile below him. Pedestrians were moving about the streets freely. No one seemed to be looking up at him.

After crawling further to the edge of the property, Adam jumped onto the wall that protected the first floor from the mountain below. He pulled himself up and over the barricade. When his feet hit the larch wood decking, he rolled forward to the gutter at the corner of the house. Using the gutter hangers as footholds, he raced up the wall to the roof of the chalet. Once he was atop the house, he looked out onto the driveway from behind the chimney. The police vehicle sat idling, puffs of exhaust blowing from its twin tailpipes. The driver was eating a sandwich and talking to his colleague beside him.

Adam removed the four screws that secured the chimney's cap in place. He'd brought a screwdriver but it was unnecessary – the screws were the pointed variety that dug into the masonry beneath them. He placed the cap on the roof, and removed a headlamp and a grabber tool with an extendable handle from his backpack. He attached the former to his forehead and slipped the latter into an open pocket along his right thigh. Then he tossed his backpack into the flue, climbed in feet first and slid down the chimney.

Once his head dipped below the top, Adam flipped on his headlamp. He exerted pressure against the flue with his arms and legs to control his descent. Soot drifted up his nose and onto his throat. He tried to suppress a cough but ended up swallowing carbon flakes instead. When the damper appeared below, he used the grabber to lift it open and slid down the rest of the way. His legs negotiated the damper easily, but squeezing his hips through the opening required some patience.

Once Adam was finally in the house, his headlamp illuminated the room. Wood paneling covered the walls. Plush upholstered chairs faced the stone fireplace. A set of antlers hung above the latter. Adam searched for the television. He found it mounted on a wall with a sound bar to the left of the fireplace. Standing beneath it, he looked out onto the room and located the four speakers that comprised the surround sound system. He placed a side chair under the far-right speaker and climbed atop it. Then he grasped the speaker with both hands and pushed firmly.

The wood panel to which the speaker was attached receded an inch into the wall and then popped out like a trap door. Adam swiveled it open to reveal the safe behind it. He input the six-digit code Nazarov had given Victor and opened the safe.

A stack of four gold bars gleamed on the left. A pile of documents in protective plastic envelopes, a safe deposit box, and an unremarkable black package lay beside them. Adam removed the package from the safe. It was sealed in a material made of waterproof black resin that resembled the smooth side of a roof tile and lent it a nuclear-resistant appearance. It weighed about three pounds and its dimensions matched those Victor had provided.

The package was in his possession.

Adam savored the moment. From his perspective, more than half the job was done. Getting out was almost always easier than getting in because of the experience gained with entry. In this case, slipping his hips through the damper opening would be relatively easy because he'd be able to push off with his thighs and explode upward.

Adam closed the safe, returned the speaker to its normal position, and climbed off the chair. He stored the package in his knapsack and slung it over his shoulder before returning the side chair to its proper location. No one was allowed in the house and its owner was his client, hence Adam didn't need to be concerned with putting things back in their proper places. And yet the thought of leaving the home in a state different from the one in which he'd found it was entirely unacceptable to him.

He spent an extra moment aligning the chair with the area rug beneath it. Smiling to himself, he turned toward the chimney to leave.

"*Assalamu alaikum,*" Terzic said.

Adam stood dumbfounded. Terzic must have been in the room the entire time or Adam would have heard him enter. And at least three policemen were guarding the chalet, not two as he'd assumed, based on the presence of only one car in the driveway.

"*Alaikum salaam.*" Adam answered, without even thinking.

Terzic's gun remained pointed at Adam as he reached for his radio transmitter.

Getting out really was usually easier than getting in, Adam thought.

But sometimes it wasn't.

EIGHT

"I WOULDN'T DO that if I were you, sir," Adam said.

Terzic hesitated, hand on his radio transmitter.

"I won't be the only one who gets in trouble," Adam said. "You're trespassing, too."

"What's that?" Terzic grinned, but guilt flickered in his eyes. "You're a thief, Mister Ziegler. I'm a soldier and a police-man." He lifted the radio transmitter to his mouth.

"The Swiss government may have seized this property but it still belongs to the owner. You're not permitted to enter the house. What are your superiors going to say when they find out you broke in here to steal from the same oligarch you're sanc-tioning because you think he's a criminal?"

Terzic continued pointing the gun at Adam. "I heard a noise. I entered the house to stop a thief. Who's going to say different? The thief who was caught in the act?"

Adam nodded at his weapon. "Could you lower that thing, please? I'm scared of guns. Like, really scared of them. They make me really nervous."

Terzic did not oblige.

"I'm sure we can help each other," Adam said.

"You know the combination to the safe." Terzic lowered the gun. "The gold bars. Why didn't you take them?"

"Not my thing—"

"The tensile strength of your knapsack not good enough?" Terzic said. He stepped back and pulled a pair of rugged-looking duffel bags from behind a lounge chair. "These will do the trick. Look, I'm a reasonable man. If you open the safe again, we can split the loot."

Adam remained silent.

"What was that thing you took?" Terzic said. "Was it jewelry? It looked like a box for a necklace. Let's see inside. Because if that's worth more than all the gold ..."

Adam considered his options. He couldn't allow the package to be opened. That would violate his contract with his client. And he couldn't help Terzic steal Sternfeld's gold. If Terzic had done so on his own, Adam wouldn't be complicit. But if Adam opened the safe for him, he'd be aiding and abetting the robbery of his client. That would be a violation of his ethical responsibility for his client's property.

That left him with only one course of action, the one he so desperately had hoped to avoid pursuing.

"I don't know what's inside the box," Adam said. "I didn't open it. It looked important and it wasn't too heavy so I just took it." He stepped forward and unzipped his backpack. "Here. Grab it and let's have a look."

Terzic holstered his gun and reached into Adam's backpack.

Adam let the bag slip from his grip and fall to the floor. He grabbed Terzic's arm with both hands and gripped it firmly.

A bolt of energy passed from his heart through his arms.

Shock registered in Terzic's expression. One beat, two beats, three beats passed. His eyes began dancing in their sockets. Adam understood. The military policeman had tried to pull away but Adam's energy had temporarily paralyzed him.

His brain was functioning but his motor skills were incapacitated.

Adam closed his eyes and steeled himself for what he knew would come next.

A seizure gripped him. His body convulsed. His entire nervous system seemed to be pleading with him, begging him to release Terzic's arm, reminding him that tapping into the man's past was not without consequences. He would pay for his actions, later tonight, and in the coming years, in ways he himself didn't comprehend – that he knew.

And then the pain subsided almost as quickly as it had come. A strange serenity enveloped Adam. He was both vaguely aware of his current circumstances and partially detached from them at the same time

Adam took a deep breath. The images followed so quickly he couldn't make sense of them. Adam let them pass. Experience had taught him that the insignificant memories would soon fade. The most enduring ones would return and persist. The deselection process ... it would take only seconds ... and if Adam remained patient, only the most indelible memories would remain

A little girl on dated skis fires a snowball that hits a boy on similar skis in the face ...

The boy chases the girl downhill on skis ...

Three soldiers with Bosnian Serb Panther patches rape a woman in a prison yard, while a fourth soldier with a NATO Peacekeeping patch smokes a cigarette and watches ...

The boy shoves the girl with both hands ...

The girl smashes head-first into a tree on the mountain ...

Rescue personnel remove her skis and secure her to a stretcher ...

A solemn-looking doctor emerges from a hospital room and shakes her head ...

A weeping couple and their son take turns pouring handfuls of sand onto a casket ...

The mother is an older version of the woman who was raped ...

Her son is the one who pushed the girl into the tree ...

Adam opened his eyes and released his grip.

Terzic, dazed and confused, pulled his arms to his chest and rubbed them.

"You didn't mean to do it," Adam said.

"What?"

"Your sister. Everyone thought she just veered off course and collided with the tree by accident. But that's not what happened. You pushed her."

Terzic's eyes widened. His jaw slacked.

"But no one saw you," Adam said. "So, you didn't tell anyone."

"How ... how can you ... how can you possibly know that?"

"You didn't want to get in trouble. Who can blame you? You were a child. Given what your parents probably went through, I bet they were pretty strict. I bet you were scared to tell the truth, that it was you who pushed your sister to her death."

Terzic's eyes welled.

"But what you didn't understand," Adam said, "was how much it would cost you in the long run to keep the truth to yourself. All these years ... the guilt ... it's eaten you up inside. How can a man forgive himself without confessing what he's done?"

Tears streamed down Terzic's face. "I can't forgive myself. Not now. Not ever."

"That's not true," Adam said. "It was an accident. You didn't mean to do it."

Terzic fell to his knees, covered his face, and bawled.

"What was her name?" Adam said softly.

"Aleza," Terzic said. He struggled to get his words out. "I miss her so much."

"I know you do."

"If I could trade my life for hers ..."

"I hear you," Adam said. He chose his words at a measured pace to give Terzic time to absorb them. "It's good you said that out loud, got it out of your system. The past is what it is. You can't change yours. I can't change mine. All we can do is move on. And as of today, you can move forward. Because the truth is out there. Someone else knows it. I know it. That means the truth doesn't own you anymore."

Terzic remained seated for a few moments as though consumed with his thoughts. Then he wiped his eyes with his bare hands and stood up.

Adam retrieved his knapsack. He looked Terzic in the eyes and channeled all his empathy.

"Be well, my friend," Adam said, and took a half-step toward the chimney.

Terzic's eyes narrowed, as though he'd just remembered how they'd arrived in the room in the first place.

"No, wait. You can't go," Terzic said. "I mean, that's a crazy way to go. I can let you out the service entrance. I jimmied the door. The boys in the car – they won't see you."

"That's okay," Adam said. "I left the chimney cap on the roof. I have to screw it back on."

"Don't worry about it," Terzic said. "I'll bring a ladder and do it for you."

"I appreciate it," Adam said. "But I have to go out the way I came in. It's a thing with me."

Adam strode toward the chimney.

"Mister Ziegler?" Terzic said.

Adam turned.

In the circular glow of Adam's headlamp, Terzic looked like a ghost who'd been resurrected.

"Who are you?" Terzic said.

Adam considered the question. "I'm just a courier. *Assalamu alaikum.*"

The doubt in his eyes suggested Terzic remained far from convinced. "*Alaikum salaam.*"

NINE

TASIA STEPPED through the side door of the FSB's headquarters in Kherson and absorbed a blast of sun and a shot of reality. Hundreds of Ukrainian citizens stood in line waiting to be summoned into one of three military tents. In the tents, Russian officers confiscated passports, took fingerprints, and downloaded contacts and photos from each person's phone onto their computers. Depending on their findings, the officers either sent the Ukrainians back home or into a fully enclosed tent for further evaluation. Russian soldiers stood guard over the proceedings.

It looked like a reenactment of Nazi Germany, Tasia thought, except it wasn't. The year was 2022. The place was Europe. It was happening again, and her country – the one claiming to be hunting Nazis – was the one filtering, murdering and shipping Ukrainians to Siberia. The entire world knew what was happening but wasn't really doing anything about it. If you added up all the countries that had imposed economic sanctions on Russia, they accounted for only 14% of the world's population.

The only countries who cared at least somewhat about

human beings who lived beyond their borders were those who believed all men were created equal. The citizens of those countries also revered the truth, and considered it the foundation of their value system. Russians referred to such people as the West and despised them for those reasons. Most Russians believed in their own exceptionalism. Deep down, Tasia thought, they truly believed they were the supreme Aryan race. And if their government routinely lied to them in pursuit of Russia's goals, they didn't give a damn – they didn't give a damn about the truth.

Tasia's problem was that not only was she supposed to be part of the Russian solution to the Ukrainian problem, she was expected to be enthusiastic about her participation. Her reality was as surreal as it was depressing.

She opened the door to the enclosed tent and stepped inside to observe an interrogation. Three Army officers sat on folding chairs behind a long table. The pair of stripes on the lead officer's uniform informed her they shared the same rank – lieutenant. He looked smug and doughy, unlike the officers who'd served in Chechnya or Syria.

Two doors marked #1 and #2 flanked the table. Door #1 led to a bus that would take the citizen to a concentration camp in Russia where he or she would be killed or re-settled in poverty. Door #2 led back to Russian-occupied Kherson, where a citizen needed a pass to walk the streets or he or she would be arrested and face possible execution.

The first subject was a middle-aged waif, barely five feet tall. Tasia recognized her. The FSB considered her one of the most dangerous people in Ukraine, though admittedly, there were several thousand of those.

There was no suspense here. The waif would be heading

out Door #1 and she would not be re-settled in Siberia. The waif was on the kill list.

She stood tall and proud in front of the tribunal, a slight bend in her right knee that added a touch of disdain to her carriage. The Lieutenant studied his laptop computer, which contained all the information that had been gathered at the previous tent. He confirmed her name and soon-to-be former address.

"What is your occupation?" the Lieutenant said.

The waif sighed. "You know everything there is to know about me. Get on with it, already."

The Lieutenant chuckled. "You're a curator at the Regional Art Museum, yes?"

The waif didn't answer.

"And you think that's a thing, do you?" the Lieutenant said. "Ukrainian art?"

"It's most definitely a thing," she said. "Like the lies that Russia tells the world about what you're doing to us."

"I beg your pardon?"

"You lie. We know that you lie. You know that we know that you lie. We know that you know that we know that you lie." The waif smiled. "And still you lie."

"Alexander Solzhenitsyn," the Lieutenant said. "Great Russian writer – of fiction. You were an activist during the 2014 overthrow of the legitimate Ukrainian government of President Victor Yanukovych. Do you dispute this fact?"

"No, I'm proud of it. Yanukovych had terrible taste. A gold toilet paper dispenser? And he was your President's puppet."

"I see. And what do you think of our President?"

"He's not as bad as Stalin was," the waif said. "But he's coming on strong. Give him a little more time."

The Lieutenant made a quick note on his computer.

"Final question," he said. "Do you sleep with women?"

"Only when I don't want to sleep alone."

The Lieutenant smiled. "And do you believe being a lesbian is a choice?"

The waif remained silent.

"Do you believe it's possible for the lesbian to be rehabilitated? By a man, or say, a highly motivated group of men?"

All the bravado drained from her face. Uncertainty and fear filled its void.

The Lieutenant looked beyond the waif and raised his voice. "Door number one."

A pair of Russian soldiers snatched the waif by her elbows and dragged her out of the tent. The spring-controlled door slammed shut behind her.

Tasia hadn't known about the woman's sexual orientation. The officer who'd searched her mobile phone in the previous tent must have found some revealing personal photos. That rendered her a triple threat – cultural, political and social. The Russian soldiers ultimately assigned to her elimination would be charged with first discovering if she had any LGBTQ contacts beyond those stored on her mobile phone. Given she was a lesbian, they might subject her to unspeakable horrors.

A wave of nausea washed over Tasia. She needed to get the hell out of there before she literally got sick. She couldn't afford to appear weak. But as she turned to leave, the next citizens entered the tent. They were a couple, most likely husband and wife if they were coming in together. But what stopped Tasia in her tracks was the third party coming in with them – a child.

He was a boy, no older than five or six.

The purpose of filtration was to identify people who could become obstacles to the Russification of Ukraine. Children didn't pose cultural, political or social threats. So, what was a child doing in the elimination tent?

Tasia changed her mind.
She decided to stay a bit longer.

TEN

TASIA WATCHED as the Lieutenant studied some entries on his computer, called the family before him and ordered the father to take his shirt off. He was a scruffy rogue, neither fat nor thin, just an average man trying to survive. As the Lieutenant stood up and peered at the man's left pectoral muscle, Tasia edged forward along the side of the tent for a closer look.

The father's chest contained a tattoo of a trident atop a shield. Known as the *tryzub*, the coat of arms of Ukraine was derived from the seal of Volodymyr, the first Grand Prince of Kyiv circa the tenth century. Ukrainian men wearing tattoos bearing patriotic symbols were automatically filtered for elimination.

"My husband had that done when he was a kid," the mother said, arm around her son. "A bunch of his friends did it, too. It's nothing. It's not a swastika or anything like that."

"I understand we have a second tattoo just like this one," the Lieutenant said. "Let's see it."

"Please," the mother said, pressing her son to her thighs. "He drew it himself in magic marker. He was trying to look like his father."

"Of course he was," the Lieutenant said.

"He's just a boy," the father said. "He didn't know what he was doing."

"Take off his shirt," the Lieutenant said.

The mother removed her arm from around her son and began to cry. Her son, who bore a close resemblance to his father, pulled his shirt over his head without further prodding. Then he moved next to his father and threw his shoulders back.

The Lieutenant glanced at the boy's matching ink. "Very nice," he said, and promptly barked his orders. "Mother, door number two. Father and son, door number one."

The mother screamed *no*. The father pulled his son close.

Two pairs of Russian soldiers stepped forward to escort them out their respective doors.

Tasia stormed between the soldiers and the family. "May I have a word with you, Lieutenant?" she said.

"Who the hell are you?" he said.

Tasia stepped closer to the table and flashed her credentials. The Lieutenant stood up, examined them, and went nose-to-nose with her.

"A child?" Tasia said.

"This is an Army operation," he said. "I don't take orders from the FSB, and I don't take orders from women."

A man cleared his throat behind them.

Tasia turned. Strelkov stood at the entrance to the tent. He removed his handkerchief from his pant pocket, ambled over to the front table, and squirted some hand sanitizer onto it. Then he rubbed the boy's chest until the tattoo was gone. When he was finished, he tousled the boy's hair and urged him to return to his mother with an open palm. Once the boy was back in her arms, Strelkov glanced at the Lieutenant and waited.

The latter managed to hold Strelkov's gaze for about three

seconds before deciding to alter his notes on his computer and reissue his orders to the guards.

"Mother and son, door number two. Father, door number one."

The family of three cried and hugged until the soldiers separated them and pushed them out their respective doors.

Tasia followed the mother and the son, eager to watch them head back to their home together, desperate for some semblance of humanity. To her surprise, Strelkov joined her.

"Thank you for doing that, Colonel," Tasia said.

"It's not the boy's fault his father's a Nazi," he said.

They walked around the corner of their building only to see the soldiers rip the boy from his mother's clutches and hand him to a third soldier standing in the doorway to an open bus. After the door closed behind them, the bus took off, leaving the mother wailing beside the remaining soldiers. As it drove by, Tasia could see through the windows – it was filled with children.

"They'll all experience a touch of pain, I'm afraid," Strelkov said. "Their fingerprints will be burned off. To permanently sever any connection to their prior lives. But it will end well for all of them. They'll all be adopted by fine Russian families."

"Outstanding," Tasia said, hiding her dismay. "Obviously they'll have much more opportunity. And they'll be so much more cultured. They'll lead better lives."

Strelkov gave Tasia a sympathetic look. "It's all right, Lieutenant Ivanova. You can be yourself with me."

"I ... I don't know what you mean, sir."

"It's only natural for you to be appalled by what you just saw. A child being taken from his parents? It's awful. Especially from a woman's perspective. You were put on this Earth to create life, to nurture it. The conflict within you is only natural.

From a political perspective, our means are essential. But from a human perspective ..."

Strelkov's honesty was so unexpected Tasia didn't know what to say. She feared he was laying a trap for her to reveal sympathy for the enemy. At the same time, she worried that she might be missing out on an opportunity to bond with a most informed and influential superior.

"Thank you for that, Colonel," she said. "That's very generous of you. In the spirit of what you say, may I be honest with you?"

"Please," Strelkov said.

"I think I need to take a walk ... to clear my mind ... so I can be more productive the rest of the day."

"That's a great idea. I'd offer to keep you company, but I'm sure you'd rather be alone with your thoughts. Perhaps another time."

He wished her a pleasant stroll and returned to their offices.

Tasia popped some grape bubble gum into her mouth and walked ten minutes to a nearby park. It was empty except for a few senior citizens sitting solemnly on benches. She walked along a narrow path that snaked its way through grass and trees until she reached a silver garbage can overflowing with refuse. Images of the boy being torn from his mother's arms played over and over in her mind. Tasia cursed under her breath, removed the gum from her mouth and slammed it against the can, leaving it stuck to the metal.

Later that evening, Tasia went for a run after dark. Returning to the park, she headed for the public rest rooms. They'd been locked since the war had started, as no one was available to clean them. Tasia jogged around the perimeter of the building twice to make sure she was alone, then slipped inside the picket fence that shielded the back of the restrooms from the public's view. She stopped behind one of the four rooms. A three-foot high tree stump sat pressed against the wall, a pile of broken branches scattered atop it.

Tasia moved the debris and slid the tree stump to the side. She lifted the plywood behind the stump to reveal a hole in the wall. Tasia crawled through the opening and used the handle attached to the back of the plywood to seal the hole. Once in the bathroom, she used the light on her mobile phone to find the toilet. The plywood she'd placed atop the seat was still there. She sat down and waited.

A few minutes later she heard a noise from the other side of the wall and the adjacent room. A rustling sound followed and a piece of wallboard between the two stalls vanished. The resulting gap was similar in size to the one that typically separated sinner from priest in a confessional.

A shadow flitted in and out of sight through the hole.

"The tunnels under Kyiv were built by the Vikings," a man said.

"Their names were Robin, Barry, and Maurice," Tasia answered.

"How are you?" her handler said. "Did something happen or do you have new information? Are you okay?"

"I'm okay, I'm okay," Tasia said. "Actually, no. I'm not okay. Strelkov is here, we're stealing your children, and there was something else I needed to tell you. But now I can't remember."

"Take your time. It will come to you."

"Oh, yeah. I remember now." Tasia took a deep breath and exhaled. "This war is shit."

ELEVEN

AFTER HE RETURNED to the hotel with the package, Adam soaked in the tub. He brought two bottles of beer from the minibar to help work off his stress.

Once he acquired someone's memories, the indelible ones became his to bear. On the night of acquisition, the horrible ones simply refused to go away. In Terzic's case, it was the sight of his mother being violated by three soldiers while a NATO peacekeeper watched.

Those images unleashed a torrent of emotions. They began with sheer hate. He wanted to find those soldiers, kill them over a span of several days, and then do something worse to that human scum-of-a peacekeeper. But his fury was a reflex emotion, and it faded after the first mouthful of beer. In its place came waves of anguish and sorrow. He didn't just think of Terzic and his mother – if he concentrated hard enough, he could actually experience their pain.

How could a human being make another suffer so much? What possessed men to violate a woman like that, and in front of her son, no less?

The simplest answer was defined by one of Victor's favorite

sayings – some people needed to die. Adam didn't disagree with that philosophy, until it inevitably morphed into a whole lotta people needed to be killed. That troubled him because it implied that more than a select group of sociopaths and psychopaths could not change. Why not?

Why couldn't more people treat others the way they wanted to be treated themselves?

Why couldn't everyone just be a better man?

That evening, Adam sent the twins a text message that he was on schedule to meet them in Warsaw tomorrow. He copied Victor on the message, per their standard procedure. Theoretically, Adam could have transferred the package to the twins in Zermatt, but Victor preferred that it stay in Adam's possession until the last possible moment. He was, after all, the most reliable and resourceful courier in the world.

The next morning Adam awoke depressed, but a shower, shave and most importantly, the prospect of the breakfast buffet buoyed his spirits. He put on a sweater and jeans, and packed his suitcase before departing to eat. He carried the package with his laptop in a briefcase with the strap secured around his neck and shoulder.

He arrived at the breakfast room at 6:45 a.m., an hour and a half before his train would depart for Zurich. As the hostess escorted him to his table, he studied the other patrons. It was still early by vacation standards, so there weren't too many of them. A platinum-haired woman in a sleek corporate suit sat with her back to the aisle, papers surrounding an open spreadsheet on her computer. An agitated middle-aged couple appeared to be giving instructions to a server in English on how to make iced tea, while two men in t-shirts and slim-fit leather jackets sat quietly sharing a plate of fruit. Adam immediately zeroed in on the hands that held their forks – their nails appeared to have been professionally cut, the fingers and palms that surrounded them soft and uncalloused. Adam doubted they posed a threat, but he would still keep an eye on them.

A server took Adam's order for spring water without bubbles and Coca-Cola Light – there was no such thing as Diet Coke in Europe because the population regarded the word *diet* to be four-letter obscenity. As it happened, Adam preferred their Light version as it went down a bit more smoothly.

After the waitress left, Adam made his way to the buffet. He took his time and built a proper breakfast, taking comfort in knowing the package was in the briefcase and with him the entire time. At home, he preferred whole grain cereal with almond milk and blueberries. But when in Europe, he always opted for smoked salmon and vegetables. To the man who was saving every dollar for his dream home in Florence, salmon was an indulgence he could not afford. But when the breakfast buffet came with the room, it was too delicious to pass up.

On his way back to his table, Adam noted that a fourth guest had arrived for breakfast. An elegant man in a blue blazer was reading an English paper and sipping coffee alone. When his eyes drifted to the man's shoes, Adam was surprised to see he was wearing blue suede Adidas Gazelles. The choice seemed off, Adam thought, but then again, older guys were combining formal and casual clothes these days, apparently not realizing how silly they looked.

Adam loved returning to his table to find his water and soda waiting for him. Such was the case this morning, and when he enjoyed his first bite of salmon, last night's anguish receded from his mind. The cola cut the salt in the fish. He continued eating and drinking until a hot flash seized him.

At first, he tried to shake off the sensation, thinking it might have been an after-shock from yesterday's encounter with Terzic. He ate more salmon and drank some more water and cola. But then the heat returned, this time with sweat on his brow. A dizzy spell further confused him, and Adam wondered if these were the initial symptoms of Covid. Whether they were or not, he needed to get back to his room and lie down, he thought.

The server had left the check in a leather folder for him to sign at his leisure. Adam fought off the urge to scribble his room number and signature quickly and first calculated twenty percent of the bill. He added the gratuity to the amount owed, and only then signed it.

By the time he got to the elevator, he was afraid he might faint any moment. He stumbled out of the lift on the fourth floor and headed down the hallway. When he finally arrived at his room, he reached into his left pocket to retrieve his keycard but it wasn't there.

A shadow descended upon him from behind. Adam sensed it hovering over him even before it spoke.

"Did you have one too many mimosas again, sweetheart?" a woman said. "Here, let me help you get to bed."

A sleek hand slipped into his right pant pocket and produced his keycard. By the time Adam had gathered himself sufficiently to try to turn and see her face, the door was open and she was pushing him inside – riding him, in a way – all over his back, it seemed.

The door clicked shut behind him. The room appeared upside down to Adam, and it was then that he realized that he'd been poisoned. He should have figured that out earlier, he thought, but there was no precedent for such a turn of events. Nothing like this had ever happened to him before.

He clutched the briefcase to his chest, felt the woman leading him somewhere. The next thing he knew he was lying on the bed, and to his complete and utter stupefaction, the woman was climbing on top of him. She straddled him, hips on his midsection, knees bent behind them. His vision was so blurry he couldn't make out her face, but the oval shape and the raised cheekbones looked strangely familiar.

His eyes fells on her platinum hair. She was the corporate-looking woman from the breakfast room, Adam realized. The woman reached up with her right hand and appeared to play with something in her hair. A few moments later, she pulled the platinum wig off her head to reveal that she was actually a brunette.

She leaned forward so close that Adam could feel her hot breath on his ears and smell the shampoo in her hair. It was a delicious honey smell, a most familiar scent from the most joyous times he'd ever known.

No, he thought. It couldn't be ...

"Adam," she sang in Russian into his ear. "It's Eva."

"What?" Adam heard his own voice, unaware he'd spoken.

"Adam," she sang again, in a tune that sounded like playful mischief. "It's Eva."

"Eva," he said, breathless, vision even more blurry. "Is it really you?"

"Does it sound like me? Does it smell like me? Does it look like me? Of course it's me."

The realization that she was alive, that she was with him here and now ... the thought of holding her in his arms and kissing her lips again ...

"Look at your ears," she said. "They're so beautiful. Why did you leave me, Adam?"

"Leave you? I ... I didn't ... I would never ... I stayed and searched ... I searched for years."

"Eva loves Adam," she sang sweetly. "Adam loves Eva. You said we'd be together forever."

"Together ..." Adam said. "Forever ..."

And then a Siberian chill iced her voice. "You shouldn't have left me, Adam."

He felt the strap of the briefcase slip over his head and a bulky object being removed from his side – his laptop briefcase, he realized – and his final thought before drifting into oblivion negated all the joy Eva had brought him a moment ago.

The package, he thought.

The package was in the open.

TWELVE

ADAM WOKE UP THOROUGHLY CONFUSED. At first, he was so drowsy he couldn't even roll to his side to find his phone on the nightstand. When he finally found the strength to do so, he realized it wasn't where he usually left it when he went to sleep. Only then did he see that the nightstand looked entirely different than the one in his apartment in Manhattan.

He wasn't home, Adam realized. He was somewhere else.

His head ached. When he tried to rise from bed, his shoulders and knees rebelled as though he'd done hard labor the day before. He staggered to his feet only to be blinded by the sun pouring in through the open blinds. He had to squint and shield his eyes to make it to the bathroom. He ran the water until it turned cold and doused his face in it. As he toweled dry, the gaps in his memory filled.

Adam rushed out of the bathroom and found his laptop briefcase leaning against the suitcase he'd packed before breakfast. His euphoria was short-lived – the computer was in its pouch but the package was gone. Eva had taken it. He found his phone beside his wallet and keycard on the desk – she hadn't taken anything else.

Adam checked the time. It was 11:48 a.m. His train to Zurich had departed at 8:13 a.m. He cursed his own incompetence. Eva had wandered over to his table and slipped something into his soda after it had been delivered, while he'd been busy gathering his precious salmon. Why hadn't he stood at an angle to the serving tray and kept his table in sight the entire time? If that was impossible, he could have at least kept an eye on the other guests, and spied the woman with the platinum hair moving towards his beverages.

Adam searched for the train schedule. He needed to get to Zurich. His ultimate destination was irrelevant. Zurich provided access to all points in Europe and beyond. Once he found the departure schedule, he called Victor.

"Why didn't you grasp the woman's arm when she was lying on top of you?" Victor said, after Adam briefed him. "You could have seen who hired her and maybe we'd know where she's going."

"Easy for you to say. I was struggling to stay conscious. I wasn't thinking clearly."

"I'll say."

"And I've told you before," Adam said. "This isn't something I can do on a whim. I have to be focused. And I doubt the memory of who hired her is a traumatic one so it would have been pretty much impossible for me to spot it. Plus, there's a cost to the process, you know. I don't like how it makes me feel afterwards."

"If we're lucky, the cost of your mistake will be the down payment the client made on the job. If we're unlucky, the cost will be measured in shovels and dirt, not dollars."

"Maybe you overestimate me. Maybe you shouldn't have pushed me. You're always pushing me, Victor."

"If I didn't, you'd never leave your apartment." Victor sighed. "You never saw this woman before this morning?"

Adam didn't answer.

"Adam?"

He still didn't answer.

"You know her?"

Victor knew all about Eva. To Adam's knowledge, he was the only person alive who knew their past.

"It was Eva," Adam said.

"Eva?" Victor skipped a beat. "Wait, you mean your Eva?"

"Yeah. My Eva."

"Oh, come now," Victor said. "That can't be ..."

"That's what I thought. But it was, and she is."

"You saw her? With your own eyes ..."

"Saw her, heard her, touched her, smelled her. She survived. I don't know how but she did. I don't know why I couldn't find her but she's here now. And she has the package, which is just surreal."

"We hope she still has it," Victor said.

"Eh, she still has it."

"Why do you say that?"

"Because this is personal," Adam said. "Not business. She's angry with me. Like, really angry. She thinks I abandoned her, which as you know, is totally untrue."

Victor took a moment to answer. "You're right."

"Thank you. I spent two years looking for her."

"It is extraordinary that she appears ten years later out of the blue and lifts the package from you. Let's just stipulate that her involvement can't be explained rationally for the time being. Any attempt to do so will only send us round and round in circles and drive us mad."

"We'll get clarity." Adam said. "Sooner or later."

"That is a reasonable expectation," Victor said. "But you know what they say about reason. The sky is not less blue because the blind man does not see it."

Adam contemplated his next move. "I wonder what the skies are like in Zurich today."

"The twins are waiting in Warsaw," Victor said. "I'll tell them there's been a delay. And then I'll call Nazarov."

As Adam gathered his belongings, he realized that the red light was illuminated on the house phone, indicating he had a message. When he called the front desk, the man told him they were holding an envelope for him.

Adam scooted down to the ground floor, began the check-out procedure and received his mail. The Zermatterhof's name marked the envelope and the enclosed stationary. After reading the message, Adam guessed the author of the note had lifted them a few hours ago from his room.

The message was written in English, in gorgeous calligraphy.

Dearest Adam,

Go to where the sun is at the center of the universe and see the amber lady. She may be holding a package for you. Hurry before someone steals it. LOL.

XO,

Eva

After completing his checkout and hailing a cab, Adam texted Victor on the way to the train station.

Contact made. En route to Copernicus Hotel in Krakow. Expecting the thief and the package.

That the sun and not the Earth was the center of the universe was a theory espoused in the 16th century by the Polish genius, Nicolaus Copernicus. His father had been a successful merchant in Krakow, a beautiful city renowned for its amber jewelry. Ten years ago, Adam and Eva had admired the hotel named after the men during a weekend trip to Krakow. They'd dreamed of having enough money to stay there some day. It was there that Eva fell in love with the jewelry for which the town was famous, and upon putting on the earrings Adam had bought her, jokingly dubbed herself the amber lady.

Later, as he waited for his train to depart, Adam reminisced about that trip. Her theft of the package notwithstanding, the thought of seeing Eva again with all his wits intact left him breathless with anticipation. As his restless mind wandered, he relived his phone conversation with Victor, and regretted the tone he'd taken with the man whom he owed so much.

An hour from Zurich, Adam sent Victor a follow-up text.

The medications aren't less inaccurate just because the old man is too lazy to check them. Make sure Nina is getting your dosages right!

THIRTEEN

ADAM TOOK the 5:25 p.m. Swiss Airlines flight from Zurich and landed at John Paul II International Airport in Krakow at 7:05 p.m.

His Uber arrived in the form of an old Ford station wagon at the designated pick-up spot. Adam groaned when his eyes met those of the lanky driver. He was one of those men that had been born smiling. Unfortunately, that meant he was probably a talker, too.

"Polish?" he said in his native language, eyeing Adam through the rearview mirror

"A little bit," Adam said.

The driver slipped the manual transmission into first gear and took off.

"You here on business or pleasure?" he said.

"Hopefully both," Adam said.

"Be careful. A man once told me, if you're lucky in life, the peaks of your professional life will offset the valleys of your personal life, and vice versa. You get both parts going the same way, might not be so much fun on the downside."

"Sounds like a man I know," Adam said.

"Take Krakow itself," the driver said. "Now is not the best time for my city. All these Ukrainian refugees have come here. More than a hundred fifty thousand so far. That's twenty percent of our population. What are we supposed to do with them all?"

Adam ignored the question, hoping the conversation would end.

"And I'll tell you something else, too. Ukraine and Poland? We have history. Bad history. On both sides. But the worst was the massacres in Volhynia and Galicia in 1943. You've heard of this?"

Adam shook his head.

"Ukrainians murdered a hundred thousand Poles over a two-month span. Ethnic cleansing, genocide, call it what you want. The most sadistic atrocities you can imagine. And never have we gotten a formal apology from the Ukrainian government."

"Well, if that's the case, my hat's off to you for taking in these refugees."

"I am so proud of my people," the driver said. "We invite strangers into our homes. We host job fairs at the sports arena. But the only jobs we have to offer are the worst kind, the kind even the locals don't want – like cleaning and warehouse work."

"I've had my share of lousy jobs," Adam said.

"Who hasn't? And that's the thing about these Ukrainians. They're educated, right? Three-quarters of them have college or technical degrees. So what kind of work are they willing to do?"

Adam waited, curious to hear the answer.

"Any kind," the driver said. "They will take any job and work like hell at it. Nothing is beneath them. They want to work. They want to show their gratitude. We're got trained engineers sweeping floors, computer experts washing garbage trucks."

"Cool," Adam said.

"And so, I realize ... this is not my grandfather's Ukraine, just as it's not my great-grandfather's Poland – I mean, we're far from perfect ourselves. And while it may not be the best time for my city, it is the very best time for my people. Because we are fighting for freedom and democracy with our neighbors. You see this, too?"

"Oh, yeah," Adam said. He wondered if Eva would be waiting for him in the lobby or sitting at the bar. "I absolutely see it."

"I am so happy. Welcome to Krakow."

A city ordinance restricted access to *Stare Miesto* – Old Town – to permitted vehicles and licensed taxis. After the driver dropped him off, Adam rolled his suitcase along a cobblestone street nestled in the foothills of Wawel Royal Castle. Its fortifications and towers loomed in the background. He negotiated a winding alley featuring historic buildings with carved stone entrances. The Copernicus appeared as an understated three-story brick home, its narrow wooden doors original to the 16th century structure.

A doorman tried to take his suitcase but Adam refused. He preferred no one touch his possessions unless absolutely necessary. He wheeled it himself down a long hallway to the check-in desk on the right. He kept his eyes out for Eva, expecting her to appear anywhere at any moment.

A man with round spectacles and a distrusting air about him welcomed Adam to the hotel. Adam supplied his passport and credit card.

"You're with us for one evening, Mister Ziegler?" he said in German.

"That's correct," Adam said, or at least so he hoped. "I wonder if you might have a message for me."

"A message?"

"Perhaps an envelope."

The man at the front desk punched some keys into his computer, then turned and shuffled through a stack of mail behind him.

"I'm afraid I don't see anything, sir."

"It would have been delivered in person, not by mail," Adam said.

"I understand, sir. If there were an envelope for you here, it would have been noted with your reservation, and placed for safekeeping behind the desk."

"I see," Adam said. "The envelope was supposed to be delivered by my friend. And now I'm wondering if we had a miscommunication. Perhaps she's staying here also. Her name is Eva Vovk."

The man checked his computer and shook his head.

"I'm afraid we don't have a guest by that name staying here, nor do we have a reservation for such a person."

Adam reminded himself that Eva had made no mention of leaving a note or staying at the hotel. She'd implied that Adam should look for her at the Copernicus – nothing more. Adam finished checking-in and dumped his belongings in his room on the third floor. He searched the bar and the restaurant for Eva, and checked the fitness facility and the pool, too.

After his search proved fruitless, Adam stepped out of the hotel and looked around the street thinking Eva might be waiting outside. He didn't find her. He searched the lobby and the bar again just in case she might have been using the ladies' room when he'd looked for her before. He also checked with the front desk again to make sure she hadn't left a voice mail. When the man informed Adam he still had no messages, Adam shuffled back outside. This time he went for a walk to get some air and contemplate his next move.

When he returned to the hotel he leaned against the wall of

a residence diagonally across the street from the entrance to the Copernicus. It was from this vantage point that he first noticed the tiny storefront not too far from the hotel, wedged between two more significant structures. A window display beside the door contained empty velvet boxes. Gold lettering atop the glass door announced the store's hours. And a hand-painted sign above the entry proclaimed the store's name:

The Amber Lady.

FOURTEEN

TASIA'S HANDLER called himself Roman. She knew that wasn't his real name. He was an officer in the counter-intelligence unit of the SBU – the Security Service of Ukraine. As a fellow intelligence professional, Tasia understood his mission. His goal was to keep her healthy and happy so that he could glean as much information from her as possible. His means knew no boundaries. His most powerful weapon was his attentiveness.

"We know about the children," Roman said through the hole in the wallboard. "Our last count was a hundred thirty thousand."

"Wait," Tasia said. "What do you mean? A hundred thirty thousand what?"

"Children. Our last count is that Russia has stolen one hundred thirty thousand Ukrainian babies and children. They've been taken to temporary camps in Russia pending adoption."

"That is insane," Tasia said. "Strelkov knew. I didn't. They must have kept it on a need to know."

"In the 19th century, Russia and America had the fastest

population growth. A hundred years later they were superpowers. In the last days of the Soviet Union, there were two hundred ninety million people. Now there's less than half that number in Russia. That's less than half the population of America today."

"Women are having fewer children," Tasia said.

"Especially white women," Roman said. "And your boss and his nationalist friends don't like that either. The mix is turning Central Asian, and they're gradually moving to cities. If nothing changes, parts of Russia will be completely uninhabited in twenty years. Which will make it vulnerable. In your Boss's eyes, a lot easier to conquer. Some people think that's the real reason he chose to invade now – that which does not grow dies."

"I remember in school," Tasia said, "teacher told us, after World War II, a German Field Marshall once said fighting Russia was like fighting a hydra – for every head he cut off, two more would appear."

"Problem is," Roman said, "the hydra became an alcoholic with low self-esteem."

"Speaking of high self-esteem ..." Tasia told him about Strelkov's assassination of the Deputy Mayor of Kherson.

Roman took a beat to process her news.

"Seven mayors missing," he said. "This is the second confirmed death."

"I'm sorry for your loss."

"Any more on Wagner? If we could get the exact names of their agents in Ukraine ..."

The Wagner Group advertised itself to be a private military contractor. In reality, it shared bases, transportation, and healthcare services with the Russian military. Within the FSB, Wagner was considered to be the Boss' private army. It specialized in sabotage and assassination.

"I told you," Tasia said. "I don't have that kind of access. I have some friends in the home office in Russia. That's the only reason I've been able to warn you when Wagner was getting ready to move on your President up to now. There's no guarantee I'll know next time."

"Maybe your friends have access to the list of names," Roman said.

"Out of the question," Tasia said. "There's going to be a purge in the FSB. The Boss is pissed off at how well-informed you guys are. If that puts me at risk, so be it. But I will not put my friends in danger."

"Okay, okay. I understand," Roman said. "Strelkov probably has access to the Wagner file."

"How do you see that working?" Tasia said. "Strelkov and I have a torrid affair. It'll start off as emotional intimacy and then turn physical. I steal the list of names off his computer while he's taking a shower, only to be found out just before my escape. And then right before he disembowels me, you come riding in on horseback to save me, twirling your Cossack axe. Does that sound consistent with your Ukrainian sensibilities?"

A chuckle was followed by a long breath. "Ninety-nine," he said, referring to her by the alias he'd given her, "that's not what I meant."

"How's Lena?" Tasia said. "Where is my sister now?"

A moment of silence struck fear in her heart.

"Roman?" she said.

Another heavy moment passed

"I'm afraid I have some sad news to share with you," Roman said. "Your brother-in-law was killed in action in Irpin five days ago."

Tasia brought her hand to her mouth.

"Oh, no," she said. "That is just the most horrible ... the most awful ..."

Lena had gotten married to a fellow soldier in the Ukrainian

Army three days after the war started. They'd been a couple since secondary school, for over twelve years. It wasn't hard for Tasia to imagine her sister's grief. Her own fiancé had been killed hiking in Costa Rica in 2019. The four of them had enjoyed a memorable vacation in Croatia together during better times.

"I want to see her," Tasia said.

"I'm afraid that's not realistic," Roman said.

"A video call?"

"Lena went right back to theater after the funeral. She's back on the front line. Satellites are listening to everything. You know that. It's impossible to guarantee a video call won't be traced somehow."

"A simple phone call, then." Tasia said.

"No," Roman said, with uncharacteristic firmness. "It is absolutely essential you have no contact with her. We simply cannot risk compromising her whereabouts."

Tasia sighed. "You'll let me know when this changes."

"Immediately."

"All right then. I'll let you know what develops with Strelkov."

"Be safe, Ninety-nine. If it weren't for you ... We have no one else like you."

Tasia thought about Lena as she jogged home. She was all the family Tasia had left. She longed to return to Croatia with her, or maybe Italy. This time, sadly, they'd both be single. But at least they'd have each other. Unfortunately, she thought, there were no realistic prospects for such a reunion.

This war really was such shit.

FIFTEEN

WHEN ADAM SAW that the *Amber Lady* was closed for the evening, he rushed back to the hotel and sought the concierge's help. Adam told him he was leaving tomorrow morning before the store opened, and that he'd promised to buy his girlfriend a ring to match the earrings he'd bought her previously. The concierge exhausted himself on Adam's behalf. He even secured the store owner's mobile phone number from the property leasing agent. Sadly, that number was no longer in service.

Adam spent a restless night in bed worrying about Eva and the package. When he woke up the next morning, he performed his usual exercise routine. After his workout, he took a long walk around Old Town. He followed the path he and Eva had taken after dinner during their visit. The medieval town's architecture had delighted her, stone and brick structures boasting turrets and watchtowers with octagonal steeples and Gothic cupolas.

Upon returning to the hotel, Adam showered and shaved. He ate salmon and cucumber for breakfast. He packed his luggage to be ready for a quick departure, and then took his post across the street a full hour before the jewelry store was scheduled to open. Adam expected the owner – or his employee – to arrive early to fill the empty boxes in the display windows.

He wasn't disappointed. An elderly man with thick glasses and furry gray eyebrows arrived half an hour early. He watched as the man filled the display cases with jewels. Adam didn't want to startle him while he was handling his inventory. Only when the owner was finished and sipping coffee behind his counter did Adam knock on the door.

The owner shuffled over and cracked it open.

"I'm so sorry to intrude," Adam said. "I was told you might have a package for me."

"A package?" the owner said.

"Yes. A small package. About this big." Adam described the dimensions of the box he'd taken from Sternfeld's safe. "It might have been left by a woman. Tall, dark hair, oval face."

"Would this be a purchase she made in the store or over the internet?" the owner said.

"It wouldn't necessarily be a purchase," Adam said. "Does the woman I described sound familiar?"

"If this isn't about a purchase, why would there be a package?"

"Her name is Eva. Eva Vovk. Did a woman by that name leave a package for a man named Adam?"

"The post office is over on *Karmelicka*. Why don't you check with them?"

"No, no ..." Adam said.

The owner closed the door and shuffled back behind his counter.

Adam returned to his vantage point across the street to gather his thoughts. He thought of Eva's message. He was certain he was in the right hotel in the right town. Of that he had no doubt. It was the remaining bit that he wasn't interpreting properly.

"... *see the amber lady. She may be holding a package for you.*"

Who was the amber lady? At first, he thought Eva was referring to herself. But as soon as he'd laid eyes on its name, Adam knew she'd meant the store. Eva liked puzzles and games. She enjoyed speaking in riddles. But if the store was the thing, why did its owner have no clue about the package?

According to the message, Adam was supposed to see the amber lady. What if the latter phrase referred to both a place and a person? By visiting the store, Adam had followed the first of those instructions, but he'd ignored the second.

Adam hustled back to the shop. The owner was wrapping a bracelet for a woman with a red neck. The process seemed interminable.

When she finally left the store, Adam stepped up to the counter.

"Ah," the owner said. "The young man and the package. Did you have any luck at the post office?"

"I'm looking for the Amber Lady," Adam said. "Is she available?"

"That would be my granddaughter," he said.

"Your granddaughter. That's fantastic. Do you know where I can find her?"

"She was meeting some tourists at Saint Mary's Basilica at 10:00 a.m."

"Thank you," Adam said. "Thank you so much. Would you happen to have her mobile phone number? As I said before, it's very important ..."

The owner smiled and shook his head – he wasn't going to give up her digits. "She may still be there, but I'd run if I were you. She's leaving town when the meeting is over. And she won't be back for a while."

Adam thanked the owner again and ran back to his room.

He grabbed his luggage, placed his key on the desk with the zloty equivalent of twenty dollars for the housekeeper, and left the hotel. Then he raced to Old Town's Main Market Square, suitcase in hand.

St. Mary's Basilica was a brick building flanked by two Gothic towers of different heights. Adam entered the church and looked around. He counted fifteen visitors snapping pictures of the high altar, studying the murals and stained glass, and praying in the pews. He watched them for a minute. They were mostly couples with a few solitary folks as well. Adam didn't see any evidence of a tour or a meeting, and the females appeared to be either too young or too old to be the store owner's granddaughter.

The church was sprawling. At the end of the center aisle, a series of stanchions connected by thick scarlet rope prevented tourists from entering the altar. Adam detected the faint echo of a man's voice coming from the left of the altar. He wound his way toward the sound until he spied a priest speaking to a group of people in a side chapel. The group consisted of five men and a woman, all of them in the prime of their lives. They stood solemnly, hands by their sides or clasped at their waists, as though the priest were conducting some sort of service.

Adam slipped his luggage onto a pew and moved close enough to hear the priest's words in English:

Lord Jesus, born under the bombs of Kyiv, have mercy on us.

Lord Jesus, dead in the arms of a mother in Kharkiv, have mercy on us.

. . .

Lord Jesus, in the 20-year-olds sent to the frontline, have mercy on us.

Lord Jesus Christ, son of God, we implore you to stop the hand of Cain, enlighten our conscience, let not our will be done, do not abandon us to our own doing.

Stop us, Lord, stop us, and when you have stopped the hand of Cain, take care of him also. He is our brother.

Amen.

The priest issued a final blessing and wished everyone good luck. The men dispersed quietly and retrieved their bags from the back of the chapel. They looked relaxed yet determined. Khaki was their favorite color. On one of the bags, Adam spied the flag of Finland. On another, a patch for the Lithuanian National Soccer team.

While the men gathered their belongings, the woman among them slipped the priest an envelope and thanked him in Polish. Then she strutted over to Adam. She cut a striking figure in custom-fit camo fatigues, standing almost eye-to-eye with him, with broader shoulders to boot. Amber dripped from her body. Earrings, bracelets, rings – the works.

"You're the recon expert," she said, in heavily accented English.

"Excuse me?" Adam said.

"You're Ziegler, yes?"

Adam hesitated. She knew his alias, he thought. How was that possible?

"Yes. I'm Ziegler," he said.

"You're late."

She reached into a crossbody bag and removed a letter-sized manila envelope.

"This is your package," she said. "Bus leaves in fifteen. I hope you're better at reconnaissance than you are at being on time."

"Bus?" Adam said. "Bus to where?"

"Ukraine, obviously." The Amber Lady looked at him as though he were an idiot. "Where else would we be going?"

SIXTEEN

WILD GRASS PRESSED the shoulders of the two-lane road. Scrub pines and conifers stretched to the horizon. The trip from Krakow to Lviv reminded Adam of his recent journey from Manhattan to the Catskills and back. But he wasn't returning home this time.

The bus was actually a late model van with seating for twelve. The Amber Lady sat alone in the first row behind the driver, who wore a red warm-up suit and a permanent sneer on his face. Adam took an aisle seat two rows behind her and contemplated his next move.

Eva had not lied. He'd seen the Amber Lady and she'd delivered a package, as Eva's note had promised. But the package was not quite the one Adam had been expecting. Instead of the item he'd liberated from Sternfeld's safe in Zermatt, Adam found a set of papers in the manila folder. They consisted of an application for entry into the International Legion of Territorial Defense of Ukraine, and a contract to be signed after an interview with an official from the Ukrainian Ministry of Defense. The package also contained a questionnaire that served as preparation for the interview that awaited the applicant in Lviv.

When he first saw the papers outside the church in Krakow, Adam couldn't believe he was actually holding them in his hands. The thought of climbing aboard the van and heading east of Poland struck him as even more absurd. And yet, Adam realized that he had no choice. Evidently Eva had a plan for him. If he wanted the package – and if he wanted to see her again – he had to play her game. If he were patient, a moment would arrive that would allow him to tilt the field in his favor, Adam thought. Such moments always arrived.

In the meantime, she was making him suffer and in no greater measure than by sending him to Ukraine. It was among the four places on Earth he was least interested in visiting, the others being Eritrea, North Korea, and Russia. And this had nothing to do with the war. His indifference toward the country preceded the current conflict.

Eva would have instructions waiting for him when he arrived in Lviv, Adam thought. She certainly didn't expect him to join the International Legion. He had no combat experience. No, the purpose of this leg of his journey was to get him into Ukraine. Eva had learned he was traveling under the name Werner Ziegler at the Hotel Zermatterhof. She was more than resourceful enough to have stolen a glance at housekeeping records, or bribed a bellhop under the guise of romantic interest.

But how did the Amber Lady discover Werner Ziegler? That part baffled him.

Adam walked up to her from behind. She sat riveted by what looked like an e-mail on her computer. Upon seeing Adam, she slammed the laptop shut and glared at him.

"Sorry to interrupt," Adam said. "There's been a misunderstanding. I'm not who you think I am. I'm no recon expert. I have no combat experience at all."

She motioned for him to sit down.

"If that's the case," she said, "why did you lie to me on the phone?"

Adam sat stunned. "I didn't speak to you on the phone."

"Uh, yeah you did," she said. "Yesterday. You don't remember?"

"I've never spoken with you before today," Adam said. He remembered Eva impersonating his voice when she made fun of things he said. "What did the person sound like?"

"Like you. Imagine that. You ... sounded ... like you."

"A bit more feminine perhaps?"

She chuckled. "I don't know about that. Maybe you sounded a bit more masculine yesterday. Maybe a little more feminine today."

That made perfect sense, Adam thought. Whenever Eva had imitated his voice, she'd always deepened hers a bit too much.

"What else did I say?" Adam said.

"Why? It wasn't you? Someone else called for you?" She shrugged. "The usual. That this was a cause you believed in and wanted to fight for. That you had recon skills and experience that could make a difference."

"Did I tell you how I found you?"

She thought about the question for a moment. "I don't think you got into specifics. That's not unusual. This is a word-of-mouth business. Ukraine told volunteers to apply at their embassies but that didn't work out too well. It was slow and not so well organized. So, soldiers started reaching out to their old commanders. Word got out. Best thing to do is to go to Warsaw or Krakow, meet up with other soldiers. Enlist as a group. People like me ... former Polish soldiers ... we help make it happen."

"Did I give you a reference? Tell you who told me to call you?"

"You told me you heard I was looking for men. That's all you needed to tell me. The reference part you're talking about ... that comes when you fill out the application and get interviewed by the Ukrainians."

Eva had found the Amber Lady and impersonated him, Adam thought. It would have been easy for her to find such a go-between if she claimed to know a capable soldier who was looking to enlist.

"My name is Amber, by the way," she said.

Adam nodded. "I never would have guessed."

She smiled and softened her voice. "You're doing the right thing, you know."

"What thing is that?" Adam said.

"Changing your mind, coming clean ... You wanted to fight for glory and honor but now you realize this isn't a game."

Adam started to protest but realized that would be futile.

"Let me ask you a question," Amber said. "Are you ready to die? Are you ready to die for Ukraine?"

"I'm not ready to die for anyone or anything," Adam said. "I've still got some things I need to do first."

"To be a good soldier, you must be willing to die," Amber said. "But you said on the phone that you speak English, Russian and Ukrainian." She switched to Ukrainian and asked him if that was accurate.

He told her it was true.

"That would make you invaluable to the humanitarian effort," she said, switching back to English. "If you really want to help these people ... if their suffering really bothers you ..."

Adam took a breath. "Ukraine is not my favorite place, for reasons we don't need to get into. But if I could personally stop the war, I would do it in a heartbeat. I can't. And in the meantime, I've got those things I mentioned. Things I've got to do."

Amber reached into her bag, pulled out a business card, and handed it to him.

"My mobile phone is on it," she said. "If you change your mind, Mister Ziegler, let me know if I can help."

Adam took the card, thanked her, and returned to his seat.

Two hours later they stopped at a petrol station. Amber told everyone this would be their last stop before they crossed the border.

Adam found a private spot in the parking lot, called Victor, and updated him.

"Start walking back to Krakow now," Victor said.

"What?" Adam said.

"Do not get on that bus."

"Why?"

"You cannot go to Ukraine."

Adam felt himself turning red. He knew he was embarking on a ridiculous conversation but he had no choice.

"Why not?" he said.

"Why not?" Victor sounded incredulous. "You're asking me why you shouldn't go to Ukraine? Are you not well?"

"I have to go. For the package."

"Nonsense. It's all about the girl."

"If I'm not a professional, I'm nothing."

"Of course it's about the girl," Victor said. "I talked to Nazarov."

"How did it go?" Adam said.

"Let's just say he's displeased. He knows we've been delayed. Which means he has to be worried that we might be lying. That we have the package, are aware of its value and might sell it to a higher bidder."

"What do you mean we're aware of its value?"

Victor hesitated. "Something I didn't tell you, because sometimes it's better to know less, is that the package may contain something relevant to the war."

"The war? How so?"

"From what I understand, it's a technology of some kind that could give one country an edge over the other. But Nazarov didn't want to bring attention to it by storming the gates with a private army, which is why he hired us, because we had a one hundred percent success rate over an eight-year period."

"It was just a matter of time," Adam said. "Only death has a zero-failure rate."

"The point is, we must assume Nazarov's not sitting around waiting idly for us to deliver."

He would have called all the hotels in Zermatt by now, Adam thought, probably hacked into their databases, too. He may have discovered that no pair of twins had been seen in Zermatt by anyone. By now he might have conducted background checks on every guest who'd stayed at the Zermatterhof, and if he dug deep enough into Werner Ziegler's life ...

"He'll be coming for you," Victor said.

"Eva's going to meet me in Lviv tonight," Adam said.

"Did she promise you that?"

Adam didn't answer.

"Because in case you haven't noticed," Victor said, "she's not the most reliable narrator."

"She's mad at me. So, she's making me do some things I don't want to do. Once I'm in Lviv, she'll show up and I'll find out how she became involved in all this. Lviv was our special place. That's where we stopped being friends and became ... you know ... a couple. It was the first time ... for both of us."

"There are places on this Earth that each of us should avoid. Where pain gathers and awaits our return. You must not go back," Victor said.

"I have no choice. I have to go back. You know that."

"It's a blatant violation of your professional code," Victor said. "You do not work east of Poland."

"I already violated that once. When I did the job in Istanbul."

"You do not work in countries without a McDonalds."

"Ukraine has over a hundred McDonalds," Adam said.

"Yes, but not in the spirit in which you chose them as your criteria. They're all closed."

"Doesn't matter. I already violated that part of my code, too."

"When?" Victor said, sounding surprised.

"When I did the job in Reykjavik. There are no McDonalds in Iceland."

Victor remained silent for a moment. "What if I ask you not to go, as a personal favor to me?"

Adam took his time answering as though his decision wasn't an easy one. That made him an even greater fraud, Adam thought.

"I didn't think so," Victor said. "At least promise me you won't go east of Lviv."

"There's not going to be any reason for me to go east of Lviv," Adam said.

"Remember you said that when she tries to lure you even closer to the front line. I don't know what she's up to, but I don't trust her. I look forward to the moment you prove me wrong."

"Me too."

Victor ended the call.

Three and a half hours later the bus cleared customs and immigration, and crossed the Polish border.

Adam was back in the place where he'd vowed to never return.

He was back in Ukraine.

SEVENTEEN

THE FIRST MANIFESTATION of war appeared within five minutes of crossing the border from Poland. Three road signs at a major intersection had been covered with black tape to disorient the enemy.

That the local population was taking such precautions even though Russian forces were nowhere near western Ukraine told Adam two things. First, Ukrainian citizens were highly motivated and organized. Second, from the locals' perspective, the eventual arrival of Russian troops was too realistic a possibility to ignore.

Adam, Amber and the soldiers arrived in Lviv at 7:30 p.m. They drove through a neighborhood with commercial and residential buildings onto a street called Pekarska. Students mixed on the grounds of a university campus. Further down the road, a couple opened the door to a restaurant to reveal a big crowd inside. On the opposite side of the street, a police car rolled along as though patrolling the area during normal times.

The van dropped them off at an uninspiring concrete corner building. It brought to mind the bland architectural element from Ukraine's Soviet past. A light shone on the building's higher floors. A dozen men and two women milled around the doorway smoking cigarettes and chatting.

"The recruitment center is on the second floor," Amber said, as the van pulled away. "City curfew is at 2100. We've got bunks for you in a building nearby. I'll take you there and get you situated. We'll regroup here at 0900 tomorrow morning. Any questions?"

"I have a question."

A teenager stepped forward from the group that had congregated beside the building. When he emerged from the shadows of a blue awning, however, Adam could tell by his narrow face and smaller jawline that he was no teen. He was actually quite a bit older than he'd first appeared, most likely in his mid-twenties. His head barely reached Amber's chin, but he looked rawboned and rugged.

"Will you marry me?" he said in Ukrainian, a twinkle in his eye.

"That depends," Amber said. "How many children do you want?"

"As many as you want."

"So, I'd be in control of the relationship?"

He flashed a knowing smile. "You have to be in control for the relationship to work."

"Oh, I like you. Come find me after we win the war."

"Sure. I'll just follow the glow."

Amber turned to Adam and switched to English. "You staying the night with us or are you on your own from here?"

"He's coming with me," the young man said, in surprisingly good English.

He bounded up to Adam and lowered his voice to a whisper. "I have instructions for you. From a tall, dark woman."

"What woman?" Adam said.

"The woman who roams with wolves."

Eva's last name was the Ukrainian word for wolf.

"Who?" Adam said.

He grinned. "Eva. Eva Vovk."

Adam led him twenty feet away from the others so they could speak in private.

"What's your name?" Adam said. He stuck to English.

"Mykhailo, but foreigners usually call me Michael."

"Mikey it is," Adam said. "How do you know Eva?"

"I don't."

"Then how did you get instructions for me? How do you know her name?"

"She knows my uncle," Mikey said. "He told me to meet you here."

"What's your uncle's name?"

"Ivan. Ivan Boyko. He's a professor at Lviv Polytechnic."

"Take me to him."

"I can't. He's out of town. But he'll be back tomorrow."

"You said you have instructions for me from Eva."

"Via my uncle. Train number forty-six arrives on platform one at 7:45 tomorrow morning. Be there."

"Will she be on the train?"

Mikey shrugged. "My uncle didn't say. But why else would she tell you to be there?"

Eva loved the railway. They'd taken the night train from Kyiv and arrived in Lviv at a similar time in the morning.

"Anything else?" Adam said.

"Yeah. She said be sure to build an appetite for sour cherry *varenyky*."

Adam recalled the last time he saw her stuffing her face with Ukrainian dumplings. Lviv was for lovers, the Prague of Eastern Europe. They'd eaten lunch at Café Centaur. Adam wondered if her favorite dish was still on the menu.

He spent the night on a bunk in a nearby college

gymnasium with the candidates for the Ukrainian International Legion. The next morning Mikey was waiting for him on the street at 6:30 a.m. Given the recent trajectory of events, Adam was pleasantly surprised he'd showed up as planned. Mikey brought Adam a bottle of water and a croissant for breakfast. Adam offered him American dollars in return.

Mikey did not refuse.

The train station was six kilometers away. After yesterday's interminable bus ride, Adam was eager to start the day with some exercise. They ate as they walked, Adam rolling his suitcase along even ground.

"Your English is so good," Mikey said. "You sound like you spent some time in England, or maybe America."

"A little bit," Adam said.

"Which place?"

"Both."

"You have any connections in the film business?" Mikey said.

"Can't say that I do. Why?"

"I'm a thespian. I specialize in understanding people's motivations. I'm going to be the next great American actor. Not a movie star. No. No vanity. All that posing is not for me. I'm going to be a craftsman. Like Ben Foster."

"Never heard of him," Adam said.

Mikey recoiled. "Never heard of Ben Foster? You don't like movies?"

"Television is better than film these days. Maybe that's why I don't know him."

Mikey shoved the rest of his croissant between his teeth and punched his phone's keypad. When he was finished, he stuck the phone in Adam's face.

The screen contained an image of an actor. Adam recognized him. He wasn't the biggest or most famous guy in his films – just the most memorable.

"*Hell or High Water*," Adam said. "I liked that one."

Mikey glared at him with such intensity Adam stepped away for fear he was going to come unhinged.

"This is Mister Pibb," Mikey said, like a Slavic version of the actor himself. "I asked for Doctor Pepper."

"So?" Adam said.

"Only assholes drink Mister Pibb."

"Drink up."

Mikey howled with delight. He offered Adam a fist bump.

Adam ignored it.

They continued walking. Mikey chattered away about his acting method, until finally moving on to a fresh topic.

"If you need anything during your stay in Lviv – things that are hard to come by in a store – I can be your man."

"What things?" Adam said.

"You know, the things that make men happy. Weapons, whiskey, weed. Other forms of medications that may not be available by prescription."

"Not my kind of things," Adam said. "But thanks."

They arrived outside Lviv station at 7:30 a.m., fifteen minutes prior to the train's arrival. Refugees from the war-torn parts of Ukraine gathered beneath tents. Volunteers with Red Cross armbands tended to them. Rows of jug-style water dispensers formed the boundaries of an improvised food court. The air smelled of fresh bread, bacon and pizza. Cars with license plates from nearby countries lined the curb – Poland, Romania, Hungary, Moldova and Slovakia.

The incoming train was from Kyiv. Adam wanted to believe Eva would be on it, but logic suggested otherwise. This was a non-stop night train, which meant all the passengers had boarded at the place of origin. Why would Eva have traveled to

Kyiv while the city was under attack? Also, she'd deceived him in Krakow. It only stood to reason that she might do the same in Lviv. But if she wasn't on the train, whom was he supposed to meet?

"This meeting is personal," Adam said, "so I'm going to go alone. Can I trust you with my suitcase?" He wanted his hands free to help Eva, and just in case something went awry, he didn't want to be weighed down.

Mikey channeled a bit more of his favorite actor. "All you had to do was ask, Little Brother." He took the suitcase from Adam's hand.

Mikey appeared too willing, just a bit too eager, and thus left Adam a touch suspicious about his motives. The *Little Brother* bit sounded off to Adam, too, for he was surely Mikey's senior by at least five years. But the proper tuning of other folks' ears was none of his concern and Mikey knew Eva's name – he had no choice but to roll with him and hope for the best.

Adam slung his laptop briefcase over his shoulder and entered the station. The platform was empty except for a pair of matronly railway employees smoking cigarettes. All was quiet and still.

Adam stood and waited.

EIGHTEEN

TASIA PULLED up to the hospital's emergency entrance in her SUV. Nikolai jumped out of the passenger side door as soon as the vehicle came to a stop. He whipped the rear passenger door open and helped one of their FSB colleagues slide out onto the asphalt. As Tasia circled around, an attendant came hurrying out of the hospital with a wheelchair.

"*Temperatura, temperatura,*" Tasia said.

It was the code word among Ukrainian first responders for injury due to shelling.

"Understood," the attendant said.

Nikolai and the attendant helped their colleague into the wheelchair. He was wearing the uniform of a member of the 28th Mechanized Brigade of the Ukrainian Army, which had been acquired by the Russian Army from a captured soldier. Meanwhile, Tasia and Nikolai were dressed in red jackets and baseball caps worn by paramedics. Huge lettering on the back of their jackets identified them as providers of emergency medical assistance.

The front desk bustled with activity. Prospective patients filled the waiting room, some with undetectable illnesses, others with obvious wounds. An admitting nurse saw the injured man's uniform and promptly called him forward to the head of the queue.

"Get him into room seven," she said to the attendant, "and get that uniform off his body."

Tasia knew the attending physician would find burns, blunt and penetrating trauma, scrapes, cuts and bruises. He'd also detect symptoms of concussion. The latter would be feigned by Tasia's subordinate, while the former would prove to be superficial wounds. Nikolai had administered them personally to his colleague, with a little too much enthusiasm.

While another nurse debriefed Nikolai on the supposed injuries and the circumstances that surrounded them, Tasia studied the hospital staff – aides, attendants and professional caretakers. Any one of them could have provided Tasia with the diagnostic service she was about to request, but only a select few would possess the information the FSB coveted. Tasia zeroed in on a nurse that walked while others ran, and answered questions as opposed to asking them. One other feature suggested she was the one for Tasia. Her shoulder-length hair featured yellow and blue streaks.

Tasia overheard someone call her by her first name.

"Gigi, can I ask you a favor?" Tasia said.

Gigi, glancing at a chart, raised her eyebrows.

Tasia looked around, as though making sure no one could hear her.

"Can you take a look at me?" she whispered. "I don't feel right."

Gigi flashed a look of concern and promptly put the chart back in its cubbyhole on the wall.

"Come with me," she mouthed.

She led Tasia to a storage room that had been modified to accommodate a bed and a cart on wheels. Hospital supplies lined the walls. Medical tools and examination devices rested on the cart.

Tasia sat down on the edge of the bed.

"What's your name?" Gigi said.

"I'm Anna," Tasia said. "Anna Kosh."

"Nice to meet you, Anna. So, tell me, what doesn't feel right?" Gigi said.

"I'm feeling anxious at really strange moments, like when nothing is happening. My partner will be driving the car and all of a sudden, I'll get scared that he's crossing the line ... that he's going to hit the car on the opposite side of the road."

"You're stressed ... not that surprising, is it?"

"I have this headache that won't go away," Tasia said, "and I woke up with a bloody nose this morning – second morning in a row – for no apparent reason. How messed up is that?"

Gigi put her hand on Tasia's shoulder. "Take it easy, take it easy ..."

"I don't have any time to take it easy," Tasia said. "That's the problem. People are getting hurt out there every second of every day. I have to be out there. I need to be out there."

Gigi squeezed her shoulder. "You have to stop and take care of yourself first before you can take care of others. You're a professional. You know that. When was the last time you ate?"

Tasia shrugged.

"Are you getting enough liquids?"

"Not since booze was outlawed."

"Ha. You've got to get more fluids. What about sleep?"

"What about it?" Tasia said. "Only the dead are sleeping in this country, thanks to that bastard in Russia."

"Let me take your blood pressure," Gigi said.

Tasia remained still and focused on what she'd witnessed in Russia's filtration camps in Kherson to try to elevate her numbers so that her purported stress appeared genuine.

"One thirty-two over eighty-two," Gigi said, when she was done. "A bit elevated. But not bad under the circumstances." She unwrapped the sleeve from around Tasia's arm. "Haven't seen you here before, have I?"

"I was a student in Bratislava," Tasia said. "I just came back a week ago. I mean, I had to come back."

"You're my hero for the day," Gigi said. "I'm going to go get you something for the headache. And for the anxiety, in case it gets worse. And some water. You've got to drink more water. Your lips are chapped."

"Thanks," Tasia said. "Can I ask a small favor, too?"

"Sure, love."

"I helped treat a platoon of soldiers a couple of days ago ... my colleagues told me they brought them to this hospital. I don't know his name ... he was kind of cute ... I was just wondering if maybe he's still here ... you know ... maybe I could pop my head in and say hello?"

A suspicious look crossed Gigi's eyes. "We don't treat soldiers in hospitals overnight. We only treat civilians. The soldier you brought in just now ... we're going to stabilize him but then he has to go. Otherwise, we're fair game for the enemy." She lowered her voice. "But I'll ask around. In the meantime, you lie down, and get some rest." She raised her voice back to its normal level. "Anna, you have to take rest when you can get rest because it might not be there when you want it." And then she whispered, "I'll be right back."

Tasia actually took the nurse's advice, closed her eyes and tried to meditate, but she had no success. She was too amped up from pretending to be someone else.

Gigi returned ten minutes later with a smile on her face.

"Good news," she said, as she closed the door behind her.

She placed a bottle of water, a cup with two pills, and a prescription vial on the table before taking a seat on the edge of the bed. Tasia never saw her remove the scalpel from the tray. Gigi was already pressing it against the socket of her right eye when Tasia saw it shimmer.

"I see a sliver of shrapnel here," Gigi said, "but don't worry. I'm surgical with the knife. I can eliminate the problem with one flick of my wrist."

The sensation of cold steel against her flesh froze Tasia in place. She carried a gun in her utility bag but it was resting on the floor beside the bed. She didn't dare move. She didn't dare say a word.

Gigi leaned into her. The yellow and blue streaks in the nurse's hair brushed Tasia's face. They were all Tasia could see – a collection of twisted and turning strands the colors of the Ukrainian flag.

"We're not going back to the way it was before," Gigi said. "Not like it was with the communists, not like it was with the Tsars. So go back to Russia and tell your Boss – it doesn't matter what you do to us or how many of us you kill. It's not gonna happen."

The pressure against her eye socket eased. The blue and yellow strands pulled away.

"I guess I was wrong," Gigi said. "There was no shrapnel there after all."

She stood by the bed, scalpel in hand.

"What gave me away?" Tasia said.

"You asked the question," Gigi said. "A real paramedic would have known not to ask about soldiers. Even if she just came back home from Bratislava a week ago. It would have been one of the first things they told you before you ever put that jacket on. You want your medications?"

Tasia actually wanted the medications and believed they were safe. If Gigi had wanted to poison her, she would have made sure Tasia had taken them first. But she couldn't take the risk.

Tasia rose from the bed. By the time she'd retrieved her bag, Gigi was standing beside an open door.

"Go home," she said.

When Tasia stepped out of the room, a doctor in scrubs stood staring at her.

"Go home," he said.

Tasia turned and headed past the station where half a dozen aids, attendants and nurses had gathered.

"Go home," they said.

Blood rushed to Tasia's face. She picked up her pace, left the treatment area and approached the lobby. It was eerily quiet. Tasia wondered – where had all the people gone?

Three steps later she understood.

They'd gone nowhere. Those that could stand where facing her. Those with open wounds were swallowing their pain. All the people in the waiting room – every single one of them – stood staring at Tasia.

A woman started the chant, and by the third chorus everyone had joined in.

"Go home, go home, go home ..."

When Tasia exited the hospital, Nikolai was standing by their vehicle. Their injured colleague was sitting in the back seat. Both of them were smoking cigarettes.

"Colonel Strelkov is going to be disappointed," Nikolai said.

"You shouldn't be worried about the Colonel," Tasia said. "You should be worried about me."

Nikolai appeared taken aback. "Why? What did I do?"

"Obviously you gave us away."

"Me? How can you be sure it was me?"

"Because they threw you out of the hospital first, didn't they? So, it stands to reason that you gave us away, doesn't it?"

Nikolai frowned, tossed his cigarette to the ground and got in the car.

They headed back to FSB offices without further discussion.

Nikolai had just revealed that he had limited career upside, Tasia thought. He didn't understand the single most important attribute for advancement in the Russian intelligence service – the need to deny all accusations at all times regardless of the truth.

NINETEEN

STRELKOV LIFTED his right arm until it was parallel with the ground, and then swung it to the right as far as possible. He repeated the process three times in hopes he'd loosen up his shoulder but the pain returned. He suffered from arthritis now and then, probably from the strain of all the shooting he'd done through the years. Recently he'd forgotten about his injuries, until his daughter went and got herself arrested in Moscow this morning.

She'd joined a protest against the special military operation in Ukraine – no one dared call it a war in Russia for fear of being imprisoned. To express her outrage, she'd held a sign for the foreign press to see. The sign contained no words – it was just a blank piece of white cardboard – because public criticism of the special military operation also had been outlawed. But the cops had arrested her anyways, as they should have done. Russia was waging war in Ukraine to recoup its rightful place as one of the premier powers in the world. Those who didn't understand that needed to be educated immediately, including his daughter.

Strelkov had spent the morning on the telephone negotiating her release. Expunging the arrest from her record was going to cost him $500. Nothing was free in Russia, especially not justice. When he'd finally spoken to her, she'd informed him that the cop who had shoved her into the police car had twisted her arm behind her back. As a result, her shoulder felt as though it had been separated. Within the hour, of course, Strelkov's shoulder was killing him in sympathy with his daughter's injury.

He was popping some Naproxen for the pain when Ivanova walked in and briefed him on the operation at the hospital.

"I was just winning over one of the nurses as a legitimate patient," Ivanova said, "when, all of a sudden, she told me to get out of the room. I couldn't believe it. She'd just come back with some aspirin and anxiety meds, so something must have happened when she left the examination room for a few minutes."

"Nikolai?" Strelkov said.

"Had to be. Or the would-be patient he roughed up. One of them must have had a tell of some kind."

"No matter. You still accomplished your mission."

"I did?" Ivanova appeared perplexed.

"They treated your colleague even though he was wearing an enemy uniform. If they weren't treating soldiers—"

"Treating a soldier's wound and hiding him overnight aren't the same."

"Then they never would have let you through the front door, and the order wouldn't have been given to get rid of the soldier's uniform. As soon as he was admitted for treatment, they gave us all the proof we needed."

"I'm not so sure about that."

Ivanova seemed reluctant to accept the truth, Strelkov thought, no doubt because she was smart enough to understand that some quality healthcare workers might perish as a result of her fine work. If only she would stop thinking of them as human beings and realize they were merely Ukrainians.

"The hospital is acting as a shield for our enemies," Strelkov said. "That justifies an attack on the building."

"But according to international law," Ivanova said, "a hospital is supposed to lose its protected status during war only if it's doing something harmful to the enemy. Does treating a soldier qualify as being harmful to the enemy?"

"It did in Afghanistan and the Gaza Strip," Strelkov said. "We're just following the precedent set by the Americans and the Israelis. No one loves to bomb hospitals like the empires of lies. I want you to be careful around Nikolai from now on."

"Why?"

"There's a leak on our ship. Everyone knows it. The Ukrainians are one step ahead of us. It's all over the internet. The entire world knows it. And now something has come to my attention about young Nikolai."

"What's that?"

"When his class graduated from the Academy, they rented Mercedes G-Wagons and paraded like fools through Moscow. It made the papers and social media everywhere."

"I remember," Ivanova said. "The Boss got really angry."

Strelkov smiled. "There's the understatement of the day. He assigned them all to Siberia. Every last one of them."

"Nikolai was part of that class?" Ivanova said. "I had no idea."

"Neither did I. The reports said every single graduate was sent to Siberia but that wasn't true. Young Nikolai wasn't banished."

"Why not?" Ivanova said.

"Because he was the only graduate who refused to take part in that nonsense."

"Good for him, right? It jives with his academic record. He was first in his class, a savant with the computer."

Strelkov shrugged. "That's what I thought, until I started to wonder. There's a lot of peer pressure in the Academy, a constant push for conformity. It's relentless. You know that. How easy is it to go against your classmates?"

"Well, when you put it that way ..." Ivanova said.

"Maybe I'm wrong. Maybe Nikolai is just smarter than the rest and knows when to separate himself from the crowd. Or maybe ... "

"Or maybe he's a bit too smart," Tasia said.

"Exactly. That's why I want you to watch him very carefully, and report to me and me alone if you see any suspicious behavior."

"Yes, Colonel," she said.

Strelkov nodded. "One last thing. I'd like you to join me this evening for a special event. It's strictly professional. You'll meet some influential visitors from Moscow. Dress appropriately."

"Thank you, Colonel. Can you tell me anything else about the event? So that I dress appropriately."

Strelkov considered her question. "Wear your Sunday best. Something you'd be comfortable wearing to church, but that might earn a second glance from an influential superior, if you know what I mean."

A demure smile crossed her lips.

After she left, Strelkov met with the officer in charge of construction. The storage area in the building's cellar had been shuttered years ago due to flooding. Strelkov ordered the engineer to create a new staircase and build a small office for him in the basement. He needed a place where he could meditate, and perform certain duties on behalf of the Russian Federation that were best fulfilled in private.

Afterwards, Strelkov found Nikolai monitoring the filtration proceedings outside the building.

"Good work at the hospital today," Strelkov said.

"Thank you, Colonel. I wish we'd been able to stay inside a bit longer."

"We rarely get exactly what we wish for in life," Strelkov said. "Which is why we must celebrate every success no matter how minor it may seem. You're lucky to have Major Ivanova as your superior. She's sensitive but strong, supremely competent, don't you think?"

"Yes, sir. I consider myself lucky, for sure."

"Good. I want you to remember the chain of command here, it's very important. But from time to time, I may need to ask you for a special favor, the kind of favor that would stay between the two of us. Can I count on your discretion?"

"Absolutely, Colonel."

"Good," Strelkov said. "I understand you're a savant with the computer. Is that true?"

"I'm no genius, sir."

"I didn't ask if you were a genius. I asked if you're as capable as your record suggests?"

"I'm capable, Colonel. How can I help?"

"I'm curious about the backgrounds of all my lieutenants. There are three of them. One of them is your superior officer. I want you to start with her. Oh, I have their FSB backgrounds. But those were created many years ago before the internet became such a trove of information. I'd like a fresh look."

"I'd be glad to help, sir."

"We'll keep this between the two of us, yes?"

"Goes without saying, sir."

"Good man," Strelkov said. "Good man."

Before eating his ham sandwich for lunch, Strelkov called Moscow and informed FSB headquarters of Ivanova's discovery.

Less than an hour later, his building shook when the missiles hit the hospital thirty-two kilometers away. Eighty-four people died in the attack, including three children.

The latter was tragic, Strelkov thought. His count of re-settled children was up over 220,000. He regretted the death of the three youngsters.

Russia needed every one of them.

TWENTY

THE TRAIN from Kyiv screeched to a halt. A hissing noise followed. A moment later, the doors slid open.

Women and children descended down the steps onto the platform. They emerged from every doorway. The adults carried luggage and babies. The children held bags stuffed with clothing. Cats peeked from knapsacks and jacket pockets. Dogs barked from their carriers.

Adam craned his neck in every direction in search of Eva, but within a minute his attempt to stand his ground became futile. People, pets and possessions packed every inch of the platform. Their voices spoke of relief, confusion and uncertainty. They moved toward the main lobby as one.

The throng swallowed Adam and pushed him backwards. His foot landed awkwardly. He lost his balance and slammed into a boy beside him. The boy careened off Adam through a narrow gap in the crowd and toppled toward the tracks below. Adam regained his footing and blasted through the opening. He grabbed the boy by his wrist and pulled him to safety.

The boy looked to be about ten years old. He wore a sign on his chest attached to a leather shoelace tied around his neck.

The sign asked the reader to help deliver the boy to a family in Poland. The family's name and address followed. The boy's expression turned from fear to hope as soon as he saw Adam reading the message.

And then it turned to one of shock, for Adam had never let go of the boy's wrist. The process had begun the moment Adam had stopped his fall.

One beat, two beats, three beats passed and the boy's eyes began dancing in their sockets. He tried to pull away but Adam's energy had temporarily paralyzed him. His brain was functioning but his motor skills were incapacitated.

Adam closed his eyes. The obligatory seizure gave way to serenity. The images came rapid-fire and faded just as quickly, until only the most indelible ones remained

A soccer star signs a ball for the boy with his parents beaming beside him ...

Soldiers wearing red and white arm bands tie his father to a tree ...

The soldiers take turns shooting at his father's head until his face is riddled with bullet holes ...

The boy runs into the house and bursts into a bedroom ...

His mother lies naked and lifeless on a bed, her neck grotesquely twisted ...

The soldiers race into the house after the boy ...

He slips through an open window and hides in the outhouse ...

A soldier with blue and yellow arm bands lifts the boy from a hole filled with human waste ...

The boy scrubs his body with soap as other soldiers hose him down ...

A group of villagers affix the sign to the boy's neck beside a train ...

The boy looks out the window of a moving train with a blank stare ...

Adam's eyes snapped open. He wanted to say something to make the boy's pain go away. He wanted to do something to guarantee the boy would never suffer again.

"Let go of his hand," a woman shouted behind him.

Adam released the boy's wrist. The woman called the boy by name, glared at Adam as though he were a pervert, and whisked the child away.

Adam pivoted toward the crowd. A forlorn-looking woman his age fell into him. He grasped her shoulders out of sheer instinct. She released the handle of her suitcase and grabbed his arm to steady herself. Adam put his hands around hers. A tattoo in the shape of a city's confines appeared below her wrist. Eight letters accompanied the drawing –

M-A-R-I-U-P-O-L.

One beat, two beats, three beats passed. The woman stood paralyzed. Adam's eyes closed. Convulsions gave way to calmness. The images came rapid-fire and faded just as quickly

The woman plays fetch with a black Labrador retriever puppy at a beach ...

A grown black Labrador retriever guards the woman and a four-year old girl, who sits coloring a book in a basement wearing pink slippers ...

Dust falls from the quaking ceiling above ...

With the ceiling no longer shaking, the woman races up the

stairs and stirs a pot of soup in the kitchen until the walls start to shake ...

The woman races down the stairs and holds the girl beneath the quaking ceiling ...

With the ceiling no longer shaking, the woman races back up the stairs to stir her soup again ...

An explosion sends the woman flying against a kitchen wall and knocks her out ...

The woman steps through rubble in search of her stairs but cannot find them ...

In her blown-out basement, she finds the torn remnant of a dog collar ...

Beyond the dog collar lies a solitary pink slipper ...

Outside a bombed-out apartment building, a burnt-out missile lies on the grass ...

The army green missile casing contains three Russian words written in white paint ...

For the Children ...

Adam opened his eyes and released his grasp of the woman.

"I'm so sorry for your loss," he said, without thinking.

Disbelief flashed in her eyes. She promptly retrieved her suitcase, squeezed into a gap among the crowd and squirmed away from Adam. He shifted his stance so his eyes could follow her out. She glanced over her shoulder at him with fear and fascination, and then continued shuffling forward with the others

"Help."

Adam lowered his gaze.

An elderly lady wearing a scarf around her head stood directly in front of him. She was carrying a single piece of luggage – a handheld brown leather suitcase from a prior century.

"I don't know where to go," she said in Ukrainian. "I don't know what to do." She reached out and took Adam's hand in both of hers. "Please help me."

Three beats passed, Adam closed his eyes, and the subsequent events unfolded as usual.

A young woman in an A-line dress poses for photographs at an art gallery beside a sculpture priced at 1,000 Deutschmarks ...

German soldiers and Gestapo officers herd citizens onto trains ...

The young artist and her daughter are among them ...

The daughter gathers with other children in a prison camp surrounded by barbed wire ...

Current-day soldiers wearing red and white arm bands carry sculptures, paintings, jewelry, a microwave oven, and a television into a living room ...

The elderly woman addresses the soldiers defiantly ...

One of the soldiers strikes the woman in the face and knocks her down ...

A tank with the letter Z emblazoned on its skirt reduces a house to rubble ...

The elderly woman looks on in tears ...

Adam opened his eyes. The elderly lady was still holding his hand, unperturbed and unafraid.

"I'll help you," he said. "Come with me."

"Where are we going?" she said.

"Outside. To find a volunteer."

By the time they worked their way out of the station, lines

had formed near the makeshift crisis center, and all the volunteers were busy. Adam looked around for Mikey, but he was nowhere to be found. There was no place to sit down.

Adam guided the elderly woman to a shady spot near the curb. Then he picked out the oldest of the volunteers, apologized for interrupting, and whispered a few words into her ear. The volunteer, who bristled at first, changed her attitude once she heard what Adam had to say.

"My name is Pasia," the elderly lady said, after the volunteer came over to help.

The volunteer asked a series of background questions. Pasia answered them.

"The most important question is, where do you want to go?" the volunteer said.

"I'm alone. I have no one. Where should I go?"

"Poland is right over the border," the volunteer said. "The Polish people are so generous to Ukrainian refugees." Then she pointed at all the cars with foreign license plates. "But there are people from other countries here, too. They have all come out of the goodness of their hearts to help."

A pair of men emerged from a hatchback with German plates. They came over and introduced themselves. The older man was an architect, the younger one a physical therapist. They discussed languages and learned that everyone spoke German.

"We have a spare bedroom in our flat in Berlin," the older man said.

"And you remind me so much of my grandmother," the younger man said.

"That is so nice of you to say." Pasia adjusted her scarf. As she lifted her arm, her sleeve pulled back to expose a portion of the concentration camp entry number on her left forearm.

When the tattoo appeared, the younger man touched the older one on the shoulder.

"If you would like to come to Germany," the older one said. "We would very happy to have you stay with us until you get settled."

"Yes," the younger one said, his tone betraying his eagerness. "You could stay as long as you need. And we would do everything we can to help you."

Pasia thanked them and turned to Adam. "What should I do? You must tell me. You're a wise young man. I know I can trust you. Should I go to Poland or to Germany?"

Adam considered her choice. "Only you can decide. Poland has been incredible, but it's taken in so many refugees. And Germany is a richer country."

"Germany? Hmm ... "

The older German stepped forward and let his arms fall to his sides. He bowed his head slightly, and then raised it and cleared his throat.

"Madame," he said, "I'm certain I speak for my entire country when I say that it would be our honor and privilege to give you a home in Germany, and we will all take very good care of you."

Pasia turned to Adam, who nodded.

"You look like nice boys," Pasia said. "Okay, thank you. Thank you. I will go to Germany. I will go home."

They said their good-byes. Pasia held Adam's gaze for an extra beat. She didn't say anything or change her expression, and neither did Adam. Then she turned and left with her new flatmates.

Adam bounded around the square looking for Mikey. He pictured Pasia arriving at her new home and walking the streets of Berlin with a smile on her face. The ether of his imagination propelled Adam to circle around the front of the station a second time before reality set in.

The refugees' memories flashed before his eyes. They played over and over in a continuous loop. The boy's memories became Adam's memories. He relived the pain of his mother's and father's murders. The woman's memories followed. In his mind, Adam became a parent. The subsequent anguish of the woman's daughter's death spurred waves of sorrow, the likes of which he'd never experienced.

What kind of world leader murdered innocent civilians? What kind of country allowed its military to label missiles intended for children? How could a government claiming to be de-Nazifying a country with no Nazis destroy the life of a Holocaust survivor?

Why couldn't everyone just be a better man?

Adam began hyperventilating. He picked up his pace and hurried away from the station. He knew what was going to happen next. Fighting the panic would only exacerbate it, and yet he could do nothing else. The more he tried to slow his breathing, the faster it became. He'd had difficulties absorbing Terzic's pain in Zermatt. The military policeman was just one man. What he'd just absorbed was exponentially more. And he had his own memories on top of it – oh, did he have memories ...

Adam took aim for the corner of a building across the street. If he could just get there before he passed out the people at the train station wouldn't see, they wouldn't laugh and jeer at him, or mock him ...

He rounded the corner and slid down against the wall so that he wouldn't fall and hit his head.

The last image he saw was an imaginary one of Eva, telling him everything would be okay, that his brain would tell his lungs to keep breathing even after he passed out.

TWENTY-ONE

ADAM AWOKE to the sound of a train's whistle.

He realized he was lying on the ground. The faint smell of Italian food drifted into his nose. An image of a solitary pink slipper flashed in his eyes, and an overwhelming sense of despair possessed him. His daughter had died in the missile attack, Adam thought. So had his dog. He could not comprehend the thought of continuing life without them

And then he remembered waiting for the train from Kyiv and realized the girl was someone else's daughter, and the dog belonged to another person, too. He wasn't a parent – he'd acquired a refugee's memory. Adam recalled the boy with the sign around his neck, Pasia, and the panic that had ensued. He was in Lviv, he thought, and Eva had not been on the train.

When he lifted his head, he realized that it hadn't been touching concrete but rather a blue article of clothing turned into a makeshift pillow. Adam sat up and unfolded a lightly insulated hiking jacket. He rubbed his eyes with his forearm and looked around.

Mikey sat shivering on a cinderblock, so low to the ground

he appeared to be squatting. The wind whipped the sleeves of his t-shirt. He swayed back and forth rhythmically as though trying to keep warm. Adam's suitcase rested beside him.

"Perhaps now you'd be interested in some of those medications I told you about?" Mikey said.

"Where were you?" Adam said. "When I came out of the station ... I looked around for you ... you weren't there."

"I was there the whole time. I saw you with the grandmother. I saw the thing with the Germans. I was in the background, like a good supporting actor is supposed to be, not getting in the way of my leading man."

Adam tossed Mikey his jacket. "What time is it?"

Mikey checked his phone. "About ten-thirty. Was Eva on the train?"

"What do you think?" Adam said.

Mikey didn't answer.

"Is your uncle back in town?" Adam said.

"I don't know. He didn't say what time he was coming back."

"Call him," Adam said. "Or, no ... better yet ... give me his number."

Mikey sent a digital copy of his uncle's contact information to Adam's phone. Adam called him and left a voice mail. The greeting that preceded the prompt wasn't personalized – it was the recording of a generic female voice asking the caller to leave a message.

After ending the call, Adam studied Mikey.

"You're telling me the truth about everything, right?" Adam said. "You don't know Eva. You have an uncle who met her, and he really is coming back to Lviv today."

"That's what he told me." Mikey didn't flinch. "You know what I know. I don't know nothing else."

Adam grabbed the handle to his luggage. "What's the fastest way to the City Centre?"

"Tram. Come. I'll show you."

The ride on the tram took two minutes. When they emerged in the center of Lviv, Adam recognized his surroundings but couldn't recall specific locations. He'd only visited the town once, and more than ten years had passed since then.

"Those sour cherry *varenyky*," Mikey said. "The ones you're supposed to be building an appetite for ... not everyone makes them. I'm guessing she had a special place in mind?"

"Café Centaur," Adam said.

"Cool," Mikey said. "There's a nice hotel around the corner from there. When soccer teams from the Premier League come to town to play FC Lviv they stay there. A lot of the players eat at Centaur. I once got David Neres' autograph there. He's the best player in the league. He plays for Shakhtar Donetsk. He escaped with some other Brazilians to Romania when the war started. I heard the Russians were after them, to take them as hostages. I heard it wasn't easy."

"It's never easy," Adam said. "That's why they call it an escape."

"I guess you're right. I never thought of it that way. You sound like you know what you're talking about."

"One thing my mentor taught me," Adam said, "if you don't know what you're talking about, it's best not to say anything at all."

They passed the Main Square and found Centaur around the corner on a cobblestone street facing a mansion that had been converted into an apartment building. The café featured a terrace with outdoor seating that spanned the entire length of the restaurant. Most of the tables were occupied. Adam rolled his suitcase under the awning beside an empty one.

He pulled a hundred-dollar bill from his wallet as discreetly as possible, folded it in half, and handed it to Mikey.

"Thanks for all your help," Adam said.

Mikey glanced at the bill. When he spied the currency and denomination, his eyes widened. He grabbed the bill and thanked Adam, so excited he could barely enunciate the words.

"I'll stick around," Mikey said. "You never know what else you might need."

"I'm good," Adam said. "I work alone. Take care, Mykhailo."

Mikey pursed his lips and dropped his head for a moment. Then he glanced at Adam one last time, nodded and left.

An impeccably mannered male server with a noticeable limp took his order for a bottle of flat water and a Coca Cola Light. A few minutes later, he returned with Adam's beverages on a tray. As he poured the drinks, Adam wondered what Eva had planned for him next. All he knew for certain was that he was supposed to be prepared to eat sour cherry *varenyky* at this restaurant.

When the server finished pouring the drinks, he sat down in the chair opposite Adam. He winced as he lowered his hips onto the seat. Dark creases surrounded his eyes.

"Hello, Mr. Ziegler," he said, in English. "My name is Ivan Boyko. I'm Mykhailo's uncle."

He offered his hand. Adam shook it.

"I thought you were a professor," Adam said.

"It's hard to make a good living as an assistant professor in Ukraine," Boyko said. "So, I moonlight here on weekends once in a while. Don't tell Mykhailo. He doesn't know. He'd get mad. Think it's beneath me."

"How did you recognize me?" Adam said.

"Eva gave me a general description."

"How long have you known her?" Adam said.

"I don't know her," Boyko said. "Not really. She called me

on the phone and asked if she could come see me during my office hours. Said she wanted to discuss my work with me."

"When was this?" Adam said.

"Oh, about a week ago."

"What kind of work do you do?"

"I teach politology," Boyko said.

"Politology?"

"The theory, analysis and prediction of political systems and behavior. You've heard of the Nuremberg trials that revealed the truth about all the Nazi crimes and atrocities of World War II? My doctoral thesis argued that Russia will eventually incite a nuclear war unless trials are held for the crimes and atrocities it committed when the Soviet Union existed."

"And Eva was interested in this?" Adam said.

"Shouldn't everyone be interested in this?"

Adam shrugged.

"If the free world had demanded a Nuremberg equivalent when the Soviet Union was disbanded in 1991, every Russian would understand the magnitude of the horrors committed by their leaders. KGB officers wouldn't be in charge of the country, and there would be no war in Ukraine. They would understand that Stalin killed more people than Hitler. That their country was poisoned a hundred years ago and they need to administer the antidote."

"So, Russia is toxic and the world is screwed. That's not news to me."

"My conclusion is the world is not screwed. My conclusion is one of hope. That after such a trial, Russia can become a democracy and a good citizen, the kind you find in Europe."

Adam considered the implications for the package. He was working for his client. His client was a Russian. What if the package really could alter the course of the war?

Not his problem, Adam thought. He was just a courier.

Victor found the business, Adam delivered the package, and the client paid the fee. That process defined his existence and he wasn't going to alter it for any reason.

Evidently Eva had developed other interests. That didn't affect him.

"I thought Eva might be a student," Boyko said. "So, I checked with the registrar, just out of curiosity. But they had no record of her. She left me some money, to pay for your meal. I put in your order when I saw you. I'll go check with the kitchen and see if it's ready. In the meantime, here's some reading material for you."

The professor lifted the napkin that covered his tray and uncovered an envelope. It was identical to the one that Eva had used in Switzerland from the Zermatterhof Hotel. After the professor left, Adam opened it and read the note.

Adam, my Adam,

After you left me, I had to rely on the kindness of strangers to survive. One such man lives in a village called Ruta. His name is Luca. I owe him so much. He's in desperate need of help to acquire a most important package. Only you can help him. No one else. Help him with his package, and I will return yours to you. But you must do it now. You must help him tonight!

XO,

Eva

Boyko returned with a plate of sour cherry *varenyky* and sour cream.

"You know, I hope you don't mind my saying this," Boyko said, "but if I had a girl like that, I'd probably do anything for her."

After the professor returned inside, Adam wolfed down his meal. He'd vowed not to go further east beyond Lviv but both he and Victor had known that was a lie. The professor's final words had rung true, just as surely as the dumplings blew his mind.

When he was finished, Adam began to work his phone in search of transportation. As he searched for a driving service, a familiar voice piped up behind him.

"I just want to remind you," Mikey said. "If you're going someplace where a weapon would come in handy, which is pretty much anywhere in this country, I can be your man. Glock 17, Sig Sauer P320, Baretta 92 ..."

Adam continued typing. "No thank you."

"Already have a gun?" Mikey said. "Cool. I've got bullets. Roundnose lead, hollow point, full metal jacket ... Anything you want, I can get it for you."

Adam punched a letter on his phone and wheeled around to face Mikey.

"Give me a break, please. I don't need ammunition, I need a ride."

"You need a ride?" Mikey said.

"I need a ride."

"Why didn't you say so? Where are you going?"

"A village called Ruta," Adam said.

"Never heard of it." Mikey worked his smart phone, then looked up. "That's fifty-six kilometers outside Kyiv. You sure about that? You know what's happening there, right?"

"Do you know anyone available for hire? I'll pay top dollar."

"You're asking someone to drive you close to a hot zone so it's gonna cost." Mikey thought about it for a moment. "But yeah. I think I know a guy. A guy who knows a guy, you know? Come with me."

They hustled to the corner nearest the Main Square where

vehicles were allowed. Mikey asked him to wait by a traffic sign while he went to see a friend.

Fifteen minutes later a beaten and battered Jeep Cherokee roared up to Adam. Mikey rolled down the driver's side window.

"All you had to do was ask, Little Brother."

TWENTY-TWO

THE DRIVE from Lviv took eight hours.

Shortly after they left the major metropolitan area, they passed a convoy of trucks sticking closely together.

"That," Mikey said, "is most likely a delivery of weapons from our good friends in Europe, South Korea, or America."

"How can you tell?" Adam said.

"Easy. Check out the license plates."

Adam studied the license plate holders of each truck as they passed them.

"There aren't any," he said.

"There you go," Mikey said.

Adam learned to keep his passport handy. Mikey had to stop at five checkpoints fortified with sand bags and cinderblocks along the way. The Ukrainian Territorial Defense volunteers at the first two checkpoints were unarmed but had cases of Molotov cocktails handy. The volunteers at the later checkpoints were heavily armed. Once they became comfortable that Adam and Mikey weren't Russian saboteurs, all the volunteers praised them for traveling such a long distance to help an old Ukrainian friend in need.

Fewer than a thousand people lived in the village of Ruta. Their homes swayed in the wind, run down cottages held together by rusty nails, warped two-by-fours, and constant prayer. Luca's property was the most dilapidated of the bunch. Bald tires, hand-held farming tools, planters, and a variety of junk surrounded his home. Even the quarter moon in the sky looked spent, a charcoal silhouette suspended in the night. Another visitor might have wondered how these people survived during the best of times, let alone during the war. But as soon as he saw Luca's yard, Adam knew how he made a living – he was a scavenger. He acquired what he could and sold it to whoever would buy.

"These are Romani people," Mikey said, as he parked the Jeep.

"How do you know?" Adam said.

"Look around you. Not sure we can trust this guy."

"Why not?" Adam said.

"They have a sketchy reputation in Ukraine."

"Why?"

"They stick to their own," Mikey said. "They don't care about the community. They don't consider themselves Ukrainian. Just Romani. Be careful, that's all I'm saying."

Adam knocked on the splintered front door gently for fear it might collapse. As he and Mikey waited, artillery fire sounded in the distance – quick, sudden blasts that reminded Adam he wasn't in Lviv anymore.

A man whipped the door open. He looked like a crazed gypsy serial killer with streaks of gray in his hair and beard. When he saw Adam and Mikey, his eyes bugged out and he dropped to his knees. He raised his arms over his head and looked up at the ceiling.

"Thank you, Lord," he said. "I asked for a savior, for a man among men, and you sent me two. I am not worthy of this gift ..."

He lowered his gaze and grinned at Adam and Mikey. "But I'll turn into a tidy profit in your name. That I promise."

He stood up and told Adam and Mikey to come in. The front door opened directly into a kitchen with a partially collapsed ceiling and piles of filthy dishes. A fluorescent light dangled from an exposed beam above. The air smelled musty and the walls contained splotches of yellow mold.

They introduced themselves. Luca offered them cabbage soup and water. They both declined.

"Another platoon is coming," Luca said. "It'll be here by tomorrow morning so we have to make our move tonight."

"A platoon?" Mikey said. "Whose platoon?"

"How do you know Eva?" Adam said.

"The Russians are down to two squads," Luca said. "Twelve soldiers. They're dug in beside the bridge. Eleven of them sleep while one patrols the perimeter of the camp."

"Eva Vovk," Adam said. "When was the last time you spoke with her? Is she nearby?"

"What exactly are you planning to do?" Mikey said.

"Give the mothers some peace of mind," Luca said.

"What mothers?" Mikey said.

"Come ... come to the other room and I will show you."

Luca led Adam and Mikey to the living room next door. He showed them a schematic of an unremarkable bridge. The Russians had taken control of it, he said. If their assault on Ukraine spread west, the bridge would prove to be a strategic asset. The mass grave could be found a quarter mile beyond their encampment along the banks of the Red Ruta River, Luca said.

"Am I getting this right?" Adam said. "You want to risk being killed by Russian soldiers so that you can steal the bodies of dead Ukrainian soldiers who were already killed by the same Russian soldiers?"

"The Russians don't care about the living," Luca said, "and they don't care about the dead. Not theirs, or ours."

"I'm so sorry," Adam said. "It's terrible. It really is. But to risk dying for the dead, that I don't understand."

"It's not for the dead," Luca said. "It's for the living. It's for the mothers."

"You mean it's for you," Mikey said. "You want us to risk our lives so you can sell dead soldiers for money, pretending you're doing it for the mothers."

Adam glared at Mikey.

"No," Luca said. "It's not like that"

"You're lucky I'm just the driver here," Mikey said.

Adam smacked Mikey in the shoulder with an open palm and continued glaring at him.

The room turned silent.

Adam turned to Luca. "You didn't answer my questions before. How do you know Eva?"

"I know her well," Luca said.

"I didn't ask you how well you knew her," Adam said. "I asked you how do you know her?"

Luca scratched his beard as he eyed Adam. "Life is so hard right now ... there's so much going on ... I forget about these things, you know? But if we took care of this business before the platoon comes, while we can still cross the bridge ..." Luca smiled. "My memory might come back to me. Yes, yes. I think it just might."

"I bet it might," Mikey said.

He looked at Adam, his eyes practically begging Adam to leave immediately.

But that, of course, was not viable course of action from Adam's perspective. This was what Eva wanted, he thought, for him to help Luca.

Adam studied the schematic. "So, what's your plan?"

Mikey rolled his eyes.

Adam glared at him yet again. "Hey. We're doing this. You don't want to be a part of it, don't be. I'll pay you for your time and you can leave now if you want."

Mikey averted Adam's eyes.

Luca outlined a cumbersome strategy that involved two of them crossing the river by raft, exhuming the bodies, and then transporting them to safety one at a time. If they executed his plan to perfection, the extraction of the dead soldiers' bodies would take six hours.

"It's a good plan," Adam said, so as not to offend Luca. "But we'd be pulling a lot of exposure."

"The mass grave is far enough away from their camp," Luca said. "Their patrol doesn't go anywhere near there."

Adam shrugged. "We'll be making noise with our feet ... with our shovels ... There's no margin for error. These guys aren't security guards who ask questions first and shoot later. They're soldiers trained to shoot and not ask questions. The longer we're out there, the greater the chances we get shot."

Luca appeared despondent.

"So how do we do this?" Mikey said. "If this is something we've got to do, then I'm going to do my fair share. But it has to be a good plan. It has to be a smart plan." He cast a look of disdain at Luca. "It can't be two fools and a gypsy con-man."

"I don't appreciate that word," Luca said.

"I don't appreciate you hustling us," Mikey said.

"Okay, okay," Adam said. "We're all on the same side here, right? Everybody has an agenda, everybody wants something. Maybe there's a way everyone can get paid the way he wants to get paid, and some good comes out of it, too."

"You think that's possible?" Mikey said.

"Everything is possible," Adam said. "Where there's a will, there's a way."

Of course there was a way, Adam thought. There was always a way. If Victor knew what he was thinking right now he would have suffered a stroke on the spot. But this is what Eva wanted, so this is what Eva was going to get.

"We have to use the only advantage at our disposal," Adam said.

"We have an advantage?" Mikey said.

"We do," Adam said. "We have speed."

"Speed?" Luca said.

"You guys are going to be the mules," Adam said.

Mikey and Luca looked at each other and then turned to Adam.

"And what are you going to be?" Mikey said.

Adam sighed. "I'm going to be the rabbit."

TWENTY-THREE

ADAM STOOD a hundred meters west of the bridge waiting for his eyes to adjust to the night. Based on his prior experiences under similar circumstances, that would take approximately twenty-three minutes. Mikey was leaning against Luca's ramshackle Tacoma pick-up truck, which was parked in the shoulder beside the road. Luca stood beside him. Mikey appeared calm while Luca kept tapping his toes on the ground.

Luca pulled out a cigarette.

"Please don't do that," Adam whispered.

Luca glanced at him.

"Bad for the night vision," Adam said.

The flash of a lighter could also be noticed, as could a burning ember or the smell of nicotine if the wind carried it towards the Russians. But Adam went with the least obvious explanation to avoid embarrassing Luca. Clearly, the man did his scavenging during the day and did not solve crossword puzzles for fun.

"So, what," Mikey said, glancing at Luca. "You got family or something?"

Luca smiled. "Two girls, two boys. My wife took them to her brother's home in Romania once the war started. My children, they said to me, *Papa, are you going to stay and fight?* And I said, yes, *your papa will stay and fight.* But the truth is I'm a coward. I can't imagine firing a gun, killing another human being. So, I do what I can for my neighbors. They know they can count on me, no matter how ugly the job is."

Mikey didn't respond, which given his attitude toward Luca thus far, suggested he approved of what he'd heard. Good for Luca, Adam thought. Self-deprecation had a way of changing people's opinions of oneself.

"Family coming back when the war is over?" Mikey said.

"Yes, that will be something," Luca said. "When they come back, I want my children to be proud of me. Proud that their father stayed. In the meantime, I hear there are telephones that let you see the person who is calling you. Intelligent phones, yes?"

Mikey pulled his mobile device from his pocket. "Smartphone."

"Yes, that one," Luca said. "If I can make enough money to buy one of those, I could see my children every day while they're gone." He shook his head. "Now that ... that would be something."

They waited quietly. Images sharpened. Branches and leaves came into focus. The individual planks that comprised the bridge popped. When twenty-three minutes passed, Adam put the binoculars back in his knapsack and strapped it to his back.

Luca and Mikey straightened. Luca tossed his cigarette and stomped on it even though he'd never lit it.

"Don't be a hero," Adam said. "You hear gunshots, get out of here. Regroup at Luca's."

"What if they take you prisoner?" Luca said.

"That's highly unlikely," Adam said.

"How can you be so sure?" Mikey said.

"They'd have to catch me first."

Adam hustled to the edge of the bridge. He took cover behind a pillar and retrieved his binoculars. He scanned the north side of the road. Mounded soil revealed a network of trenches that stretched beyond his sight. A sentry sat on the bulging roots of an oak snacking on something, rifle leaning against the tree beside him. None of the remaining eleven soldiers were visible.

Adam's confidence rose a notch. The Russians soldiers were expecting reinforcements, not hostilities. They were resting accordingly.

Adam put the binoculars away and scampered the length of the bridge. He slowed down at the far end, just long enough to estimate some distances for future reference. The nearest trench could be found two hundred feet away on the other side of the road. The sentry was sitting a hundred feet beyond it.

A glorious soundtrack accompanied Adam's visual reconnaissance. Water cascaded below him. It was much louder than he'd expected. It drowned out his heartbeat and the sound of his own breathing. It would mute the sound of his footsteps and his shovel, as well.

Adam circled around the southeast corner of the bridge and descended to the river bank. Luca had told him to look for a mounded ridge twenty feet away from the river's edge. Adam followed the river and found it a quarter mile away from the bridge. The mass grave presented itself in the form of a rectangle three times the size of a coffin. The sight of the mounded dirt was preceded by the arrival of a most unpleasant odor.

Adam pulled out the work gloves and the folding shovel Luca had provided from his knapsack and began to dig. The shovel moved the moist earth easily. He worked the entire area, removing six inches of dirt at a time. When he was finished with his first pass, he took the shovel and thrust it deeply into the ground. On his first two tries, the blade sank freely into the earth. On the third try, it hit something another six inches below the ground.

Adam continued to clean the area. The more he progressed, the worse the stench became. The shovel came into contact with something hard on several occasions. When he'd cleared another six inches of dirt throughout the area, Adam folded the shovel to form a ninety-degree angle and used it as a hoe to pull the loosened dirt to the sides. Twenty minutes after he'd started, the outline of two bodies appeared.

Adam brushed dirt away from the corpses with his gloved hands. A pair of legs in camo pants revealed themselves, but they didn't belong to the same person. Similar sightings followed. Arm and legs had become intertwined, and Adam had to untangle them to separate the bodies. By then the stench had become so bad he was taking shallow breaths. Adam wished he had some menthol he could have applied under his nose.

And then he saw the first soldier's face. Insects emerged from the white foam gathered at his lips and disappeared into his bloated nose. His cheeks appeared disproportionately large, the skin green and slick.

Adam threw up onto the ground beside the grave.

When he was finished, he kicked the shovel aside in frustration and hurried away from the burial site. He bounded to the river's edge, splashed some water on face, and focused on his breathing for thirty seconds. Then he took a deep breath and returned to unearth the remaining five bodies.

Adam realized that he'd completely messed up his projections. He'd thought he'd be able to carry two of the bodies at a time, the way he'd done in Siberia, when the transport plane had crashed in Buryatia. But those people had been alive. They'd been able to lean their bodies into him so that he could stand up with one on each shoulder. In this case, he was dealing with dead people and dead weight. There was no way he'd be able to lift a second body while already holding one. As a result, he'd have to make six runs instead of three.

He hoisted the first body over his shoulder and raced back towards the bridge. He paused after ascending the hill when his eyes were at bridge-level. When he detected no change to the Russians' positions, he turned left and sprinted across the wooden planks.

Five minutes later, Luca and Mikey removed the soldier's body from his shoulder and placed it in a black bag.

"How was it?" Mikey said.

"So far so good," Adam said.

He turned and raced back to the burial ground.

The four ensuing trips mirrored the first one, except for the time it took for Adam to complete the runs. Fatigue gradually set in. Each run was successively slower. Unearthing the bodies and moving five of them had taken ninety minutes. But he had only one body to go, Adam thought. Even if that one took half an hour round-trip, he would have bested Luca's plan by four hours. His strategy had been the right one.

As he approached the bridge with the sixth body slung over his shoulder, Adam saw smoke rising from a cluster of bushes along his path. He stopped and listened, but the sound of water rushing and his lungs working prevented him from discerning any noises. He took ten additional steps forward and stopped to listen again.

He heard two distinct voices, he thought, both male

A Russian soldier emerged from the thicket. He held a joint instead of a rifle. He stared with disbelief at Adam.

Adam bolted right and raced toward the road. Three seconds later a whistle shrieked from where the soldier had been standing. One short, one long ... one short, one long ... The alarm had been sounded. The sentry would be rushing to wake the other soldiers ...

Buryatia flashed before his eyes. A burning plane ... gasoline trickling from the fuel tank toward the fire ... eight passengers trapped, some of them injured. As a teen, Adam had always been the fastest skater on the ice, but it was at that moment in Siberia that Adam learned there was something profoundly different about him. It was then that he discovered that when his fight or flight instinct kicked in – when his life was threatened – he could move at a speed beyond the capability of a normal human being.

Adam burst onto the road and turned left.

A soldier stood before the bridge. He aimed his rifle.

A shot rang out.

Within a nanosecond of the trigger being pulled, Adam sprinted across the road into the Russian camp. The bullet sailed behind him. Three or four soldiers had climbed out of their encampments. They appeared to Adam as faint images, tall reeds in an open field. He passed two of them so quickly their eyes couldn't follow him, and then saw a third Russian standing dead ahead, rifle raised. He fired, but by the time the bullet exited the barrel Adam had leaped into a trench.

He landed five feet away from a soldier stirring from sleep. Adam vaulted onto the soldier's body with his right foot and catapulted himself forward. He tore through the maze of trenches, body slung over his shoulder, pivoting at corners and annihilating the straightaways at an unfathomable pace.

He made certain to execute turns that kept him moving

south by southwest. When his gut told him he was close to the bridge, he jumped up to ground level and slowed down to study his location. He heard shouting and screaming coming from all directions.

A Russian soldier wheeled toward him, ten feet away, pistol in hand. Adam powered forward and slammed into him with the dead soldier's body. The armed soldier toppled to the ground. His gun flew out of his hand.

Adam took aim for the far side of the bridge, and in a count of three ... two ... one ... obliterated the distance in between. Halfway to the other side, however, he had a strange sensation that he'd passed a living thing – an animal, perhaps, crouched low to the ground ...

Adam continued shredding distance beyond the bridge until the gunshots became echoes in the distance. He slowed down long before the pick-up truck came into sight to prevent Mikey and Luca from seeing him at top speed. When he arrived, however, Adam saw that Luca was alone.

"Where's Mikey?" Adam said.

Luca nodded toward the bridge. "I told him not to go."

Adam realized it was Mikey he'd seen at the bridge.

Luca and Adam lifted the corpse into an open body bag. As Luca slipped an errant arm into the storage area so that the zipper could close, Adam spied a patch with red, blue and white colors.

"Wait a minute," he said. "These are dead *Russian* soldiers?"

Luca shrugged. "The Ukrainians took their dead with them when they retreated to Kyiv. The Russian soldiers ... they threw their own into a mass grave. But even Russian soldiers have mothers."

A minute later, Mikey showed up with a rifle slung over his shoulder, spent and out-of-breath. He was looking at Adam as soon as he arrived, and continued firing glances in his direction as he walked around, hands on hips, gasping for air, trying to catch his breath.

Adam had seen that look a few times before.

It was the look of someone who'd seen a demonstration of skills beyond the capability of a human being.

TWENTY-FOUR

ADAM WAS TEMPTED to pepper Luca with questions about Eva as soon as they drove away, but his instincts told him to wait. Luca was determined to sell the dead bodies this evening. While Mikey drove, Luca placed a call on his vintage flip phone from the passenger seat beside him. A terse and coded exchange ensued between him and another party. The only thing Adam comprehended was that they were headed to a rendezvous point twenty-four kilometers northeast, closer to occupied Russian territory.

"What I don't understand is this," Mikey said. "The Russians are going to pay you for these bodies, right?"

"Unless you want to buy them," Luca said.

"Funny," Mikey said.

"Then why aren't you laughing?" Luca said.

"I am on, the inside," Mikey said. "Why would they do that when their own soldiers knew where they were since they're the ones who buried them? I mean, it's ridiculous, right?"

Luca told Mikey to take a turn onto a primary road with wider lanes.

"The Russian Army thought they'd take Kyiv in two days,"

Luca said. "So, they came here with no plan for what to do with their dead – they didn't expect to have any. Some soldiers just leave their brothers where they fall. Others bury them. Now the bodies are starting to add up and there's still no plan. But mothers are asking questions. And now that mothers are asking questions, someone in Russia cares. And when someone cares about a product, there's profit to be made."

"Enter Luca," Mikey said.

"I am who I am," Luca said.

"Yes, you are," Mikey said.

"You've done this before?" Adam said.

"With bodies?" Luca said. "No. This is a first."

"So how do you know you can trust these people you're meeting tonight?" Adam said.

"I've dealt with them before," Luca said. "Agricultural goods, mostly. They're kind of a middle-man for the government. They know me. It's good. It should be good. I think it will be good."

Adam caught Mikey's eye in the rearview mirror and could tell they were thinking the same thing – it was entirely possible that the most dangerous part of the evening had yet to arrive.

The location of the rendezvous did not allay Adam's fears. They turned onto an access road and drove three kilometers to an abandoned paper mill. Light came from a fire burning inside an industrial barrel in front of the main building. Two hulking Mercedes SUVs gleamed on one side. A military transport vehicle with a canvas cover idled on the other.

Five rugged-looking men were sitting on square crates around the fire, rifles and vodka bottles by their sides. A sixth man, the only one who'd shaved any time recently, sat apart from the others on a metal folding chair. He was drinking from a thermos.

As soon as Mikey pulled in, two men came over with their

weapons and motioned for him to park fifty feet away from the other vehicles. They told everyone to step out of the truck, and all three of them obliged.

"Luca, Luca," one of the men said, "who are these assholes?"

Luca introduced Adam and Mikey. The first man patted them down, while the second searched the truck for weapons. They took Mikey's rifle and promised to return it after the meeting. Afterwards, they examined each of the body bags together. When they were satisfied, they told Adam and Mikey to get back in the car, and motioned for Luca to come with them.

Mikey climbed back into the driver's seat and Adam sat beside him.

"Keep your window rolled down," Adam said, "and don't say a word. Just listen."

The armed Russians flanked Luka as he stood before the others near the fire.

"Luca, Luca," one of them said. "Who's the dumbest guy in any room?"

Luca widened his smile and spread his arms out wide. "Luca is."

The men laughed and drank from their bottles.

"Luca, Luca," another man said. "If you had to give my rifle a blowjob to get this deal done, would you do it?"

"No problem," Luca said.

More laughter.

"Luca, Luca," the man said. "Get down on your knees and show me how you'd do it."

Luca dropped to his knees and pretended he was performing oral sex on a man.

The Russians cheered.

"Luca, Luca," a different man said, "if my rifle wanted to fuck you in the ass, would you let it?"

Luca smiled. "No problem."

"Luca, Luca," the man continued, "Take off your pants and stick your ass up in the air. My rifle wants to see if you've got back."

The men howled.

Luca obliged.

They cheered as he undressed, and whistled as he followed the instructions he'd been given.

"Luca, Luca," the man added, "with your ugly ass so high in the air, tell me why we should do this stupid deal with you."

Luca, still in his underwear and on all fours, rotated in the dirt to face him. "You should do this stupid deal for the mothers."

The Russians turned somber.

"Get the bodies," said the man drinking from the thermos. "And pay him. Come on, let's go."

"Okay, Bertie," his men said.

Luca gathered the clothes he'd removed. "Thank you, Bertie."

The Russians removed the bodies from the pick-up truck and loaded them into the military transport vehicle. Afterwards, Luca followed one of the men to one of the SUVs to get paid.

"The things a father will do for his children," Mikey said. "All this just so he can earn enough money to buy a smartphone and see his kids every day."

Adam wondered about the circumstances surrounding Luca's meeting Eva and saving her life. He could not wait to hear the story.

"By the way," Mikey said, staring at the scene outside. "What did I see out there at the bridge earlier tonight?"

Adam had been waiting for such a question. "I don't know. What do you think you saw?"

Mikey paused. "I think I saw .... I think I saw something supernatural."

Adam waited a beat. "That happens. Think about all that you've been through recently. A man starts to see things. You just need some rest."

"Is that all it was?"

"I think so."

"Okay, Little Brother. If you say so."

When the Russian arrived at the Mercedes, he opened the driver's side door. Adam assumed he was reaching inside to get an envelope for Luca. Instead, he spoke to someone in the vehicle and closed the door. A moment later he opened the rear door, and two men in military uniforms stepped out. Zip ties bound their wrists. Both sported black eyes and scratches on their faces.

Luca guided the two men toward his Tacoma. When they crossed the path of his truck's headlights, the patches on their right shoulders shown in the night. They featured the blue and yellow colors of the Ukrainian flag.

"You were right," Adam said. "It's all about his children."

"Oh ... my ... God," Mikey said.

He jumped out of the SUV, brandished his pocket knife, and freed the Ukrainian soldiers from their restraints. After hugging the men, Mikey gave Luca an enthusiastic high-five. Afterwards, Luca bounded up to Adam's window.

"Six of their dead equals two of our living," Luca said, eyes blazing. "Tidiest profit I ever made."

Adam privately rescinded his previous assertion that Luca didn't solve crossword puzzles in his free time.

The Russians returned Mikey's rifle and they drove to Luca's house. Mikey and Luca seemed giddy. They inquired about the soldiers' backgrounds. Adam enjoyed listening. At some point Luca started singing the Ukrainian national anthem. That the soldiers and Mikey joined in didn't surprise Adam as much as the gusto with which they all sang.

When they got to the house, Luca pulled out a bottle of American scotch and poured glasses for everyone to celebrate. Adam didn't drink hard liquor but knew better than to ruin the atmosphere by refusing to partake. He sipped a little instead, and hid his disdain for the iodine taste. After various toasts, Luca looked at Adam.

"And now please raise your glasses to Mister Werner Ziegler." He described Adam's retrieval of the bodies, though he didn't know the true magnitude of the danger Adam had encountered, or the abilities he'd needed to survive. "Without Mister Ziegler's help, you would not be here this evening, and you would not be free men."

The soldiers stood up.

"Thank you, Mister Ziegler," one of them said.

"We are forever in your debt, Mister Ziegler," the other one said.

Adam fumbled for a response. Only one phrase came to mind.

"*Slava Ukraini*," he said. Glory to Ukraine - the century-old symbol of Ukrainian resistance and sovereignty – had become the official greeting of the Ukrainian Armed Forces.

"*Heroyam Slava*," said the soldiers, Mikey, and Luca. Glory to the Heroes.

They drank together in Adam's honor.

When Luca left for the kitchen to find snacks, Adam followed him.

"We have to talk about Eva," he said.

"I met her about a year ago," Luca said. "She'd found some cigarettes. They'd fallen out of a truck and she was trying to sell them. To some men like you met tonight. They wanted a little extra from her to get the deal done – if you know what I mean – and she refused. I was there with some pills that had fallen off a different truck, and so I helped her out."

"How did you help her?"

"I distracted them. I got their attention, made them laugh. They paid us, we left. We scavengers ... we have to stick together. She gave me ten percent of her take for helping. So, when she called me the other day asking for a favor, how could I refuse?"

"What favor? What exactly did she ask you to do?" Adam said.

"She told me Lviv was sending a man named Werner Ziegler to help me with the thing we did tonight."

"Lviv was sending a man?" Adam said. "What does that mean?"

Luca shrugged. "I needed help, so I went to a guy I know who's a volunteer in the Territorial Defense Forces. He said he'd get me someone. A day later, Eva called. She said you'd be coming."

Eva had joined the Ukrainian Territorial Defense Force, Adam thought. There was no other possible conclusion. That was why she'd been interested in Boyko's work, and how she'd re-connected with Luca. She was no longer the girl he'd known as a teenager. She had a cause.

"What else did she say?" Adam said.

"That once we were done, I was to take you to see the Farmer."

"Who's the Farmer?"

Luca shrugged. "The Farmer ... is a farmer. He grows wheat. He's having trouble with his harvest. Eva said you're the only person she knows that can help him. Once you've helped him, she said he has some kind of package for you. That's all she told me. Does that make sense?"

"Where does the farmer live? Is he closer to the front line or further away?"

Luca didn't bother answering.

Sure, Adam thought. Her instructions made sense the way everything had made sense since she'd poisoned him and stolen what he'd been hired to retrieve – they were consistent with Victor's fear. She was leading him to war.

"It doesn't matter where the Farmer lives," Luca said. "You know it, and I know it. You're going wherever she tells you to go."

"You think so?" Adam said.

This house stank, he thought, and so did this little man. Why was he wasting his time on a manipulative girl he'd known a decade ago and some gung-ho Ukrainian nutcases?

"I know so," Luca said.

"Oh, yeah?" Adam said.

"Yeah."

"How can you be so certain?"

"You forget," Luca said, gathering some chips and pretzels. "I've met your girl."

TWENTY-FIVE

TASIA SAT in the front pew of the eighteenth-century Ukrainian Orthodox Cathedral next to Strelkov. That wasn't exactly where she expected to be when he'd invited her to a special event. It turned out that when he'd told her to dress for church, he hadn't been kidding. In fact, a prominent Russian Orthodox bishop had arrived for the night and was about to deliver a special blessing to the FSB and Russian military personnel on hand.

The local priest didn't have much to say in the matter. He was an influential man in Kherson, hence the Russian Army had kidnapped him upon arrival. He was presently in the FSB complex being tortured into submission. Strelkov wanted the priest to sign a confession that he was an instrument of a Ukrainian government bent on Russian domination. The priest, of course, was refusing to admit to a complete lie. Last Tasia knew, her colleagues were beating him in the chest with a lead pipe and threatening to kill his family if he didn't cooperate. It was only a matter of time until he signed.

The bishop came out wearing a resplendent green robe, a white headdress embroidered with gold crowns, and a gold staff.

The Russian Orthodox Church and its leaders could acquire all the gold they wanted. During his rise to power, the Boss had awarded them a rare tobacco license that allowed them to import duty free cigarettes for profit. All it took was for the Church to continue supporting him no matter whom he robbed, imprisoned or poisoned.

"The West is involved in the systematic genocide of Russia because we will not host a gay parade," the bishop said. "Because we will not degrade our way of life the way they have. Ukraine is the vehicle for this genocide. Our humble and peace-loving people have been fleeing Donbas from Ukrainian oppression for years. Fortunately, the rule of our leader is the rule of God. With his guidance, we will exterminate the Ukrainian Nazis as we exterminated the Nazis of the past. And the united people of Russia, Belarus and Ukraine will come together as one, the way God intended. And our external enemies, who speak in foreign tongues, led by one oppressive force, will be vanquished forever."

The bishop retrieved an icon that depicted the reported appearance of the Virgin Mary to Russian soldiers on the eastern front during World War I. He descended from the altar and presented it to Strelkov.

"May this icon protect you and all our soldiers as you battle evil. I bless you and all your military operations against the Ukrainian Nazis, in the name of the Father, the Son and the Holy Spirit, amen."

"Amen," the faithful said.

Strelkov bowed as he accepted the icon, visibly moved by the bishop's words.

After the ceremony, those in attendance gathered across the street in a house Strelkov had seized from a doctor. The latter had mysteriously disappeared after a search of his home computer had revealed that the assistant to a member of the Ukrainian President's cabinet was his second cousin.

"There are three bedrooms upstairs," Strelkov said, as officers enjoyed drinks and hors d'oeuvres. "Meet me at the one at the far end of the hallway."

Tasia tried to hide her disappointment. Until this moment, he'd proven to be a murderer but shown no evidence of being a philandering pig. To make matters worse, he reeked of cigarettes and booze. Evidently, he needed to self-medicate like everyone else.

"No, no," Strelkov said, smiling. "By now, you know me better than that, Tasia. I've turned that bedroom into my office."

Tasia smiled. "This sounds urgent."

"It can't wait. Go now. My computer's on. There's a folder on the desktop labeled *NLO*. I want you to study it and tell me what you think. I'll be up in five minutes. I have to talk to the guy from Wagner first – he's not staying long."

Strelkov slipped away and joined two men, one an Army Major and the other a civilian whom Tasia didn't recognize. He wore a slim-fit khaki suit with black combat boots. Probably the man from the Wagner Group, she thought. Tasia swirled her glass, took another sip of the delicious Divnomore Cabernet, looked around to make sure no one was watching, and escaped up the stairs to Strelkov's office.

Modular shelves crammed full of books and souvenirs lined three of the walls. A signed photo of Strelkov receiving a commendation from the Boss was the only item on the fourth wall. It faced an antique Louis XV writing desk with a desktop computer. A screensaver with a photo of a woman and three children flashed on the oversized monitor. So that was Strelkov's wife, Tasia thought. She looked ten years older than him and wasn't smiling in the picture.

Tasia sat down in the matching antique chair and hit the

space button on the keyboard. The computer desktop material-ized. It featured a snow-capped mountain scene from the Caucasus in Krasnaya Polyana on the Black Sea. A dozen or so blue folders appeared. One of them was labeled *NLO*. This was also the title of a popular Russian magazine that dealt with para-normal phenomena and ufology. The acronym was comprised of the first letters of the Russian words for incredible, legendary, and obvious.

As Tasia moved the cursor to access the file, she spied another folder of paramount interest. That folder was titled *WAGNER*.

There it was, she thought, a gift from heaven, most likely the exact information the Ukrainians were desperately seeking – the name and location of all the assassins that had infiltrated Kyiv before the war started. All Tasia had to do was duplicate the folder and move it to the thumb drive in her pocket.

And yet the ease with which this opportunity presented itself suggested caution. What could possibly be so urgent that Strelkov couldn't wait until they were back in the office tomorrow morning? Perhaps multiple cameras had begun filming her from the moment she'd entered the room. Perhaps they were imbedded in a book, a piece of pottery, or one of the many knickknacks in the shelving that surrounded her.

Tasia used the mousepad to discover the cursor and promptly directed it onto the *NLO* folder. She clicked on it without further hesitation and waited for the file to open. That was the smart move. She'd been tempted to sneak a peek at the *WAGNER* folder's contents. But if this were a trap to expose her as the mole in the Russian FSB, the files probably contained a list of false names purposefully crafted to deceive the Ukrainians.

The possibility of a trap didn't alarm Tasia. Everyone – even the Boss – knew a double-agent was supplying the Ukrainians with timely intelligence from within the FSB. That meant everyone was a suspect. An FSB agent woke up worrying her coffee might be poisoned and went to sleep wondering which of her colleagues hated her the most. This was simply business as usual.

When the *NLO* folder finally opened, a video file popped up. Tasia clicked twice.

An image of a wooded area appeared. It featured two trenches in a clearing that met at a ninety-degree angle in the shape of an L. Two Russian soldiers also appeared in the image. One sat in a distant trench with his legs in the air, while the other stood closer to the camera, aiming his pistol at something beyond the camera's field of vision.

The bar on the video player indicated the clip was seven seconds long.

Tasia hit the play button.

A jittery close-up of river rocks accompanied the sound of rushing water. A man shouted *get him, get him* in Russian. A second man screamed *I'm trying.* The river rocks gave way to random flashes of sky, asphalt and woodland, as though the film-maker was struggling to aim his camera. Then the image stabilized.

A blur zipped around the trenches. A Russian soldier raised his pistol, but by the time he aimed it, the blur was beyond him. A second Russian soldier fell backwards as the blur flew past him. The blur descended into the trenches, veered left, and vanished from the camera's field of view.

The filmmaker adjusted his aim. A quick shot of a military vehicle and two more soldiers followed, and then the blur reappeared momentarily as it headed towards a bridge on the horizon. After it faded into thin air, the film clip ended.

Tasia's first impression was that the film was complete nonsense. She continued playing the clip over and over again to see if she'd missed something until Strelkov bounded into the room. He pressed the door shut behind him.

"You saw the video?" he said.

"Ten times," Tasia said. "It's so amateur I can't stop watching it."

"That's what I thought when I first saw it."

"When you first saw it?"

"Let's watch it again together," Strelkov said.

Tasia played the clip again

"What do you think you saw?" Strelkov said.

"Someone trying to make the worst horror movie ever made," Tasia said. "Either some film students posing as soldiers or some soldiers posing as film students. And some really low-budget special effects."

"The blob is really bad, right?"

"I called it a blur. Really bad."

"That's what I thought, too. Until I slowed down the frame speed by a factor of four." Strelkov made some adjustments on the video playback software. "Now play it."

The adjustment in speed brought the blur into focus. It no longer resembled an amorphous shape. It now looked like a man carrying a wounded soldier while moving at warp speed.

"Is this for real?" Tasia said.

"Of course not," Strelkov said. "It can't be real. I took some measurements. The man is moving at forty-eight kilometers per hour with the video at quarter speed."

"Meaning what, he was really moving at a hundred ninety kilometers per hour? Twice as fast as a cheetah?"

"I love the cheetah," Strelkov said. "Is there a more beautiful animal?"

"Where did this come from?"

"A platoon at an encampment at a bridge we control eighty kilometers or so outside Kyiv. It's probably a camera malfunction or some sort of prank. A lot of these soldiers are kids. They may be bored, homesick ... they spend all their time on their computers these days. They're more than capable of making this up. To them it's entertainment. But to us ..."

Tasia raised her eyebrows.

Strelkov shrugged. "We have to be vigilant on all matters no matter how preposterous they may seem. The margin of error in our business ... the smallest oversight could prove to be costly."

"You actually want me to look into this?" Tasia said.

"Bring in a couple of the soldiers – the one who took the video and one of the other two. Sit them down and have a conversation with them. The revealing kind, conducted in your inimitable way. I'm sure it will leave them with a story to tell their families the rest of their lives, if they survive this special military operation. Do that, just to make sure ..."

"To make sure?" Tasia said.

"You know what I mean," Strelkov said. "Make sure it's nonsense and that the Americans haven't created some other-worldly technology."

"Why the Americans?"

Strelkov laughed. "What, if that's a real human being moving at a hundred sixty kilometers per hour, you think a so-called Ukrainian could come up with something like that? Now that's some real nonsense."

Tasia returned the video clip to its original speed and watched the blur appear and disappear like a faint flash of light.

"One thing we know for sure," Strelkov said. "The day there's a human being like that out there and he's running *away* from our soldiers, that's the day we're in trouble."

If only such a man existed, Tasia thought.

TWENTY-SIX

THEY LEFT for the farm at sunrise in two vehicles. Luca led the way in his pick-up truck, while Mikey followed in his Jeep.

Adam sipped tea out of a paper cup beside Mikey and stared out the side window. Adam loved the first light of day. Dew glistened atop wildflowers. Patches of fog rolled by. It was the perfect time to meditate. He wanted nothing more than to close his eyes and contemplate Eva.

How had she learned about the package? If she knew it could alter the course of the war, and she'd joined the Territorial Defense, why hadn't she given it to the Ukrainians? Or had she? If she hadn't, was her reluctance a function of money? Perhaps the scavenger had a cause, but the scavenger was still a scavenger. Or was she holding onto the package because of him? Was she concerned his loss of the package could put him in jeopardy? That was the explanation he so desperately wanted to believe.

All these questions he would have loved to have pondered. But he couldn't, because Mikey was blasting a Ukrainian war song with an incredibly catchy one-word refrain. Adam asked

Mikey to turn down the volume. He did so, and then began singing along.

Invaders came to us to Ukraine,
New uniforms, new machinery
But their inventory has melted
Bayraktar ... Bayraktar

Their arguments, all kinds of arms
Powerful rockets, steel machines
To all their arguments, our response is
Bayraktar ... Bayraktar

"Bayraktar?" Adam said.

"Unmanned combat aerial vehicle," Mikey said.

"Drone?" Adam said.

"Turkish drone. The best in the world. The CEO of the company, Haluk Bayraktar, said he'll never sell Bayraktar to the Russians."

"Good man," Adam said.

"Great man. A Ukrainian soldier wrote the song when the war started. In two hours. Since then, a million downloads and dance versions in all kinds of languages."

"Dance versions?" Adam said.

"We fight, we sing, we dance, and then we fight again. The Russians – they fight, they whine, they sulk, they die. And that's how it's going to be until the invaders are gone."

Mikey glanced at Adam and continued singing along. He looked happy and confident, just like the singer sounded, in contrast to the song's lyrics. Adam returned his gaze to the windshield.

A dense patch of fog rolled in. Visibility turned to zero.

Red lights shone from the tail of Luca's pickup.

"Watch out," Adam said.

Mikey slammed the brakes. The Jeep skidded and collided with Luca's truck. Adam's head snapped back. They'd slowed down sufficiently to blunt the impact, but there was no question the bumpers had been dented.

"My friend's gonna kill me," Mikey said. He exited the Jeep before Adam could unclip his seatbelt. "What the hell, Luca?" he said, as he disappeared into the fog.

Adam stepped out onto the asphalt and followed Mikey through the mist.

Two Russian soldiers greeted him with pistols drawn. A third soldier stood beside them with a knife conspicuously strapped to his calf. Mikey and Luca faced them, hands behind their heads.

Adam thrust his open palms into the air.

The senior of the bunch trudged forward. Grime covered his cheeks. A cigarette dangled from his lips. He was the only one of the three with a stripe on his uniform, and the only one who looked over the age of twenty.

"Anyone else in the car?" the officer said.

Gunshots rang out.

Adam ducked. Mikey and Luca fell to the ground.

The other armed soldier was firing through the fog in the direction of the vehicles.

"Stop," the officer said.

The other armed soldier fired two more rounds.

"What the hell are you doing, Marat?" the third soldier said.

"Shut-up, Solomon. I'm shooting them before they shoot us," Marat said.

"Before who shoots us?" Solomon said.

"There's no one else," Luca said.

"There's just the three of us," Mikey said.

"You're going to end up shooting one of us," Solomon said.

"No one's shooting anybody," the officer said. He glanced at Marat, head hanging at an odd angle, as though he could barely hold it up. "Holster your weapon."

Marat returned his stare and spit on the ground.

"Be smart, Marat," the officer said. "And if that's not realistic, think of a smart person, and ask yourself, what would he do under the present circumstances? And then do what he would do."

"Fuck you, Konstantin," Marat said.

"Ah, yes. Too late," Konstantin said. "The Boss has fucked us all."

Marat sneered and put his gun away.

"Sorry about the shooting," Konstantin said, lowering his gun to his side. "And the damage to your cars."

Adam turned. The fog had rolled by. Cracks in the shape of a spider surrounded a bullet hole in the windshield of Luca's truck, and the Jeep's right headlight had been shot out. Judging by their reactions – or lack thereof – neither Mikey or Luca were concerned about their vehicles at the moment.

"And sorry for stopping you like this," Konstantin said. "Do you guys have any food or water? I wish I didn't have to ask, but we're hurting badly here."

"I have some cottage cheese cookies," Luca said. "And some biscuits. No water but there's tea in my thermos. You're welcome to it."

"I've got some candy bars," Mikey said. "And some Fanta."

"You have Fanta?" Konstantin managed half a smile, his teeth stark white against the dirt on his face. "That is *fantastisch*." He turned to Adam.

"Half a cup of tea," Adam said. "That's all I've got. Yours if you want it."

"That's very kind of you," Konstantin said. "Yes, to the

cookies and candy, and of course, the Fanta. But we'll pass on the tea, thank you very much. Caffeine dehydrates and that would be counterproductive. Would you be so kind as to get us what you can spare, please?"

As Adam turned, he noticed the tank for the first time. It had been there the entire time – a track-driven, olive-colored beast – but Adam had been too consumed with the scenario at hand to focus on it. Konstantin had parked it on the side of the road heading in the opposite direction. It was the first tank Adam had ever seen in his life. Its presence on a country road was as stunning as the precision with which Konstantin had positioned it – in a manner than would allow traffic to flow freely in both directions.

Adam gathered the Fanta and the food into a canvas bag and brought it to the soldiers. Konstantin gave each of his men a can of soda, some cookies and a candy bar. He allotted the same to himself and returned the rest in a bag to Adam.

"We don't want to take all your stuff," Konstantin said. He made eye-contact individually with Adam, Mikey and Luca. "Appreciate it."

Marat and Solomon cracked their sodas and dug into their snacks where they stood.

"We have an appointment," Adam said. "And we're running late. Is there anything else we can do for you?"

Konstantin took a swig of Fanta Grape and appeared to reflect on the question. "I don't know." He turned to his men. "Is there anything else we need?"

"Directions to Kyiv," said Marat.

"Interesting," Konstantin said, under his breath. "That assumes we actually want to get to Kyiv." He raised his voice. "Anything else?"

"Yeah," Solomon said. "I want to talk to my mother."

Marat glanced at him with no visible reaction – or apparent

judgment – and continued eating. Meanwhile, Konstantin sighed, as though the request was absurd and inappropriate, and yet he sympathized with it.

"She thought we were going on maneuvers for two days," Solomon said. "That's what we were told, so that's what I told her. She has no idea where I am. She must be going crazy by now. It's not right, Captain. I want to talk to her. I need to talk to her."

Konstantin contemplated the request for another moment, and then turned to Adam, Mikey and Luca.

"We had a phone," he said. "A smartphone. For all of one day. That phone was so damn smart – all it took was twenty-four hours in the tank with the three of us for it to realize it needed to get lost if it wanted to survive. And so, it did. It got lost. Any of you gentleman have a phone we can borrow to call Moscow?"

"No problem," Mikey said. "Permission to reach in my pocket."

"Permission granted," Konstantin said, twinkle in his eye.

Mikey pulled his phone from his pocket and held it up for all to see. "My provider is from the west of the country. There are some access codes you have to enter for Russia. I can make the call for him if you want."

"That would be greatly appreciated," Konstantin said.

Mikey stood up. Solomon placed his soda and biscuits on the asphalt and met Mikey in the middle of the road. Given the current scenario, Adam would have expected Mikey to appear eager and earnest. But such was not the case. Mikey tapped digits into his phone slowly and methodically, with a calm expression on his face.

"Put it on speaker," Konstantin said. "We all need a feel-good moment, don't we?"

Mikey activated the speaker and held the phone in the air for all to see.

After three rings, a woman with a high-pitched voice answered. Solomon spoke to his mother, who cried with joy once she was certain the voice on the other end truly belonged to her son.

"Where are you, kitten?" she said.

"Somewhere near Kyiv," Solomon said.

"Kyiv? Did you say Kyiv?"

"They didn't tell us we were coming here. They didn't tell us we were going to war. I didn't know or I would have told you so you didn't worry. They made us invade Ukraine, Mama."

"Are you okay?" his mother said.

"No, Mama. I'm not okay. They made us invade Ukraine."

"Yes, but are you okay? You're not hurt, are you?"

"No. I'm not hurt."

"Are you getting enough to eat?"

"Mama, did you not hear what I said?" Solomon said. "They made us invade Ukraine. Some guys have family in Ukraine. I've got friends in Ukraine. And we're here to kill them."

A pause followed. When his mother didn't answer, Solomon looked at Mikey as though they may have been disconnected. Mikey glanced at the screen, shook his head and shrugged.

Three beats later, his mother spoke again.

"Now you listen, son, and you listen carefully. The Americans have been making biological weapons in Ukraine for years. And they were on the verge of giving them nuclear weapons, too. Ukraine was planning to invade Russia. Do you hear me? You're there on a special military operation to save our country."

Solomon frowned. "Mama, you're talking crazy. None of that is true."

"Don't you tell me what's true."

"If you had friends in the West, you'd know."

"Don't talk to me about the decrepit West," his mother said. "The West is our enemy. Your generation is spoiled and naïve. You're hopeless unless there's an adult standing by to tell you the truth. To tell you what you don't want to hear."

Solomon shook his head.

"There is no such thing as a Ukrainian," she said. "The people who call themselves Ukrainians are Russians with ponytails. They're serfs, nothing more."

"The hell you say, Mama."

"Kill that *khokhol*," she said. *Khokhol* was an ethnic slur that referred to the tuft of hair Ukrainian Cossacks wore on an otherwise shaved head.

Solomon's eyes watered. "Please don't say that, Mama. I called to let you know I'm okay. And now your words are hurting me more than this war."

"You're a Russian soldier now. Act like one."

"Mama, you're on speaker, you know."

"What? Who's listening? Are you with a *khokhol*? Do you have your knife? You never go anywhere without your knife …"

"Mama, please …"

"Take your knife"

"I have to go now, Mama"

"And kill that *khokhol*."

Mikey's eyes shot up. He glanced at Solomon and then at the knife attached to his pant leg.

"Mama, you don't know what you're saying," Solomon said.

"He's your enemy. He wants to destroy you, your family, your country"

"Mama, I can't"

"Take your knife and stab him deep in the heart. Kill that *khokhol*."

Marat flung his soda can aside. "Screw you, Solomon," he said. "I'll kill him."

Marat raised his gun, aimed it at Mikey, and marched toward him to get a clear shot.

Adam sprang forward.

A gun fired.

Marat collapsed to the tarmac. Blood poured from the side of his head.

Adam's momentum carried him three steps further. Mikey stepped back, phone in hand, as Luca hit the ground again. Solomon stood still, staring at his comrade's corpse. Adam finally came to a stop. He turned.

Konstantin lowered his pistol, lips pressed tight.

No one moved or said a word.

"Solomon? Solomon?" His mother's voice cracked the silence. "Kitten, are you there?"

Three beats passed and she repeated her plea.

Solomon, tears rolling down his face, walked over to Mikey, who raised the phone for him to speak.

"I'm okay, Mama," he said.

"Praise be to God," she said. "Did you kill that *khokhol*?"

Solomon considered his answer.

"Yeah, Mama," he said. "I killed that *khokhol*. Good-bye, Mama. I'll call you soon."

Solomon nodded at Mikey, who ended the call.

Konstantin holstered his weapon. He ambled over to the others, scratched his chin, and glanced at Adam.

"You guys know someone who might want to buy a tank?"

TWENTY-SEVEN

STRELKOV REVIEWED the latest statistics about the number of Russian generals killed thus far during the special military operation. Ukraine claimed they'd killed twelve, the West said it was seven, and now the Army had confirmed that twelve Russian generals, in fact, had been killed in action.

That was a staggering number. As a proportion of the troops deployed and time passed, such a death rate was consistent with what Russia experienced during the end of World War II. The Ukrainians couldn't find a general at a banquet honoring the entire Russian high command without the Americans' help. It was time for Russia to deploy its full arsenal of weapons to end this operation before turned into another Afghanistan.

A knock on his door startled him.

Nikolai apologized. Strelkov asked him to come in and close the door behind him.

"I've made some progress on the assignment you gave me," Nikolai said.

"Before you say another word," Strelkov said, keeping his voice down despite the door being closed, "where is Lieutenant Ivanova now?"

"She just went for one of her walks. If it's a short one, she'll be back in twenty to twenty-five minutes. If it's a long one, forty-five minutes to an hour."

"What do you have for me?"

"Her father, Dmitri Ivanov, was a diplomat for twenty-five years for the Soviet Union. His longest time in one place was in France – twelve years. Six years in Germany, seven in Italy. When he was stationed in all those places, he paid a private instructor to help learn the local language, and in each country, the instructor was the same person."

"Wait, let me guess," Strelkov said. "It was a woman."

"Very good, sir."

"What was her name?"

"Daria Privalova," Nikolai said.

"Ukrainian?"

Nikolai nodded.

"Well, that's interesting, isn't it?" Strelkov said.

"There's more. She owned a home in Lviv. Ivanov traveled to Lviv no less than fifteen times during his career, always under the guise of some sort of conference on diplomatic relations. But there's no record of him ever speaking at such an event, or paying for a hotel."

"And all the while he was married, with child."

"He was," Nikolai said.

"Well, like I said. That's interesting. But you might have a harder time finding a high-ranking diplomat that didn't have a mistress in those days. You've cast some doubt on the man's honor, Nikolai, but you haven't proven anything, let alone discovered something compromising."

"I was just getting to that part."

"There's more?"

"The woman, Daria Privalova, had a child. Her name is

Lena Privalova. She's Alpha Group, dedicated special forces of the Ukrainian Security Services."

"What?" Strelkov sat up. "Are you telling me Lieutenant Ivanova may have a half-sister who's an SBU agent?"

Nikolai held his gaze.

"Have they ever met?" Strelkov said. "Because – if they're half-sisters, they may not even know each other. Is there any evidence they ever met?"

"Not yet," Nikolai said. "But here's my thinking on that. The father and both mothers have passed on. Neither of the women had a sibling born to her mother. So not only are they sisters ..."

"They're all the family they have left," Strelkov said.

"And with all the DNA-based family searches being so popular, it's not hard to imagine one used such a service and found the other."

"It's not hard to imagine at all. Not at all. But that's all we're doing right now – imagining various scenarios. Imagine if you or I were in Lieutenant Ivanova's position. We wouldn't want to be accused of a crime we didn't commit."

"No, sir."

"Evidence," Strelkov said.

"Already on it, sir. If I find something, you'll be the first to know."

"And the second, and the third, and the last."

"Yes, sir," Nikolai said. "That was understood."

Nikolai left the office.

If Ivanova was the traitor supplying the Ukrainians with timely information, he'd have to deal with her himself, Strelkov thought. He'd never survive an inquiry into her treason even if she'd committed the majority of her crimes under someone else's watch. When in doubt, the FSB pursued the kitchen-sink solution and eliminated all of the traitor's supervisors. By doing so, the general giving the orders was also seizing the opportunity to eliminate ambitious men who might someday become a threat to his own career.

Strelkov had spent so much time away from home he knew his way around a kitchen all too well.

And he, too, was particularly fond of a nice kitchen sink.

TWENTY-EIGHT

ADAM WATCHED Luca negotiate a deal between the Ukrainian government and the Russian soldiers using nothing more than his flip phone. In exchange for their tank, Konstantin and Solomon became prisoners of war. They agreed to be taken to a camp where they would receive three meals a day and be treated in accordance with the Geneva Conventions. In addition, after Ukraine won the war against Russia, they would be awarded citizenship and ten thousand dollars each to start new lives in their new homeland.

Konstantin and Solomon considered this a good deal, infinitely superior to killing innocent Ukrainians for a leader who didn't give a damn about his own soldiers' lives, or being incinerated by a Javelin anti-tank missile at any moment. The Ukrainians considered it a great deal – the tank had cost four million dollars to build in 2020.

"It's a T-14 Armada," Mikey said, once they were back in the Jeep and on the way to the Farmer's house.

"I thought you dealt in Glocks and Full Metal Jackets," Adam said.

"American tanks have a four-man crew. Russians said, that

is some old-school crap. We'll show you how it's done. So, they built the T-14 for a three-man crew with an autoloader. Lighter weight, less manpower, technologically superior. How can it not be better, right?"

"Right."

"Wrong," Mikey said. "The autoloader takes ten seconds to get a round off. The fourth American soldier takes only four to five seconds to get his round off. You see the lesson in this?"

"All good things don't necessarily come in threes?"

"It's one thing if American technology is faster than yours," Mikey said, "but when one of their soldiers is faster than your technology, you've got problems. That's why Russians talk a big game, but when they're on the same battle-field with the Americans – like in Syria – they never, ever, mess with them."

"You seem to know a lot about military things," Adam said.

Mikey steered the Jeep around a broken and burned-out armored vehicle with a machine gun on top.

"My father was a colonel in the army," he said.

"Was?"

"He died in the war at Donbas a couple of years ago."

"Sorry for your loss," Adam said.

"They were all military guys on my father's side of the family – or the underground resistance – going back for a century."

"How about you?"

"Me?" Mikey said.

"Yeah. No interest in continuing the family tradition?"

"I knew what I wanted to be by the time I was twelve after my first time on stage in a school play. I was the honeybee in a Ukrainian fable. I didn't have any lines but I put a buzz in the crowd."

"I have no doubt," Adam said. "So, what do you do – or

what were you doing before the war? Were you in school or taking acting classes or something?"

"I was in Lviv Polytechnical," Mikey said. "Where my uncle teaches. But it wasn't for me. I dropped out after a year to be a man of the street, so I can observe life, and deepen my ability to understand the motivations of my characters."

"What did your mother say about that?" Adam said.

"I don't know," Mikey said. "She stopped talking to me."

"Huh. No mother in your life. I know the feeling."

"Really? Why? What did you do?"

"I was born," Adam said.

"What?"

"She died after giving birth to me."

"Oh," Mikey said. "Sorry, man. Where was this?"

"On planet Earth, in a remote location, where previously extinct species won't drink the water. Can't this thing go any faster? We're late, you know."

Mikey pressed the gas pedal.

They traveled southeast for an hour to the village of Pyrohovtsi, stopping at two more makeshift Ukrainian checkpoints along the way. They arrived at the farm just before noon without Luca – he stayed behind with the Russian soldiers.

A single-story thatch-roofed house stood before a barn and other small farm structures. To their left, a tractor lay tipped on its side in an endless field of wheat. Not a person or other piece of equipment could be seen on the property.

"Problems with the harvest?" Mikey said, as he killed the engine.

Adam scanned the horizon for signs of life. "That's what Luca said."

They stepped out of the SUV.

"Does this feel like problems with the harvest or something more?" Adam said.

"I'm taking my rifle," Mikey said.

"No guns, please."

"No can do, Little Brother. But don't worry. I'm a decent shot. My father made sure of it."

Adam took comfort from Mikey's revelation about his family's military history, and believed him when he said he knew how to use the weapon.

They marched along a fieldstone path toward the front door.

A bloated madman in overalls emerged from around the house wielding a scythe.

"I'm the grim reaper," he said in Russian, "and I'm going to eat your livers for dinner. But first, I'll have your Russian heads for breakfast."

"We're not Russian, we're not Russian," Mikey said. "I'm from Lviv." He pointed at Adam. "And he's from Munich."

The Farmer frowned. "What are your names?"

Mikey and Adam introduced themselves.

The Farmer let the scythe slide through his hands. When the handle hit the ground, the curved blade came to rest beside his head. His eyes widened as he glanced at Adam.

"You're the healer?" he said.

"The healer?" Adam said.

The Farmer nodded. "Luca said he was sending a healer. That he was a friend of a fellow scavenger – a woman. That a man from Lviv would be bringing him."

Adam didn't know what to say. The Farmer was staring at him, waiting for his answer. Adam got the impression that if he didn't identify himself as the healer, the Farmer would have no interest in talking to him.

"If I'm the healer," Adam said, "does that mean you have something for me?"

"Of course," the Farmer said.

"And what would that thing be?"

"Instructions."

"Instructions for what?" Adam said.

"Instructions for where she'll meet you."

"Where who will meet me?"

"Luca's friend," the Farmer said. "The female scavenger. When I text a message that your work is done here, I'll get your instructions."

Adam paused. If the Farmer was sending a text, that meant he had a phone number. It wasn't necessarily Eva's number, but it was still something.

"She's coming here?" he said. "In person?"

"That I don't know," the Farmer said. "But I was told she's waiting for my text."

"Then yes," Adam said. "I'm the healer. I understand you're having trouble your harvest? Your wheat field sure looks good to me." The words sounded ridiculous as they rolled off his tongue. He knew nothing about harvests let alone how to solve agricultural problems.

The Farmer appeared confused. Then he laughed. "Trouble with the harvest? Is that what Luca told you? That's an interesting way to put it. Yes, that harvest is a problem, too. You boys come with me. I'll show you. You want something to drink first?"

The Farmer served them some refreshing *kvas*, a sweet and sour drink made from rye bread, malt and honey. Afterwards, he led them out back.

"The Russians stole everything," he said, opening the door to an empty barn. "My sower, my harvester, three tractors – and you saw what they did with the fourth." He pointed toward the field. "They got drunk one night, drove it out there, and tipped it over. All the gasoline and oil spilled out ... They took my cows, horses, pigs and my chickens. I had fifty tons of grain in my elevator. Gone."

"How could Russian soldiers take all that?" Mikey said. "They come with trucks, or what?"

"The soldiers came first. That was chaotic. Then the trucks with Crimean license plates. They were more organized." The Farmer closed the barn door and gazed at his field. "I was a metallurgical engineer for a material sciences company in Donbas until 2014. Then I quit my job, bought this farm, and moved here. My daughter and I speak Russian. We don't speak Ukrainian. I never thought of myself as a Ukrainian. I didn't identify with the culture. It didn't matter to me. But now, that's all changed."

"The war is horrible, I know," Adam said. "It's unbelievable that it's happening. But I'm not sure what I can do to help with your harvest."

"You can't do anything," the Farmer said. "Until I get my equipment back – or someone helps me get new equipment – my farm is dead. But there are worse fates in life. And, so it is here, for me. It's not this harvest I need help with."

Adam and Mikey exchanged bewildered glances.

"You have another harvest?" Mikey said.

"My fifteen year-old daughter," the Farmer said. "Her name is Teresa. It's a Greek name. It means *harvest*."

Typical Eva, Adam thought. More word play.

"Look," Adam said, "I'm not a doctor. I'm just a caretaker for the elderly"

"My wife divorced me three years ago," the Farmer said. "If she'd wanted to marry a farmer, she said, she wouldn't have married me. My daughter is all I have. It hasn't been easy. And now, since the Russian soldiers left, she won't come out of her room. She won't talk to me. I leave food outside her door and all she does is nibble on the bread. It's as though she's trying to starve herself."

"Did the soldiers stay in your house?" Mikey said.

"Yes," the Farmer said, "but it's not what you're thinking. No one laid a hand on her. She was barely out of my sight the entire time they were here. And the soldiers had decent matters. Especially their commander. He was professional."

"What kind of girl was she before ... before all this?" Adam said.

"The happy go-lucky kind," the Farmer said.

Mikey cracked a smile. "Not a care in the world," he said, in his best Ben Foster.

"That was her," the Farmer said. He looked at Adam. "Please, Mister Ziegler. I was told the healer has a way ... a way with people. Will you talk to her? Please ..."

"I've never done anything like this before," Adam said, "and I haven't spoken with someone as young as your daughter since I was her age. So please don't get your hopes up. But I'm willing to give it a shot."

The Farmer eyes welled. His lips moved as though he wanted to say something but couldn't find the words.

"How do you plan on introducing me?" Adam said.

"I'm going to tell her you're a healer," the Farmer said.

"And how are you going to get her to open her door to a stranger, when she won't even open it for her own father?" Adam said.

"I'm going to tell her that if she doesn't open it, I'll break it down," the Farmer said.

Adam nodded with as much deference and respect as he could muster.

"I understand," he said. "It's your home, sir. And your rules. But I'm not sure either of those strategies are going to help us."

The Farmer studied him. "You have a better idea?"

Adam shrugged. He asked Mikey to wait in the Jeep for him. He was reluctant to leave but Adam insisted. After Mikey left, he shared his suggestions with the Farmer.

"A bit devious for a healer, aren't you?" the Farmer said.

"You mean I should be honest and straightforward to succeed in my mission?" Adam said. "How's that working for the people of Ukraine these days?"

"Hmm," the Farmer said. "You might be for real after all. Follow me."

They headed towards the house.

TWENTY-NINE

TASIA SAT beside Nikolai in the same interrogation room where they'd interviewed the Deputy Mayor of Kherson. They both looked like undertakers in black suits and ties, and white shirts. That they were both dressed the exact same way was not a coincidence. Tasia had made arrangements with Nikolai ahead of time. She wanted to project an atmosphere of impending doom.

One of Tasia's other subordinates escorted a soldier into the room. His first name was Tolkyn. He walked with a swagger and did a double take at Tasia when he saw her. A grin spread across his lips as he sat down across the table from them. Either he was pleased to see a woman, Tasia thought, or anticipating an easier interrogation because of her presence. Given the way he slouched in his chair with his legs splayed open, she bet on the latter – or both.

"My father's a member of the Duma," he said, referring to the Russian Federation's legislature. "Just in case you didn't know that."

Tasia pressed her lips together and bowed her head. "Wow.

I mean, my father doesn't even pay any attention to Russian politics." She glanced at Nikolai. "How about yours?"

"Nope," Nikolai said.

"My father's name is Zeus," Tasia said. "He spends his days ruling the universe. How about yours?"

"My father's name is King Kong," Nikolai said. "He spends his days kicking ass in the universe."

Tasia smiled at Tolkyn. "See? You really are the man. We're nobodies." She turned serious and nodded at the small blue and white cooler, the only item on the table. "What do you think is in this cooler?"

"I don't know. Beer?"

"He's connected and smart," Tasia said. "Right you are. It's Ukrainian beer. Obolon, to be exact. It's cold, crisp and refreshing. Would you like a can?"

"Hell yeah, I'd like a can."

Tasia slid the lid open, tipping the cooler toward her so that only she and Nikolai could see what was inside. She removed an ice-cold green and silver can and slid it across the table to him. Afterwards, she hid the cooler beneath the desk and glanced at one of the cameras mounted discreetly where the walls met the ceiling. As soon as she found the camera's eye it turned red, implying one of her subordinates had turned it on.

"I love the sound of the flip-top snapping open," Tasia said. "Don't you?"

"You mean this noise?"

Tolkyn cracked the can open and winked at Tasia. Then he sipped and slurped the beer.

"Ah," he said. "That is so good." He measured Tasia, at least the part of her that was visible above the desk. "You know, there's other noises I like even better."

"Is that a fact?" Tasia said.

"Like, what kind of noises?" Nikolai said.

Tolkyn raised his eyebrows twice and grinned, then took another long swig of beer.

"Who cares what you like," Tasia said.

"Let the record show," Nikolai said, "That the subject just directed a lewd and lascivious comment toward Lieutenant Ivanova. It was a sexual provocation no doubt fueled by his outrageous consumption of alcohol."

"What are you talking about?" Tolkyn said. "You gave me this beer."

"That's a lie," Tasia said. "And the video recording will prove it."

"What video recording?" Tolkyn said.

"I'm sure your commanding officers will have something to say about this," Tasia said. "Insisting on bringing alcohol to an interview with the Federal Security Service under the supposed protection of your father, the lawmaker. And speaking to an officer the way you just did."

"This is complete crap. No one's going to believe it."

"Believe what?" Nikolai said. "That you're drinking enemy beer while wearing the uniform of a Russian soldier?"

Tasia said, "Didn't the Duma just introduce legislation that anyone caught drinking Ukrainian beverages is subject to a fine and up to ten years imprisonment?"

"Didn't your father tell you that?" Nikolai said.

Tolkyn pushed the beer aside. He straightened in his chair, placed his legs squarely beneath the table.

"Look," Tasia said, in a softer tone. "This doesn't have to be about you. Everything that's happened here ... everything that's been said ... it can all go away."

"Like it never happened," Nikolai said.

"What do you want?" Tolkyn said, finally sounding like a politician's offspring.

"We want the truth about the video you took near the

bridge," Tasia said. "And we want every part of your story to match up with what the other soldiers are telling our colleagues as we speak."

"There can be no discrepancies," Nikolai said. "If you lie to us about the smallest detail—"

"If you omit the smallest detail," Tasia said, "you're going to jail and your father's career will be over. You're a smart boy. You understand this is one of those moments in life, don't you?"

"None of this was necessary," Tolkyn said. "All you had to do was ask."

"No harm done yet, right?" Tasia said. She held his eyes and pointed her finger at him. "Go."

"We were coming back from the river—"

"We?" Nikolai said.

Tolkyn gave them the other soldier's name.

"And there he was, right in front of me."

"Who was there?" Tasia said.

"The guy. The guy with the corpse over his shoulder."

"Wait," Tasia said, "you saw this man, face-to-face?"

"Sure," Tolkyn said.

"What did he look like?" Tasia said

"It was a corpse?" Nikolai said. "You sure about that?"

"He was six feet tall," Tolkyn said. "Maybe a little taller. Skinny, but strong."

"What do you mean, strong?" Nikolai said.

"Like an athlete," Tolkyn said. "I mean, he was carrying a body over his shoulder but he was walking like it was ..."

"Yes?" Tasia said. "Like it was ...?"

"Nothing," Tolkyn said. "He was carrying it like it was less than a sack of potatoes."

"Did you see his face?" Nikolai said.

"No. It was too dark. As soon as we saw each other, he took off. I got my phone out, but he moved so freaking fast that by the time I could point the camera at him he was just a blur. I've never seen anything like it."

Tasia and Nikolai probed about the stranger's appearance but Tolkyn didn't have any more details to offer – except one.

"The only thing I can tell you about the guy is this," he said. "He was probably an American."

Tasia remembered Strelkov's prediction, which he'd made in jest. "Why American?"

"He was wearing Danner Mountain Light II hiking boots," Tolkyn said. "Made in America. Very expensive. Very hard to find."

"Come on," Nikolai said. "It was too dark for you to see the guy's face but you recognized his shoes?"

"When I pulled my phone from my pocket, the screen lit up his foot for a few seconds. Sleek profile. Best for narrow feet. Stitchdown construction. Vibram Kletterlift Outsole. Gor-Tex all the way. My dream shoe."

"What were you doing at the river?" Tasia said.

Tolkyn hesitated for a split second, but that's all it took. Tasia knew he was hiding something.

"We heard noises," Tolkyn said, "so we went to check it out."

"But you weren't on watch at the time," Tasia said, "were you? Another soldier was on watch. So, I'll ask you again, what were you doing at the river?"

"Remember what the Lieutenant told you," Nikolai said. "If your story doesn't match what the others tell us, that's the last cold one you're going to be enjoying for a long time."

Tolkyn took a deep breath and rubbed his cheeks with his hand.

"Okay," he said. "We were smoking weed."

Tasia rolled her eyes. "Oh, for God's sake"

"It was for the stress," Tolkyn said. "I have a prescription.

You don't know what it's like out there. These Ukrainians ... they want to kill us."

Imagine that, Tasia thought.

"So, you were stoned when you saw the guy, the corpse, and the hiking shoes," Nikolai said. "You realize this makes you the best witness in the history of the world, right? What an idiot."

"I saw what I saw," Tolkyn said.

"Did you doctor the video in any way?" Tasia said.

"What? Doctor it? Why would I doctor it? Even if I wanted to, I wouldn't know how to do that."

Tasia asked Nikolai if he had any more questions. When he said he didn't, Tasia excused Tolkyn from the room.

"What's going to happen to me?" he said before he left.

"Next time, don't accept beer from strangers in black suits," Tasia said. "Off you go, back to the trenches."

The next soldier up was from the Russian Republic of Yakutia in the Siberian Far East. His first name was Boydoy. He trudged into the room.

"Have a seat," Tasia said. She lifted the cooler onto the table. "What do you think is in here?"

Boydoy shrugged. "Food?"

"You are correct," Tasia said. "Would you like a Ukrainian donut? They're filled with jams. I have apricot, strawberry and plum. They are delicious. A woman in town makes them. She's known as the princess of *pampushky*. No filtration for her, you know what I mean?"

"No," Boydoy said. "I'm okay."

"Please," Tasia said. "Take advantage of this moment. In an hour, you'll be back in the fray. How about apricot?"

After some more uncertainty, Boydoy finally said yes. Tasia lifted the cover to the cooler, removed an apricot donut and a napkin, and slid it across the table to him. She and Nikolai watched as he practically cried after the first bite.

"Right?" Tasia said, smiling as she hid the cooler.

"Good," Boydoy said, mid-chew. "Very good. Thank you."

"No one deserves it more," Tasia said. "You guys are out there without proper food or fuel. And still you're holding your own."

"You guys are our heroes," Nikolai said. "And we're behind you all the way. But we need your help. We need to know everything you know about that video clip from the other night."

"Actually, we already know everything," Tasia said. "We just need your account to corroborate what the other soldiers told us. And please understand – omitting something is the equivalent of lying to us."

"I don't lie," Boydoy answered.

Boydoy gave them his account of what transpired. His pace of delivery gradually picked-up until he was practically racing to finish.

"Sorry," he said, when he was done. "Can I use the bathroom?"

"The bathroom?" Nikolai said.

"I don't know what happened."

"Are you suggesting that delicious donut did this to you?" Nikolai said.

"I've really got to go." He started to get up from his seat.

"Sit down," Tasia said. "Bathrooms are for honest people. Not for liars."

"You're not going anywhere, liar," Nikolai said. "The door's locked from the outside."

"But if I don't go now ..." Boydoy said.

"A film of you crapping your pants will be posted online for everyone to see," Tasia said. "Your platoon, the entire Russian Army, the Republic of Yakutia and all the eligible women within." Tasia raised her index finger and pointed it at Boydoy. "Tell me everything I need to know. Now. Go."

"Tolkyn deals drugs. Half the guys in the platoon were stoned that night. The *NLO* made six trips, not one. He carried six dead bodies. Not one. And he wasn't alone. He had protection on the bridge. A man with a rifle. He was a soldier. A professional. That's all I know."

Tasia and Nikolai both sat mute as they digested everything they'd just heard.

"The dead bodies," Tasia said. "Were they Ukrainian soldiers? From the battle you had days earlier?"

"The Ukrainians took their dead with them," Boydoy said. "Those were our soldiers. We didn't know what to do with them so we put them in a mass grave. Bathroom?"

Tasia raised her hand for him to stay. "One last thing. You said he had protection on the bridge. A man with a rifle. What made you think he was a professional?"

"I could tell by the way he moved, how he held his gun. But even more than that, it was just the way he carried himself. He was so ... calm." Boydoy pleaded with his eyes. "Can I go now, please?"

Tasia looked up at the camera. "Open the door," she said.

The door buzzed open.

She nodded at Boydoy who made like the *NLO* out of the interrogation room.

"Why would this guy – whoever he is," Nikolai said, "why would he want the bodies of dead Russian soldiers? He must be Russian."

"A Russian in American boots?" Tasia said.

"Who else would want dead Russian bodies?" Nikolai said.

"That is what we're going to find out."

THIRTY

ADAM STOOD beside the Farmer as he knocked on his daughter's bedroom door.

"Teresa, open the door," he said, "and come out. We have a guest in our house. I have to introduce you to him."

Teresa didn't answer.

"Remember what your mother taught you," the Farmer said. "You must be gracious to guests in your home. You must treat them better than you treat yourself. That's what it means to be European."

The Farmer paused and waited for a sound from the other side of the door.

None came.

"Our guest is a young man from Munich," he said. "He needs your help, Teresa. He's looking for a girl. He wants to show you a picture ... see if you recognize her ... ask you some questions. It's his long-lost love. Imagine that. A young man from Munich coming here in the middle of a war looking for his girl ... shouldn't we help him?"

The Farmer paused again, and another moment of silence passed.

"I'm going to go to the kitchen now," he said, following the script that Adam had suggested, "and let you talk."

The Farmer gave Adam an uneasy nod and lumbered away.

Adam leaned into the doorway so that his voice could be heard without raising it.

"When I was your age," Adam said, "pretty much everyone in school hated me – my classmates, the older kids, the younger kids, the teachers, even the people who cleaned the bathrooms. There were a few exceptions – there's always some kind people no matter where you go. But for the most part, they hated me. They hated that I existed. Doesn't matter why – the reasons don't matter.

"Lunch time became the thing. There was this gang. Their leader was a girl a year older than me. Her name was Renata. She and her friends – they lived to terrorize me. They started this competition – who could throw the grossest thing at me while everyone was watching. They started with water balloons, moved on to raw eggs, and ended with horse manure. One of them brought a bucket of it to school and dumped it over my head from behind.

"Eva was a year ahead of me. She was different – the way I was. After lunch that day we all went outside to play and Eva beat the tar out of that kid that dumped the manure on my head. Kicked him in the balls, kneed him in the head, flattened his nose. I guess she felt sorry for me – I guess she understood what I was going through. No doubt she thought of me as a little boy back then, but I was completely in love with her from the moment I saw her. Eventually we became adults and the relationship changed the way I always dreamed it would.

"And then I lost her."

Adam stopped speaking.

Three beats later he heard a thump from inside the room, as

though something – or someone's feet – had fallen to the floor. A shuffling noise followed, and then a bolt slid out of a cylinder.

The door swung open. A lanky teenager – all skin and cheekbones – leveled her doe eyes at him.

"What do you mean, you lost her?" Teresa said, twirling strands of her regal blonde hair.

"Can I come in?" Adam said.

Teresa stepped aside and let him into her room. It featured splashes of bright colors with cozy accents – a fake fur rug, gauzy curtains and fuzzy throw pillows on the single bed. A vast collection of stickers, magazine cut-outs and pictures covered an entire wall – all of them consisted of images of popular female social influencers.

"I lost her," Adam said. He quickly moved to the diagonal corner furthest from her bed to maximize her personal space. "We were on the run. Some men were after us – they thought we had something worth stealing – but we didn't. We got separated. I stayed and searched. For three years. But I never saw her again. Until a few days ago."

Teresa sat down on her bed. "Where did you see her?"

She brought her knees to her chest and wrapped her arms around them as though she was trying to disappear into a shell of her own making.

"In Krakow," Adam said.

"Oh my God. I so want to go there ... And then what happened?"

"She made her way here. I haven't seen her again but others have."

"Meaning, you lost her again."

"Yeah. Pretty much."

Adam removed Eva's passport photo from his wallet. It had been taken when she was twenty. He took three steps toward

Teresa's bed and held it out with a straight arm so as not to perturb her by coming closer. He knew there was no chance she'd recognize the photo, but he had to humanize Eva as much as possible to win Teresa's trust.

"Whoa," she said, studying the photo with a look of awe. "She has an unbelievable Fibonacci ratio."

"Fibonacci ratio?" Adam said.

"Golden Ratio," Teresa said. "The length of a person's face divided by its width. It measures facial symmetry. The perfect number is 1.6. Then you measure from your hairline to the spot between your eyes, from the spot between your eyes to the bottom of the nose, and from the bottom of the nose to the chin. The closer the numbers, the more beautiful the person. Even Leonardo da Vinci said so. When I start making my own money, I'm going to make my face as perfect as I can. But your girlfriend ... your girlfriend was born that way."

"She'd be twelve years older than that picture now," Adam said.

Teresa let her eyes linger on the photo an extra moment. "I wish I'd seen her in person so I could take her picture and show it to my plastic surgeon someday. But no, I've never seen her."

Adam collected the picture and returned it to his wallet.

"What are you going to do next?" she said.

"Keep searching. What about you? What are you doing to do next?"

"Me?"

"You have dreams," Adam said. "You're obviously a smart person. You must have a plan. But you're not eating or leaving the room or talking to your father. What's up with that?"

"So that's why you're here. My father brought you. What are you, some sort of therapist? Is any of that story true or did you make it all up just to win my trust?"

"Every single word I told you is true," Adam said. "Let me ask you a question. Are you a spiritual person?"

"Excuse me?" Teresa said.

"Do you believe there is something more to a person than a brain and a body?"

"Anyone paying attention to the way Ukrainians are fighting knows there is."

"Then hold my hand and trust me," Adam said.

"You want me to hold your hand?"

"You've heard of palm readers, right? Well, I'm something like that, but not quite the same."

"For real?"

"I want you to trust your instincts. Do you trust me, Teresa?"

Adam stepped over to her bed and held out his hand.

Teresa hesitated, then reached out and grasped it.

One beat, two beats, three beats passed. Teresa sat on the bed awake and aware but unable to move. Adam's eyes closed. Convulsions gave way to calmness. The images came rapid-fire and faded just as quickly—

A woman sneaks out of a farmhouse at daybreak, wheeling luggage to a luxury sedan as Teresa watches from her bedroom window.

The Farmer sobs as he drains oil from one of his tractors, unaware his daughter is hiding in the barn and watching him.

Teresa sneaks out the window. She meets another girl her age and a handsome Russian soldier outside the farmhouse.

Six Russian soldiers rape Teresa's friend as she watches, bound and gagged to a chair.

A Russian soldier with two stripes and stars on his uniform breaks up the gang rape and berates his subordinates.

The handsome Russian soldier who lured Teresa from her home whispers something in her ear and frees her.

"What did that Russian soldier say to you before he let you go?" Adam said, after releasing Teresa's hand.

She stared at him, mouth agape.

Adam repeated his question.

"He called himself Blu," she said dreamily, as though in a trance. "He was so gorgeous. I'd never met a boy with a perfect Fibonacci ratio. I wanted him to be nice. I wanted it so badly."

"I know," Adam said.

"He told me if I told anyone about what they did he'd come back and kill me and my father. He said he'd tie us up and douse us with gasoline and light a match and no one would miss us because we were just *khokhols*."

Adam regarded Teresa as an underage girl, but the circumstances required him to consider her from the Russian soldier's point of view.

"I get it," Adam said, "but I wonder if we can improve on your plan."

"What plan?" Teresa said.

"Starving yourself isn't healthy and probably won't get the result you want. Don't take this the wrong way, but you'll still be pretty. Those clothes you're wearing ... they probably used to fit you snug, now they're a little loose, but they're still not helping you. You'd feel less of a target if you started wearing some of your father's old shirts and some baggy pants."

Teresa squirmed

"But the real problem is your hair," Adam said.

"What's wrong with my hair? It's the only thing about me that I like."

"That's what I mean," Adam said. "It's a magnet, don't you

think? And if you're trying to repel something, isn't it counter-productive to hold onto a magnet?"

Teresa's face flushed.

"Does your father have a set of hair clippers?" Adam said.

She looked horrified.

"I take that as a yes," he said.

She stared at him. Her expression gradually appeared more reflective.

"You're not going to tell my father about ... about what happened," she said.

"Neither are you," Adam said. "Agreed?"

Teresa nodded.

They went to the kitchen. The Farmer cried when his daughter appeared. He started to hug her but stopped himself as though he didn't want to push his luck. Adam pulled the Farmer aside and asked him to get his hair clippers.

"Why?" the Farmer whispered.

"I think your daughter might prefer to attract less attention for the time being, at least until the war is over."

The Farmer looked aghast. "Why? Did something happen I don't know about?"

"Yes, sir," Adam said. "Her imagination ran away with her."

"Ah," the Farmer said, with a sigh of relief. "Her imagina-tion. The mind wanders. Anxiety sets in. Now I understand. I'll get the clippers."

While he searched for them, Teresa kept busy by texting furiously. She smiled as she did so, and gradually appeared more excited. When her father finally returned, he set a dining chair near an electrical plug and asked his daughter to take a seat.

"I want him to do it," Teresa said, looking at Adam.

"Oh, no," Adam said. "I have no experience with those things. I'll mess it up."

"That's kind of hard to do given you're giving me a buzz cut, don't you think?" she said.

"I still might find a way."

"Stand back, Papa. Mister Ziegler is going to do this or I'm going back to my room and I'm not eating or coming out for the next week."

The Farmer handed Adam the clippers. Adam draped a clean towel over her shoulders and started cautiously at the base of her neck. By the time he was done, two of Teresa's girlfriends had arrived. She had texted them that she was about to shave her head. Adam cut her friends' hair also, only to have nine more girls show up. An hour later the Farmer was filling up a contractor bag with hair while Adam's customers vied for the title of least attractive girl in the room.

Adam waited impatiently for the Farmer to finish his sweeping. He'd done his bit and now he wanted the instructions he was owed. When the Farmer stepped out of the house to bring the bag of hair to one of his barns, Adam followed.

Teresa intercepted him before he got outside.

"I owe you an apology," she said.

"For what?" Adam said.

"I lied to you earlier."

"About what?"

"Your girl – Eva. I told you I've never seen her. That wasn't true."

"What?"

"I didn't want to get involved – I didn't want more drama. Not after everything we've been through. But now ... I didn't want you to leave without knowing the truth."

"You've ... you've seen Eva ... in person?" Adam said. "When was this?"

"A few days ago. After the Russian soldiers left. She was

here with some Ukrainian soldiers. My father said one of them was a colonel, I think."

"Your father saw her, too?"

"He met her," Teresa said. "I saw him shake her hand. But here's the thing. It was her – it was the person you saw in Krakow, I'm guessing – but it wasn't Eva. It was – Almost Eva."

"I don't understand," Adam said.

"It wasn't her. It was a woman that looked like her. She has to be the woman you're looking for. I mean, like, what are the odds there'd be another person that looks so similar in the exact place where you are? But it wasn't your Eva. I don't care if ten or twenty years have passed since that picture was taken. It wasn't the same girl."

"How can you know that? How can you be so sure?"

"Because I know faces. The Fibonacci number was off. She wasn't a 1.6. She was a bit less, meaning her face wasn't quite as long for its width. And the distance from her nose to her chin was a bit short compared to the higher points on her face. She wasn't as symmetrical. Not the same person. If the girl in your photo is Eva, this was Almost Eva."

Adam stood flabbergasted. He remembered his phone conversation with Victor after he'd informed his uncle that Eva had robbed him. Victor had asked, *did you see her with your own eyes? Saw her, smelled her, touched her,* Adam had answered, dismissing any suggestion that the woman was an imposter. But in fact, he'd been drugged at the time. How could he have been certain he'd seen her?

"Some of my friends," Teresa said, smiling and glancing at the floor awkwardly, "they'd like to thank you in person ..."

"I would love to meet them but I've got to go," Adam said. "I'm so sorry. I really am. Take care of your father, Teresa. A person is lucky if she has someone who'll take a bullet for her. I don't have anyone like that in my life. You do."

She didn't respond. Instead, she stood there in place, chin up, and watched him leave.

Adam marched out the front door. Mikey, leaning against the Jeep, spread his hands out wide as though asking what was going on. Under different circumstances, Adam might have smiled at him. No doubt the procession of teenage girls to a farmer's house forty-eight kilometers from a war zone had been quite a sight. But Adam was preoccupied, and not simply with Teresa's suggestion that the woman he was chasing was Almost Eva. One of the images he'd acquired kept flashing in his eyes.

Rape, Adam thought. He couldn't seem to get away from it, nor could he comprehend it, not the act itself or the men who committed the crime. Victor really was so right. Some men needed to die – period. And in this scenario, he could not deny the absolute truth – all the men were Russian soldiers.

"That woman was your girl?" the Farmer said, when Adam repeated what Teresa had told him. "I had no idea. I shook her hand, don't even remember her name – not sure she ever mentioned it. Come to think of it, I don't think she said a single word. She came with the officer from Territorial Defense when I called for help."

"The colonel?" Adam said.

"That's right. I assumed she was his assistant or something. I wanted the government to know I'd been robbed. Luca arranged for him to come. If she was your girl, why didn't she just stay? What's this all about between the two of you?"

"I'm trying to figure that out myself. Can you show me the number you're supposed to text?"

"Sure," the Farmer said, pulling out his mobile phone. "Why don't you watch while I send the text."

The Farmer called up a number he'd saved under the name *healer* and texted a single word.

Done.

A response arrived twenty seconds later. The Farmer read it, frowned, and handed his phone to Adam.

Dearest Werner (ha),

The Mystic is waiting for you at our favorite remote location, where previously extinct species won't drink the water. The Russians are intent on destroying the only place where the two of us ever felt as though we belonged.

It's up to us to save it.

Hurry!

XOXO,

Eva

"What is this place she speaks of?" the Farmer said.

"A special sanctuary," Adam said.

He thanked the Farmer for his hospitality and raced to the Jeep.

"Where are we going?" Mikey said, once they were both inside.

"North," Adam said.

He called the number that Eva had just used but it rolled to voicemail without a single ring.

"North can mean a lot of things," Mikey said. "Can you be more specific?"

"North of Kyiv toward the Belarusian border."

"The Belarus border?" Mikey said. "They have troops stacked there, you know."

"Don't worry about it," Adam said. "There's no chance the Belarusian troops are going where we're going."

"How can you be so sure?"

"Because apparently the Russian troops have already taken control of it," Adam said.

"Oh, great," Mikey said. "That's a relief."

Adam sent a text to Eva's number. In the text, he asked her a question that only the real Eva could answer.

"Prove to me you are who you say you are. What was our doctor's name?"

Adam didn't expect an answer.

He didn't get one.

THIRTY-ONE

TASIA WINCED as her head smashed against the roof in the back seat of her SUV for the third time in the last minute.

"You're killing me here," she said, firing an angry glance at Nikolai in the rearview mirror.

He seemed to be aiming for the craters in the dirt access road, though admittedly, they were everywhere.

"You have to ask yourself the question," Tasia said, "is the joy you get from watching your superior suffer worth getting re-assigned to a fish farm in Chukotka, where the highlight of your day will be staring through a pair of binoculars at the Bering Sea, knowing Alaska is somewhere out there but you'll never see it, because you'll be stuck at that fish farm for the rest of your life?"

Nikolai took his foot off the throttle. "Sorry, boss."

"Don't call me that. You know I hate that."

"Sorry, boss."

"What's wrong with you today?" Tasia said.

"I guess ... I guess I'm a little edgy. We're in enemy territory."

"And where do you think we are the rest of the time? Our private yachts in Croatia? Get used to it. We're not leaving for years, if ever."

The access road led to an abandoned paper mill. A chill-looking guard with an assault rifle stood beside two sawhorses blocking the entry. Beyond him, a team of armed men examined crates of boxes in the back of a delivery truck.

Nikolai came to a stop. He and Tasia rolled down their windows. The guard stooped to glance at both of them.

"You folks lost?" he said.

"I'm here to do a deal," Tasia said.

"A deal?" the guard said. "This is a mill, not a flea market."

"Tell Bertie I'm here," she said. Bertie, of course, had no idea who she was or why she was there. "He's expecting me."

"You have an appointment?"

"No," Tasia said, offering her business card through the window. "He does. With a prosecutor, a judge, and a prison cell. Unless he meets with me now. And tell him there's no escape. The eye in the sky is literally watching us as we speak. And if anything were to happen to either of us, you'll all be reduced to charcoal in a matter of seconds."

The guard marched over to the others, handed the card to a man drinking from a thermos cup, and spoke with him. He glanced at her vehicle, passed the business card around to the other four men, and talked to them. While the guard headed back toward the entrance, the others closed the back of the delivery truck and secured it with a lock.

The guard moved a saw horse and let them pass. Nikolai parked as far away as possible from two freshly detailed Mercedes SUVs per Tasia's instructions. One of the vehicles was silver, the other black.

"I have a rule," Bertie said, when Tasia and Nikolai stepped out of the vehicle. "No guns in my office."

"My weapon is in the trunk," Tasia said.

"I'm an officer of the FSB," Nikolai said. "I don't surrender my weapon to anyone."

"My office, my rules," Bertie said. "You came here on your own. You weren't invited."

Tasia nodded at Nikolai, who stored his primary weapon and the backup he kept holstered to his ankle in the trunk.

"Thank you," Bertie said. "Step into my office."

They sat on boxes and cartons near a burned-out drum that appeared to be used for fire in the evening. Some of Bertie's men drank water from gallon jugs, others from liter bottles of Coca-Cola.

"We don't care much for cops," Bertie said. "Any kind of cops. Do we fellas?"

"Tasia, Tasia," one of his men said. "Who's the dumbest woman here?"

"How would I know?" she said. "I don't know which of your girlfriends is inside."

The men remained stone-faced.

"Tasia, Tasia," another man said. "If you had to give me a blowjob to get this deal done, would you do it?"

"How could I?" Tasia said. "I didn't bring my magnifying glass with me."

None of the men reacted except for Bertie, who chuckled.

"Tasia, Tasia," a third man said, "if my rifle wanted to fuck you in the ass, would you let it?"

"You need to see an optometrist," Tasia said. "You have me confused with one of your friends here."

Bertie laughed out loud. The other men found nothing amusing about her answer.

"What is it you want from us, Lieutenant Ivanova?" Bertie said.

"First, I'll tell you want I don't want. I don't want to put you out of business. I'm not here about your black market activities. Your deals don't interest me – except for one. My sources in the Army tell me you traded two Ukrainian POWs for the bodies of six of our deceased boys the other night. I need to know the name of the man who arranged that deal with you. I need to know the name of the Ukrainian who made it happen."

"You're asking a lot," Bertie said. "He's an important source to us. We've done a bunch of deals with him. If you're looking for him, that he means he might disappear for a while, or even longer. Am I right?"

Tasia didn't answer. Nikolai also remained mute.

"If we were to lose him as a source," Bertie said, "it would stand to reason that we should be compensated for the profit we lose. It's only logical, right boys?"

A murmur of assent rose from his men.

"I have every intention of compensating you for your cooperation," Tasia said.

"Phenomenal," Bertie said. "That's all we ask." He smiled and rubbed his hands together. "What was the figure you had in mind?"

Tasia did the math in her head. "Six figures," she said.

Bertie's eyes widened. "Six figures? In American dollars?"

"No," Tasia said. "I mean, literally, six figures." She pointed at Bertie and each of his men, and counted. "One, two, three, four, five ... and the chill guard at the entrance. Six figures."

Bertie frowned. "What are you talking about?"

"I'm going to compensate you with your lives. I'm going to let you continue living. To be specific, I'm not going to have the drone that's close by eradicate the six figures that are lit up like Christmas trees on the pilot's computer screen in Moscow right now."

Bertie and his team exchanged uncertain glances, until – one-by-one – they started laughing.

"You're crazy," Bertie said. "If you weren't already employed, we might ask you to join our team."

"Bully for me," Tasia said.

"What you didn't think through when you planned this charade is that we're protected," Bertie said. "Who do you think gave us those two Ukrainian POWs to trade? Who do you think has our back on all our transactions?"

Tasia smiled. "I bet it's the same organization that's given me access to the satellite that's watching us and the drone that's waiting for my command. Same Russian Army, different set of officers, as in, mine have more stripes and stars on their shoulders. Allegiances shift during war, you know? But hey, talk is cheap." Tasia glanced at the two Mercedes. "Which color do you prefer, silver or black?"

"Excuse me?" Bertie said.

"Silver or black? Pick one."

"Why?" Bertie studied her. "What are going to do? Place a call to someone on stand-by to press a button? Even if there is such a person – and I doubt it – do you really think we're going to let you make that call?"

"Why would I need to call someone when they've been listening to this entire conversation?" Tasia said. "Can't make up your mind? No problem. I'll decide for you. Black cars look better in the shade. We'll keep the black one. If you have anything valuable in the silver Mercedes, I highly recommend not making a run for it. I don't think you'll make it."

Bertie studied her for a beat, then smiled at his men. They chuckled and put on happy faces, too. Still, Tasia thought, never had six men with assault rifles appeared more uncertain.

"So, what's going to happen?" Bertie said. "Is it just going to go *poof*?"

A missile came zipping in from above. It crashed into the

silver Mercedes and exploded. When the dust cleared, Bertie and his boys sat staring at a metallic ball of fire.

"He lives in a village called Ruta," Bertie said, without taking his eyes off the flames. "I don't know his last name. Just his first name. It's Luca. His name is Luca."

THIRTY-TWO

ADAM PULLED into a filling station to refuel the Jeep. He'd taken over from Mikey to give him a break after three hours of driving. Two other cars and an ambulance occupied the other bays.

"You want an energy drink or something?" Mikey said, after filling his tank.

"Water," Adam said, as he looked for a shady spot from which to make his phone call.

"Something to eat?"

"Not for me. I eat once a day."

"What if this turns out to be your only chance to eat today?"

"Highly unlikely," Adam said. "Unless we're caught or killed. And if that happens, it won't matter, will it?"

"You realize that's like promising me that we're going to a place where there's going to be dinner. And I mean like, a hot, home-cooked meal."

Adam stared at him for a few beats. "Do you hear me disagreeing?"

Mikey smiled. He sang under his breath as he headed toward the store. "Bayraktar ... Bayraktar ... Bayraktar ..."

Adam followed him and continued walking beyond the entrance to the store to get some privacy. He kept his eye on the Jeep from behind a dumpster, and placed his call out of earshot of all the other patrons.

Victor picked up after the first ring. That meant he'd been holding the phone in his hand – probably sleeping with it – in hopes that Adam would call.

"How's Nina doing with the meds?" Adam said.

"Terrible," Victor said. "She's confusing the dosages and thinks punctuality is a sign of weakness. I need my full-time caretaker to return to New York City immediately. Status?"

Adam provided Victor with an abbreviated version of the events since they'd last spoken.

"Where are you right now?" Victor said. "East of Lviv?"

"About an hour away."

"Away from where? From Lviv?"

"Not exactly," Adam said. "From my destination."

"Which is?"

"A remote location, where previously extinct species won't drink the water."

Victor took a long, audible breath. "I'd tell you that an idiot has borrowed your brain, but given he has it, that wouldn't do much good, would it?"

"Anything new from Nazarov?" Adam said.

"I was going to ask you that."

"If I'd seen or heard from him, you'd know."

"And the package?" Victor said.

"That's a good question. I assume she still has it, or she's given it to the Ukrainians."

"Why do you say that?"

"I think Eva joined the Ukrainian Territorial Defense." Adam explained her interactions with Professor Boyko and the Farmer.

"I disagree," Victor said. "Eva's a Russian national. She was born in Russia. Her father was an elite Russian soldier."

"But she moved to Ukraine"

"The body may move but the heart can remain," Victor said. "If she's not merely a courier – just like you – it's just as likely she's a Russian asset posing as a Ukrainian sympathizer. But let me be clear about one thing. She hasn't given the package to the Ukrainians or the Russians. Of that I'm certain.'"

"How can you be so sure?" Adam said.

"Because if she had," Victor said, "the tide of the war would have shifted in one direction or the other. And it hasn't."

"The package – the technology you said is in it – it's that important?"

"I think so."

"Care to elaborate?" Adam said.

"Absolutely not. The less you know, the better off you are, just in case you fall into the wrong hands, which is to say, anyone's hands."

"You think she's holding onto the package because she's playing a game with me?"

"Don't you?" Victor said.

"I did, but now I'm not so sure."

"Why? What's changed?"

"I'm no longer certain she's really Eva," Adam said. "I'm not sure who I saw that morning in the hotel. I mean, she identified herself as Eva, and she looked just like her, from what I could tell, in the state I was in at the time, but I was in a state at the time. That's the cold, hard, truth. And now I'm wondering if it was all wishful thinking."

Adam had expected a wave of humiliation to wash over him after expressing his uncertainty to Victor. Instead, he felt relieved. He proceeded to explain Teresa's insistence that the woman she'd seen resembled Eva but wasn't her.

"That's hardly conclusive," Victor said. "She's a girl, not a plastic surgeon. And she was drawing conclusions from a ten-year old photograph. My original statement holds – this woman's involvement cannot be explained rationally. Not yet. But it will be eventually. And now we can add to my thesis. We can't be certain of her identity. She's either your Eva, or someone pretending to be your Eva. How does that sound?"

"True facts," Adam said.

"My concern," Victor said, "is that based on the trajectory of this journey you're on, you're going to end up on a battlefield in Donbas with a sign on your forehead that says *aim here*. Surely you can see that with each passing hour you're getting closer and closer to that place?"

"It doesn't matter. If there's a chance she really is Eva, I have to know. It doesn't matter what the risks are, or what price I'll have to pay. I lost her in Siberia, Victor. I can't lose her again. At least I'm not traveling alone this time ..."

"Not alone?" Victor sounded alarmed. "What do you mean you're not"

A crash in Victor's apartment drowned out his remaining words. A man shouted something indecipherable, and a loud slamming noise followed.

"Victor?" Adam said.

Adam heard Victor's muted voice in the distance, as though he'd left his mobile phone behind. "Leave it to the Russians to break in when all they had to do was knock," he said.

A smacking noise preceded a loud thud.

"Victor, are you there?" Adam said.

The clatter of footsteps grew louder. Adam heard breathing on the other end of the line, and then the call went dead.

Adam immediately called the twins who'd scaled the cliff in the Catskills, but they didn't answer. Adam was leaving a voice-mail for the second one when Mikey emerged from the convenience store. A pair of zip ties secured his wrists behind his back. Two Russian soldiers dragged him across the asphalt, one holding each arm. They appeared to be whispering into his ears as they walked, and judging by the hate in their eyes, they weren't sweet nothings.

After the soldiers stuffed Mikey into the back of the ambulance, one of them climbed inside with him, while the other got behind the wheel and took off.

Adam prevented himself from running to the Jeep, lest the soldier driving the ambulance see him in the rearview mirror. The walk was interminable. By the time Adam started the engine, the Russians were out of sight.

Adam sped out of the station and gave chase. The package was in the open, Eva's true identity was now uncertain, someone had broken into Victor's home and beaten him, and Russian soldiers had lifted Mikey and were taking him God knew where.

But if disaster were the sum of chaos and opportunity, there was good news among all these developments, too. Such a conclusion sounded preposterous but Adam knew it to be so. He knew it to be so because Victor had taught him

The greatest opportunities presented themselves when all hope was lost.

And Adam was on the verge of losing all hope.

THIRTY-THREE

TASIA SECURED Luca's phone number from Bertie. He answered her call with one word – *what?* She introduced herself in Ukrainian as Tina, a fellow entrepreneur. Most importantly, she informed him that Bertie had given her his number.

"Bertie vouches for you?" Luca answered, over the phone.

"He does," Tasia said.

"We'll see about that," he said, and promptly ended the call.

An hour later he called back.

"Bertie vouches for you," Luca said. "He says you have something that fell of a truck?"

"Not quite. I have something that fell off a cart, that fell off a truck, that fell off a train."

"That's a lot of falling."

"Valuable things can do that," Tasia said. "On account of the interest they attract. Especially if they're really valuable things."

"A lot valuable things start their journey on the train. I like the train."

"I love the train. Watching the countryside go by through the window. This one had armed guards."

Luca whistled. "That sounds like a train with some important cargo."

"The pharmaceutical company thought so," Tasia said.

Luca turned serious. "Medicines?"

"A man could open his own hospital. In town, or in the field."

Luca paused. "Why am I so lucky? Why didn't you deal directly with Bertie?"

"The train's point of origin was Saint Petersburg," Tasia said, "the headquarters of Russian Pharmaceutical Technologies. It's one thing to sell foreign goods to the Russians, but it's another to sell their own stuff back to them. I'm guessing the Russian Army might not be so keen to pay a premium to get the goods they already paid for."

"They might be more inclined to remove the middle-man," Luca said.

"No good deed goes unpunished."

"Isn't that the truth."

"I think the Ukrainians will offer the highest price for this cargo," Tasia said. "Don't you?"

"I can meet you tomorrow."

"Sorry, my friend. It has to be today."

Luca paused again. "Well, maybe I can shift some things around. After all, I shouldn't let my schedule stand in the way of a good deal – or some good people getting their medicines. If it has to be today, then it has to be today. Tell me what you've got and let's talk price."

After their discussion, they agreed to meet in the parking lot of a primary school eight kilometers outside of Ruta. Tasia and Nicholas arrived an hour early in three vehicles with six additional men. School was in session. Luca had insisted they meet at lunch time for a reason – children were playing dodgeball outside under the supervision of their teachers.

The combination of Bertie's endorsement, Tasia's phone call, and the presence of children and teachers on a playground most likely gave Luca the impression that he was safe. When Tasia opened the door to the van to show him her purported wares, he didn't expect to see an empty cargo area, or receive a stun-gun to his neck.

Eight hours later Luca was sitting in the interrogation room in Kherson, wrists cuffed and feet shackled. Strelkov had instructed Tasia to handle the interrogation alone, without Nikolai. From this point forward, he said, the two of them would handle the *NLO* case personally. Strelkov said he wanted to prevent *this oddity* from becoming a distraction for the entire unit. The fewer eyes on the matter, he reasoned, the better.

Tasia brought Luca water and a plate of cookies. He ignored them even though he'd had nothing to eat or drink since his capture.

"A man stole the bodies of six dead Russian soldiers from a mass grave the other day," Tasia said, her laptop computer on the table before her. "You traded those bodies to Bertie for two Ukrainian POWs."

Luca continued staring at the table, as he'd been doing since his arrival.

"The American that dug them up and carried them over the bridge ... what was his name?" she said.

Luca remained mute.

"You're going to tell us everything we want to know, one way or another, and you know that," Tasia said. "But your pride keeps you from making the smart move, which is to talk now, feast on these delicious homemade cookies, and move on with your life. Don't make me subject you to the most horrible thing you can imagine. I'll get no joy from it."

Luca responded in a monotone. "Go to hell. I've left my

body. It wasn't that difficult. Look at me. Who would miss it? For me, it no longer exists. So go ahead – do what you want to it. You'll get nothing. Just wait. You'll see. Nothing."

"Luca," Tasia said. "My dear, naïve Luca. Who risks his life to trade dead soldiers for living ones? Only a good man would do that. And you are such a good man. I know you are. But you misunderstand. No one's going to lay a hand on you. Did you know your wife has a strong social media presence?"

Luca looked up.

"It's true," Tasia said. "That's how she stays in touch with her family."

"Impossible," Luca said that. "We don't have money for that."

"Your name is Luca Badzo. Father of Luminata and Rafael. Husband of Elena, maiden name Karela, sister of Nicu."

Luca frowned.

"Nicu Karela," Tasia said. "Your brother-in-law. Attorney in Bucharest. He has money for that. He can afford a smartphone." Tasia opened her laptop and played a video that had been added two hours earlier. "Here he is, taking the dog for a walk with your wife and your children. Luminata and Rafael. Luminata – that means *little light* ... from the Romanian *lumina* ... doesn't it?"

Luca pressed his eyes shut and began to sob quietly.

"Tell me what I need to know and your family will be unharmed," Tasia said. "But tell me the truth and only the truth, because if it turns out you're lying ..."

Luca took a deep breath and gathered himself.

"His name is Werner Ziegler," he said. "He's German, not American."

"Is there anything special about him?" Tasia said.

Luca shrugged. "He's brave, smart, strong."

Tasia waited for him to say more. "That's it? Nothing else unusual about him?"

Luca appeared confused. "He's searching for a girl."

"What girl?" Tasia said.

"I don't know," Luca said. "Some girl. His girl."

"Does she have a name?"

"Eva. Her name is Eva. And he's traveling with another young man by the name of Mykhailo."

"What's his last name?" Tasia said.

"Don't know the last names," Luca said.

"How did you find these guys?" Tasia said. "And, at the risk of repeating myself, please remember the video. If I turns out you lied, and I have to ask you this question again, there will be one fewer people in the next take, but your brother-in-law will still be there."

Luca gave her the name of his contact in the Ukrainian Territorial Defense. Afterwards, she asked him to describe Ziegler and his travel companion. She followed up with a few repeat questions to see if his answers were consistent, and mixed-in her most important query to bring as little attention to it as possible.

"By the way," Tasia said, "where was this Ziegler headed?"

"To see the Farmer," Luca said. "There was a note from his girl that if he wanted to see her again, he needed to help the Farmer."

Tasia pressed him for details regarding the Farmer. Luca told him all he knew. Of that she was certain.

"My family," he stammered, when she was finished with her questions. "My wife and my children ... please ... most Russians are Christians ... I'm begging you ... in the name of all that is holy."

Tasia wished she could have comforted him. But what could she have said that was true? That Russia wasn't killing children?

That was a lie. That Russia wasn't kidnapping children? Another lie. That she could assure him his wife and children wouldn't be harmed? That, too, was a lie, because any human being who stood in the way of Russia's quest for world domination was a potential victim no matter where he lived.

And then Tasia caught a glimpse of her reflection in the two-way mirror and was reminded of her own true nature. She was an FSB officer. She, too, was built, trained and programmed to lie.

"Your family won't be harmed," she said to Luca. "That I promise you."

He thanked her profusely, his sobs coming in fits now, louder than before.

Tasia couldn't wait to get out of the room, and if she could have showered before meeting with Strelkov, she would have done so.

"The name of his contact from the Territorial Defense checks out," Strelkov said. "He's known to us. He's on our list." Strelkov raised his eyes from his laptop computer. "Do you believe this gypsy?"

"No father wants his children slain," Tasia said. "Least of all a Romani. They're all about family. Should we keep him in a cell until we find the Farmer and confirm Ziegler met with him?"

"I don't think that's necessary," Strelkov said. "If he is lying and risking his children's lives, then he'll let them all die before telling us anything. But, I don't think he's lying either."

Strelkov stood up. Tasia noticed the bulge in his pocket, the one where he carried his knife sometimes.

"I'll take care of it from here," Strelkov said. "Give me the keys to his restraints. I want to say hello to him personally, if you know what I mean."

Tasia handed him the keys and marched down the hall

toward her desk. She heard Strelkov enter the interrogation room and the sound of his voice.

"Hello, Luca. My name is Colonel Strelkov. I'm here to free you from the Russian chains that bind you. You're from Ruta, yes? I hear it's lovely there. Any good restaurants? You locals ... you know all the secret handshakes."

It was a familiar refrain, Tasia thought. She remembered all too vividly what came next.

Tasia picked up her pace. She passed her desk and took aim for the exit. Five more steps and she'd be out the door and running. Faster, she told herself. Faster, lest she heard the scream, the blood-curdling scream that was imminent ...

One step, two steps, three steps—

Too late.

Luca howled and wailed.

Tasia flung the door open, but instead of the white clouds floating in the clear blue sky, all she could see was Luca's fate.

THIRTY-FOUR

ADAM SPED along the single lane road. He passed a truck overflowing with hay and two passenger cars. Three other vehicles drove by him in the opposite direction. Still, there was no ambulance in sight. His fear that he'd come upon it too quickly and alert the driver of his presence quickly gave way to despair that he'd lost Mikey for good. And all the while he wondered if Victor was still alive.

He entered the outer limits of a city called Tsarstvo eight kilometers from the gas station. A multi-lane highway ran along the edge of town. Strangely, there was no visible traffic on the freeway in either direction. In fact, all of the streets within his peripheral vision appeared empty. Perhaps the Russians had arrived in Tsarstvo, Adam thought. The two soldiers who'd lifted Mikey certainly weren't alone.

Adam cruised into the city. A park with a basketball court sat empty. Further down the road, the railroad station came into view. It appeared meticulously maintained, its green copper roof dazzling against freshly-painted brown window arches. And yet Adam didn't see any people inside, despite the presence of half a dozen cars in the parking lot.

Further on, the cityscape began to change. Vacant lots gradually gave way to a consistent mix of homes and businesses. A row of houses faced a fire station and an office building with flat roofs. Across the street, in front of one of the houses, a black and white cat was sniffing up a storm near a drain sewer.

A barefoot old man in underwear burst out the front door. He teetered down his walkway, calling to his pet.

Adam pulled over and got out of the Jeep.

"Domino," the Grandfather cried in Ukrainian. "Domino, come here. Come to Papa."

But the cat made a beeline toward Adam as soon as it saw him. Adam petted the cat, which promptly lied down on his shoe.

The Grandfather approached tentatively.

"Who are you?" he said, in Russian.

"I'm a tourist," Adam said, in Ukrainian. "From Germany."

"Oh, thank God." Then he frowned and switched to Ukrainian. "Wait. Did you say tourist? You're touring? Now?"

"You're the first person I've seen since I drove into the city. Where is everyone? Are they gone or just hiding?"

"Yes," the Grandfather said. "And you would be wise to do the same."

A storm door squeaked open and slammed shut behind them. Adam turned and saw an old woman clutching the fringe of her oversized plaid robe so that it covered every sliver of her neck.

"Who is he?" the Grandmother said.

"A tourist," the Grandfather said. "From Germany. I think he's lost."

"Lost?" the Grandmother said. "How is that possible? He missed the turn to Slovakia?"

"Careful," the Grandfather said. "He speaks our language."

"Really? Oh, well in that case, you better bring him inside. Quick, before we all end up touring the after-life."

The Grandfather lurched forward to scoop up his cat but it did a figure eight through Adam's legs and came to rest on his other foot, away from his owner's reach.

"Domino really likes you," the Grandfather said. "And Domino doesn't like anyone. Do you work with animals?"

"I used to," Adam said. "You know, the usual, herding reindeer and the like. You want me to pick her up?"

"If you would be so bold."

Adam scooped up the Grandfather's pet, squished it gently against his body the way cats liked, and brought it into the house. The front door opened directly into a living room. The shades were drawn and the lights were off. A dozen photos of two young men in various stages of life rested on a bookshelf. The men appeared to be in their forties at their oldest, posing with women and children at a beach. Swaths of black cloth covered the upper corners of each of the picture frames.

The Grandmother took the cat from Adam, scolded it, and then showered it with pets and kisses.

"The Russians are coming," the Grandfather said. "They've taken Tsarstvo."

"They just haven't gotten to our part of town yet," the Grandmother said.

"But they will," the Grandfather said.

"We have to get to the basement," the Grandmother said. "But first, how can we help you? Domino likes you. Domino doesn't like anyone. What are you doing here? There's a war in this country. You're mad for coming here. But you don't look mad. You look like a man with a purpose."

"I'm looking for my friend," Adam said. "I thought he might have come this way."

"Your friend lives in Tsarstvo?" she said.

"Not exactly," Adam said. "I saw him in the company of two men who I thought might be headed to a place where there are Russian soldiers."

"What made you think that?" the Grandfather said.

"The Russian uniforms they were wearing," Adam said.

"Russian soldiers took your friend?" the Grandmother said. "Oh, my. Where did this happen?"

Adam described the gas station and its location.

The couple exchanged a knowing glance.

"What is it?" Adam said.

"It's best you leave," the Grandfather said. "I know this must be difficult to hear."

"It's hard to let go of someone you love," the Grandmother said.

"But it won't help him any," the Grandfather said, "if you're ..."

Adam waited for his wife to finish the sentence but neither of them spoke.

"If I'm what?" Adam said.

"The Russians are taking prisoners to a place from which there's no return," the Grandmother said.

"What place?" Adam said.

"You mustn't go there," the Grandfather said.

"What place?" Adam said.

"You must go home, dear," the Grandmother said. "You must have family. You must have people who care about you"

"Thank you," Adam said. "You're both very kind. But I'm going to find him no matter what it takes. It'll be safer for me if you help me get to where I need to go."

The couple looked at each other again. The Grandfather held his wife's eyes until she finally shrugged. Then he pulled some paper and a pencil from a drawer, and drew Adam a crude map with directions to his destination.

"Why are you so certain this is the place where they took my friend?" Adam said.

The Grandfather said, "This is the place where they take prisoners for interrogation. Mostly young men they think may have served in the military, community leaders, anyone who looks suspicious, and anyone they don't like."

"My husband is being polite," the Grandmother said. "What he's trying to say is that this is the place where the Russians take prisoners to torture and execute. They're using pliers, hammers, and saws. That is what we've been told."

Adam stared at the map her husband had drawn. A large X marked Adam's destination. According to the Grandfather, the area contained barracks, large playing fields, and a man-made lake.

"Does this place have a name?" Adam said.

"It does," the Grandfather said. "You'll see signs for it when you get close."

"Signs?" Adam said.

"It's called Summer Camp," the Grandmother said. "The Russians have taken your friend to Summer Camp."

THIRTY-FIVE

ADAM PARKED the Jeep in the woods three kilometers from Summer Camp. The grandfather had drawn a route to avoid the roads surrounding the Russian stronghold in Tsarstvo. Adam, however, was equally concerned with his exact place of arrival. With the couple's help, he modified their directions to place him at the least likely arrival point, the furthest and most inconvenient for any visitor, and the one the Russians would most likely be ignoring.

He took his backpack and hiked a kilometer to the far side of the lake at Summer Camp. The sheer size of the body of water stunned Adam – a complete walk around the path that surrounded it would have spanned at least ten kilometers. Adam avoided the exposed walkway and maintained a quick pace through the forest that surrounded the water.

When he arrived at the far side of the lake, he took cover behind an oak tree, pulled his binoculars from his knapsack, and studied the Camp's layout. The entrance was directly in front of him, about a quarter mile away. Three soldiers sat with their backs against a military transport truck. They were smoking and drinking from their canteens, their rifles propped up against an armored vehicle blocking the road. To his left, no more than a hundred feet away, stood a rectangular building that comprised the kitchen, commissary and dining hall. To his far right were the barracks, fifty meters away, three single-level dormitories with pitched roofs. His hope – and fear – was that Mikey was being held captive in one of those buildings.

A group of five Russian soldiers were playing with the swing sets in the central field. They took turns seeing which of them could spit the furthest from his highest elevation, with the losers forced to drink from their bottles. Beside them, four others were playing tether ball with a peculiar twist. One of the soldiers was placed along the arc where the ball traveled, and the player's objective was to connect the ball with that man's head. Those who succeeded continued to play, while those who missed were forced to drink. Meanwhile, the walls of the dining hall pulsated from the bass of some Russian hard rock music with occasional bursts of laughter and shouting rising above the din.

Everyone and everything in sight was drunk. Three soldiers staggered out of the dining room to smoke their cigarettes outside. That brought the number of Russians outside the buildings to twelve, excluding those guarding the entrance at the far end of the campsite. Adam needed all of those men to move indoors, or for night to fall. Until that happened, he couldn't approach the barracks safely. He was confident he could negotiate the distance to the barracks in three blinks of an eye, but he'd be completely exposed during his run.

Adam watched and waited. Over the course of the next hour, a total of ten soldiers emerged from the three barracks. Some trudged along while others stumbled toward the dining area. They all used the latrine behind the kitchen before disappearing into the mess hall. Two soldiers reappeared carrying plates and bottles. They marched back into the far barracks, the only sober-looking individuals Adam had seen.

The tether ball and swing set competitors eventually retired to the mess hall. Only the never-ending procession of chain-smokers remained outdoors. If chain-smoking were an Olympic relay event, the Russians would win gold every year prior to being disqualified for some ethical violation. While a threesome puffed away, the door to the dining room cracked open, and a booming voice ordered the remaining soldiers to come inside for a briefing. The smokers tossed their cigarettes to the ground and stomped them out. When the screen door to the mess hall swung shut behind them, Adam took off.

He covered the distance to the back of the barracks in three seconds. A tank sat parked behind the buildings. Beside it was the ambulance. Adam recalled his promise to Mikey that they would enjoy a hot meal once they arrived at their destination this evening. The sight of the ambulance reminded Adam that the day, as it turned out, was far from over.

The barracks contained windows and doors in the back. He crept to the window closest to him. Voices sounded from the far barracks. Two – no, three men – speaking Russian in conversational tones.

The voices became more animated, then rose to a crescendo and ceased. Three beats later a shout and a scream were followed by the sound of glass breaking and a loud scraping noise, as though something were being dragged against the floor.

Adam looked up, noted the recesses among the wooden planks, and promptly scaled the wall to the roof of the barracks closest to him.

The door to the far barracks flew open.

Adam hovered at the edge, prepared to pounce.

Mikey raced out the door, paused to get his bearings, and continued running beyond the barracks, away from the center of

Camp. Adam jumped to ground and whistled like Victor. Mikey slowed down enough to turn. When he saw Adam running toward him, he tried to turn around completely, tripped over his feet, and fell.

"I can't believe you're here," Mikey said.

A black and blue welt covered his left eye. Dried blood covered his nose, chin and shirt.

Adam offered him a hand.

"You okay?" Adam said.

Mikey rose under his own power.

"Yeah," Mikey said.

"Can you run?" Adam said.

"Not like you," Mikey said.

Adam led the way. He pushed Mikey to his limit to get them out of danger as quickly as possible. Once Summer Camp was out of sight, he slowed down to a measured pace. They didn't speak until they arrived at the Jeep and Mikey's breathing had returned to normal.

"I can drive," Adam said.

"No way," Mikey said. He opened his palm for Adam to toss him the keys. "I already screwed up by letting those jerks take me. I've got to do the job you're paying me to do."

Adam didn't argue. He removed his backpack, climbed into the passenger seat and gave Mikey directions that would put him back on the road they'd left to stop at the filling station.

"What happened in the convenience store?" Adam said, after they began their drive.

"I made a stupid mistake," Mikey said.

"What was that?"

"I said hello."

"Not to the soldiers," Adam said.

"I didn't even see those bastards. They were looking at ice

215

cream behind a display case with paper towels and stuff. I said hello to the guy at the counter."

"Why was that a mistake?"

"Because I said hello in Ukrainian. And my accent is from the west of the country. And I'm in the eighteen to thirty range, which make me military age. Boom. That's all it took for them to kidnap me."

They came upon an intersection. Adam told Mikey which way to go.

"So, what happened then?" Adam said.

"They brought me there," Mikey said. "Took my phone, checked all my contacts and phone records – but don't worry. You're not on it. Then they started asking me questions about my past, who I know in the military, that sort of thing."

"And things got rough," Adam said.

"And things got rough."

Adam remembered informing Victor that he wasn't traveling alone in Ukraine. Victor had reacted with immediate suspicion.

Adam glanced at Mikey's blood-stained shirt. "How did you get out of there?"

"Once they knew I was from Lviv," Mikey said, "they kept coming back to whether I knew anything about strategic routes from the West. I mean, it was stupid – how would I know anything about how military supplies are getting into Ukraine? I'm a freaking nobody. I'm an actor, and I'm not even that."

"Don't sell yourself short."

"I told them to get me a map and I started making stuff up. They kept drinking and eventually they bought it. I kind of got the sense that it didn't really matter to them if I was lying. What they wanted was information that they could give to a superior and say, *hey, we got this on our own. It might be true. it might not be. But we got it.* I don't think they really cared if I was telling the truth or not. Like, they don't really care if they win this war. You know what I mean?"

"How did you overpower them? They must have tied you up, right?"

"Once I started feeding them a good story they could tell their superiors, they eased up. They brought me some food and water. Man, I can't believe how dry my mouth got. That was the most scared I've ever been in my life, and I thought I was going to die from thirst. They took the cuffs off my wrists so I could eat – you know, the plastic kind. We'd kind of gotten friendly by then. When two of them started having a philosophical conversation about the war and things got a little heated, I made my move."

"What move?" Adam said.

"I bottled one of the guys, lifted the table and smashed it against the other two, knocked them over and got out."

Adam glanced at Mikey's knuckles. They appeared unblemished and unbruised, wrapped comfortably around the steering wheel. Mikey looked Adam's way as he was measuring his hands.

"I knocked one of them out with the table," Mikey said, "not my fists. And kicked the other guy with my boot when he was down."

"Ah," Adam said.

"You don't believe me," Mikey said.

"I didn't say that," Adam said.

"You didn't say it, but I could tell you were thinking it."

"What would you think if you were in my shoes? The odds of escaping from captivity from the world's second most powerful military can't be high. But you managed to do it. What rational person wouldn't question that?"

"Second most powerful," Mikey said, "that's funny."

"Plus, the truth is … I've only known you for a few days."

"They were drunk," Mikey said.

"Which is another way of saying, I don't really know you at all."

"And getting drunker."

"You could be working for the Ukrainians – your uncle, Eva, the Farmer ... or the Russians – your escape was against all odds no matter how you describe it, especially for an actor in training. Or you could be working for a private party—"

"I'm working for you," Mikey said. "I'm your driver."

"Lots of people have multiple employers."

The cabin turned silent except for the road noise.

"I'm your friend," Mikey said.

"I don't have any friends," Adam said.

Tires crushed pebbles along the tarmac.

"I'm your brother," Mikey said.

"I don't have any family," Adam said.

They hit a clear stretch devoid of debris.

"I'm your protector," Mikey whispered.

"That's the best." Adam chuckled. "Do me a favor – stop protecting me, please."

They took a left and a quick right and entered a familiar neighborhood.

"This is where I got the intel on your whereabouts," Adam said.

"How did that happen?"

"A cat dressed like James Bond helped me out."

"Huh?"

A bizarre sight interrupted Adam's train of thought. A man had thrust his head and torso into a drain by the side of the road, or so it appeared. Only his legs were visible.

"You see that?" Adam said.

"See what?" Mikey said.

A fire station and an office building appeared ahead on the

right. Across the street, two Russian soldiers were dragging a middle-aged citizen into an open garage. His hands and feet were cuffed.

"You see that?" Mikey said, slowing down.

"Yes," Adam said.

"I thought you said there were no Russians here."

"There weren't."

Three gunshots followed. They came from the area of the garage they'd just rolled past.

"They're here now," Mikey said.

"That guy was in plain clothes," Adam said. "He looked like a regular citizen."

A black and white cat came racing from behind a house.

"Domino," Adam said.

"Yeah," Mikey said. "They're falling right before our eyes."

The cat galloped to the edge of the road. As it sniffed around the drain, the Grandfather came running out of his house again to capture it.

"No, no, Grandfather," Adam said. "Get back in the house."

"You know him?" Mikey said.

"Him and his wife – I wouldn't have found you without them."

A Russian soldier came racing from an adjacent property. Instead of a rifle, he held a machete. He arrived at the sidewalk with his weapon raised at the same time as the Grandfather and delivered a single blow to his neck.

Adam looked away at the last second.

"Oh my God," Mikey said.

"What the hell?" Adam said.

"We have to get out of here," Mikey said. "Seat belts."

They strapped themselves in. The engine's roar got the Russian soldier's attention. He turned, dropped his machete, reached for the pistol in the holster by his side, and began walking towards the Jeep.

"Hang on," Mikey said.

He swerved left, aimed for the soldier, and mashed the pedal.

The soldier raised his gun.

The Jeep crashed into the soldier's chest and sent him flying across the yard to the adjacent lot.

The seat belt pressed hard against Adam's throat. He struggled to catch his breath.

Mikey jammed the transmission into reverse and sent the SUV hurtling backward over the sidewalk and the median, and back onto the street.

The Grandmother emerged from the house. She shouted her husband's name, took three steps toward the drain, saw his decapitated torso, and erupted in hysterics. She dropped to her knees, covered her face with her hands and sobbed.

"Kill me," she shouted, to no one in particular. "Kill me now."

A gunshot rang out.

The Grandmother's' head exploded.

Adam looked around. He caught a glimpse of the sniper lowering his rifle across the street atop the fire station.

"Motherfucker," Adam said.

He opened his door.

"What are you doing?" Mikey said. "Do not get out of this car."

Mikey pressed the throttle. The Jeep's tires sought traction.

Adam's feet kissed the ground before the vehicle surged. The car's momentum threw him off-balance. He rolled to the side as he fell, snapped back to his feet and exploded toward the fire station. He heard the brakes screech and Mikey scream *no*, but by the time the echo of that word had subsided,

Adam had used the downspout to vault to the top of the building.

The sniper was rising to his feet, shocked, and turning the barrel of his rifle.

Adam, moving like a blur, thrust his right foot into the man's chest. It connected with the rifle first, sent it flying out of the sniper's hands, and propelled him ten feet backward. Adam was moving so quickly that he caught up to the sniper before he could right himself and gave him a second snap-kick. It catapulted the sniper another ten feet backward. This time he slid across the black rubber membrane over the edge of the roof.

When Adam arrived at the far end of the fire station, he found the sniper clinging to the cover of a vent protruding from the wall a few inches below the roof.

"Help," the sniper said, in Russian.

He was no conscript torn from his mother's arms like Marat, the tank crewman. The cracks and crevices in his face and the specks of gray in his beard spoke of experience.

"Didn't want to shoot civilians," the sniper said. "Orders. Orders is orders but I shouldn't have done it. Second chance? Please ..."

Adam's fury subsided. He'd never taken a life and the thought of doing so for any reason – under any circumstances whatsoever – revolted him. He'd lost his way for a moment, he thought.

Vengeance was not his. Violence was not in him.

Adam squatted down, braced himself for the added weight, and offered his hand.

The sniper grabbed it.

One beat, two beats, three beats passed. The Russian soldier hung from the vent in a trance.

Adam's eyes closed. Convulsions gave way to calmness. The images came rapid-fire and faded just as quickly

. . .

*A wide-eyed boy devours cotton candy beside his mother as
camels parade by at the circus ...*

*The boy plays with a tennis ball and a hockey stick while his
mother drinks vodka in her vegetable garden behind their house
...*

*The boy hides in a tree watching his father through binocu-
lars as he makes love to a woman who is not his mother in the
bedroom of a different house ...*

*The boy sits on the roof of a house watching his father
through binoculars as he makes love to a different woman in
another house ...*

*The boy climbs a telephone pole to watch his father through
binoculars as he makes love to yet another woman in the bathroom of yet another house ...*

Adam opened his eyes and pulled the sniper to safety. The
Russian soldier laid there disoriented and confused for a few
seconds. Then he brought his knees under his chest and sprang
to his feet. He pulled his pistol from under his hoodie, a note of
triumph in his expression.

He aimed the gun at Adam, finger on the trigger—

A gun fired.

The sniper dropped his weapon and fell to his knees.

Adam took one step forward and gave him a final thrust kick
to the chest. The sniper tumbled over the edge of the roof and
fell with a muted thud.

Adam glanced below.

The sniper laid dead on the road in a pool of his own blood.

Across the street, Mikey stood by watching Adam, rifle in
his hands.

Adam descended from the roof the same way he'd arrived.
As he hustled to the Jeep, he noticed the cat sitting beside the

grandmother's corpse. Adam ran over, scooped it up, and climbed into the SUV beside Mikey.

They didn't say a word to each other until they were past the filling station where they'd stopped initially, and back on the road north towards their original destination. The memories Adam had acquired from the sniper didn't register with their usual intensity. They flitted in and out of his imagination as a sideshow to the cumulative horror he'd just witnessed. Adam dismissed the notion of thanking Mikey for saving his life – the thought of acknowledging anything other than the slaughter of the elderly couple at that moment was simply unpalatable.

Another time, Adam thought. Another place.

Instead, he petted the cat in his lap until he finally decided that he simply had to ask Mikey a question.

"Why?" Adam said.

"Why what?" Mikey said.

"Why murder civilians? That couple had to be in their freaking eighties, for God's sake."

"Did it seem like random violence to you?" Mikey said.

"It seemed like senseless murder to me. But yeah, I guess you could say that."

"There's nothing random about it," Mikey said. "That guy with the machete? He had a black and red patch with a skull on his uniform. That's Wagner Group. The Russian President's private mercenaries. They must have a plan to terrorize our population into submission."

Adam shook his head.

"Not gonna work," Mikey said.

Adam tried to think of something sympathetic or intelligent to say. He was in Mikey's homeland and these were his fellow countrymen. But all he could think of was Victor's pet phrase, the one he'd been repeating to himself since he'd entered Ukraine.

"Some people really do need to die," Adam said.

As recently as this morning, Mikey might have channeled some Ben Foster in response to that statement. But Adam got the sense those days had passed and he would never hear such an affectation from him again.

Mikey stared through the cracked windshield at the empty highway ahead.

"Then die they shall," he said.

THIRTY-SIX

TASIA BOUNDED into Strelkov's office late morning to give him the news.

"We picked up the Farmer and his daughter," she said. "Army has them. They'll be here in four hours."

"Well done," Strelkov said. "That gives you time to check out another medical center. This one is smaller. We have an informant at the clinic. A phlebotomist. An easy mark. We turned her by promising not to draw a blood sample large enough to fill the Black Sea. She says three soldiers in blue and yellow came in for treatment in the middle of the night yesterday and they're still there. Drinking borsch that the Russians invented and calling it Ukrainian. Just cause for re-settlement, if ever there was one."

"How do you want me to play it?"

"Same as last time, but leave the lame behind, no? Just you and young Nikolai. The ambitious always find a way."

"I'm looking forward to speaking with the Farmer," Tasia said.

"I know you are. This is the most excited I've seen you since I arrived."

Tasia shrugged. "I'm curious."

"As you should be," Strelkov said. "The NLO is a welcome diversion from all the necessary social adjustments we're implementing here. Especially for a woman. Let me know how it goes at the clinic."

After her meeting ended, Tasia grabbed her knapsack and skulked her way to a supply room that contained cleaning equipment and toilet paper. The room was located in the unpopulated half of the building, almost a full minute's walk from the offices. Tasia stuffed two rolls of toilet paper in her knapsack. Technically, she was stealing state property and could get into trouble for what she was doing, but she didn't care. Deliveries of personal supplies to FSB officers were less reliable than Russian state media news reports.

As she approached the nearest exit, she was surprised to hear two men speaking to each other in hushed tones. She walked around the corner and found two engineers hanging a door over an opening in a wall that hadn't existed last week. In the gap between the door and its frame, Tasia spied a staircase that led below.

"What's this?" she said, stepping up to take a closer look. "I didn't know there was a cellar over here."

One of the engineers blocked her path, head hung low with a sheepish look on his face.

"Sorry, Lieutenant. We have orders. Only Colonel Strelkov beyond this point."

"No worries," Tasia said. "Be careful of the spiders down below. Ukrainian spiders – they're all poisonous. They told you that, right?"

She left the men slack-jawed and uncertain if she was joking or not.

On the way to the park, Tasia wondered why Strelkov needed a private torture chamber. There could be no other reason for building a room in a cellar no one even knew existed. She'd seen him in action with his knife. The private cellar suggested he was comfortable doing much worse things to another human being. He carried himself with a religious air that suggested otherwise, Tasia thought, but then she remembered the bishop's blessing of all violent acts against the Ukrainian Nazis. Everything was fair game for everyone, especially those who saw halos over their own heads.

Once she arrived at the park, Tasia left a wad of apple bubblegum in the usual place. Afterwards, she returned to work and caught up on some reports she needed to file. Three hours later she ambled out of the office to get some air again. She performed her usual ritual to make sure she wasn't being followed, and then snuck into her lavatory.

This time, Roman was already waiting for her on the opposite side of the wall.

"The tunnels under Kyiv were built by the Vikings," he said.

"Their names were Luciano, Placido, and Jose," Tasia answered.

"How are you, Ninety-nine?"

"Conflicted."

"How so?"

"Strelkov is a serial killer, our Boss is systematically eradicating a nation, most of the world doesn't really care, and I see starving animals and stolen children in my dreams. But I'm actually working on something genuinely interesting right now, which distracts me from the reality that my life and – and life on this planet as we all know it – is circling the drain at an accelerating pace. What news of Lena?"

Roman paused before answering. "Your sister is well. I asked about her today, as soon as we got your signal. Still working, still on her mission, but she's well."

"When can I talk to her?" Tasia said. "I think we've reached the point where that's going to have to happen before you ever see me in this room again."

"Now, now, that's not fair. First off, I can't see you in that room any more than you can see me. And second, no one's keeping you and Lena apart for any reason other than your mutual safety. You're both on the front lines. You're both in danger. Now is not the time for emotion. Now is the time for prudence."

"To hell with prudence," Tasia said. "Any day could be my last day. I'd rather be killed having seen my sister one more time rather than die being prudent."

"There's reason to be optimistic here," Roman said.

"How optimistic?"

"That's hard to say. Two weeks? Maybe less."

"No one wants to disappoint," Tasia said. "The smart man always sets the bar high so he can beat expectations. Are you a smart man, Roman?"

He chuckled. "A cautious man builds in a margin of safety in his estimates."

"So, if a reckless man had to guess when I might speak to Lena, what would he say?"

"I knew a reckless man once," Roman said. "But then he went and got himself killed. If he were sitting on this toilet, he might tell you you'll be speaking to Lena in less than a week. Three days, tops."

"Tops?" Tasia said.

"That's what he would say. But the man's dead for a reason. I personally wouldn't believe a word of it. Anything new on Wagner?"

Tasia told him about the evening with Strelkov, the priest's blessing of Russian atrocities against Ukrainians, and the timely appearance of a Wagner folder on his computer in plain sight.

"There's a purge under way," Roman said.

"I know."

"No. Not just inside the FSB. At the highest level of your Boss' cabinet, and beyond. We think he's about to make a monumental change."

"What change?" Tasia said.

"We think he's going to strip the FSB of all its power in Ukraine and give it to the GRU."

The GRU was a special branch of military intelligence. It wasn't just an intelligence unit. It was, in its own right, militarized. While the FSB gathered information and shared it with the Army, the GRU acted upon its own discoveries with no internal checks or balances.

"That makes sense," Tasia said. "They're experts in biological warfare. They did the chemical poisoning in Salisbury, England, on that Russian double agent and his daughter. The one that killed a random British citizen. If all else fails, that could be in the cards here."

"If the FSB is fired in Ukraine, your betters in Moscow are going to be looking for someone to blame. And they won't have to look hard."

"Every FSB officer in Ukraine will be fired," Tasia said. "And then worry about what's in her tea for the rest of her life, if she manages to survive the year."

"We would extract you before that ever happened," Roman said. "That goes without saying."

"And yet you felt the need to say it," Tasia said.

"Without the help of foreign intelligence, we could have never survived the war this well, this long. Getting a consistent flow of intelligence depends on treating those agents properly. It's crucial we treat you like the priceless asset that you are. It's crucial for our country's survival. That's why I'm stating the obvious – because you are so, so important."

"If I see an opportunity to get something on Wagner ... "

"I know you'll do your best. What's this thing you're working on that's so interesting?"

Tasia briefed Roman on the NLO. To her amazement, he didn't laugh or express amazement. He listened patiently as he always did, until she revealed that a scavenger named Luca had revealed the NLO's name.

"You know this man's name?" Roman said.

"I offered Luca a trade he couldn't refuse," Tasia said.

"What name did he give you?"

"Werner Ziegler. The NLO is German, and his name is Werner Ziegler."

A moment of silence passed. The NLO's name seemed to hang in the air, and for the first time since she'd started her investigation, a moment of clarity hit Tasia and took her breath away.

The Ukrainians knew about the NLO, too, she realized. And if they were taking him seriously, that suggested they had their own set of evidence. Was it possible that a human being could actually move that fast?

"I need to debrief you as soon as possible after you meet with this farmer and his daughter," Roman said. "Preferably tomorrow."

"You're telling me your side thinks this man could be for real, too."

"Who else knows about Werner Ziegler?"

"Strelkov and one of my boys. He's been helping in the investigation but he doesn't know what it's about. He hasn't seen the video."

"Good. Try to keep it that way."

Tasia tried to find out what Roman knew about the NLO, but he evaded her questions. They wrapped up their meeting with Tasia departing first.

After securing her hidden entrance in the rear of the restroom, she followed her usual routine to exit. When she emerged onto the sidewalk, a military police vehicle screeched to a halt along the road that abutted the park. Four men got out of the vehicle and marched towards her.

Tasia changed directions by forty-five degrees but continued moving at the same pace. She looked straight ahead as she walked, careful to neither look them in the eyes to attract their attention, or lower her head as though she were hiding. The men, however, remained in her peripheral vision the entire time. Five steps after Tasia changed course, they did the same.

If she could have outrun them and hidden, she could have arranged for extraction via an established procedure. But two of them looked exceptionally fit and moved on the balls of their feet. One of the others would have radioed for help. Word would have spread. In less than an hour, half the FSB and military police in Kherson would have been searching for the traitor, Anastasia Ivanova.

One of the men tapped the other on the chest. They looked directly at Tasia and broke into a jog.

Tasia resisted the temptation to run – there was no point in even trying.

The foursome came upon her—

And continued onward. One of them blurted out *there he is,* and they took off running after their target.

Tasia continued along her modified route until she reached the road. Before turning left to head back toward FSB headquarters, she glanced to her right to check for traffic.

She spotted him behind an oak tree, a hundred fifty feet away. He was holding his mobile phone in his hand as though he were taking a picture. The phone's camera was aimed at the public restrooms.

The man holding the phone was Nikolai.

THIRTY-SEVEN

TASIA TOOK cover behind a shed that had been a newspaper stand prior to the Russian invasion. Her vantage point offered some protection. She could see her colleague clearly, mostly from the rear, but with a slightly favorable angle that also revealed his camera. Nikolai, however, would have had to look over his shoulder or turn to catch a glimpse of her.

He had followed her from the office – that much was obvious. How had she failed to spot his tail before entering the lavatory? She'd grown complacent and taken her safety for granted – that was the only logical explanation.

He'd undoubtedly snapped some pictures by now, but he probably hadn't shared them with anyone yet for two reasons. First, he wasn't done taking shots. Second, he'd want to present them in an organized fashion, accompanied by a memo. If he were exposing a traitor, he'd want credit for his work. To get credit for his work, he'd want it memorialized in writing so that someone else didn't steal it.

Tasia needed to get rid of the pictures before he had a chance to share them with Strelkov or anyone else. She also needed to make him stop taking more pictures immediately.

She emerged from her hiding spot and headed straight toward Nikolai. She pretended to be studying the architecture of an apartment building along the road across the street. Nikolai had probably seen her by now and knew she was acting – there was no reason for her to be walking further away from the office – but that didn't matter at this point. The game was afoot and they both knew it.

"Hey," he said, once she was within earshot.

Tasia looked right and feigned surprise.

"Hey," she said, smiling. "What are you doing here?"

His arms hung loosely by his side, hands in his jacket pockets. He'd slipped his phone into one of them before she'd turned, Tasia thought. Perfect.

"I was working at my computer and I just hit the wall," Nikolai said. "The stress just got to me and I had to get out. I'm sorry I left my desk. I just … I just had to get out."

"Don't apologize," Tasia said. "Make it a routine. We have to plan for the long haul. Neither of us is going anywhere. Russia is here to stay, right?"

"Damn right, boss."

"Come on. Let's head back and get ready."

"Ready for what?" Nikolai said.

"A new op. I'll tell you about it on the way."

They hiked ten minutes to the office.

"When are we doing this?" Nikolai said, after she briefed him.

"Now," Tasia said. "Just the two of us."

"Just the two of us?"

"That's right. Colonel's orders. But we're going to mix it up."

"How's that?" Nikolai said.

"You're the senior officer when we go in."

"I'm in charge?"

"Correct," Tasia said. "You'll question the staff, see where it leads."

"But that means ... that means ..."

"I'll be in the injured soldier, which means I need you to rough me up."

"Oh, wow," Nikolai said. "I ... I don't know if I'm comfortable with that."

"Why? Because I'm a woman?"

"I didn't say that."

"Would you have a problem with this assignment if your senior officer was a man?"

"I don't have a problem with my senior officer being a woman"

"Then you have no problems inflicting some injuries on me?"

"I ... I guess I'll find a way."

"Ni-ko-lai," Tasia said. "I knew I could count on you."

They changed into authentic shirts and pants of fallen Ukrainian soldiers. The female soldier's shirt and pants fit Tasia reasonably well. Nikolai wasn't as fortunate – he had to roll up his pant legs and would have needed pads to fill out the shoulders.

After they were dressed, they moved to the FSB's makeshift medical examination room. Nikolai held the small bucket of dirt she'd asked him to gather from outside. Tasia stood in front of a mirror and smeared some on her face and uniform.

"What do you think?" she said.

"Your boots," Nikolai said. "They look like they've been hiding under a desk."

"I polished them when we got back from the paper mill," Tasia said. "They were filthy. No one with filthy boots ever got promoted in the FSB. Remember that. But good catch."

She smeared some dirt on her shoes.

"I think you've got the easy part," Nikolai said. "As for the rest, you want to start at the top or the bottom?"

"Bottom," Tasia said. "Let's save the real fun for last."

"Knee or ankle?" Nikolai said.

There simply had to be some swelling for the examining nurse to take a sprain seriously.

"Left ankle," Tasia said. "But it's got to be low, low grade. Like, really low. I need to be able to move."

"Don't worry. I've got my stomping down to a science."

He slammed his boot onto the junction of Tasia's foot and ankle, but pulled back once he connected with her bone.

Tasia cursed, winced, and hobbled around the room until the pain subsided.

"What next?" Nikolai said.

"Left eye," Tasia said. "But don't even come close to breaking anything. All I'm looking for is a little swelling, a little discoloration."

Nikolai shook his head. "I have to draw the line there. I can't punch a woman – I mean I can't punch you in the face. Demote me, send me to Siberia, whatever. I can't do it."

"What if I tell everyone you're a traitor to your country?" Tasia said.

Nikolai smacked her in the eye, though he pulled his punch instead of following through.

Tasia didn't flinch or lose her feet. She simply brought her hand to her face to make sure nothing felt broken.

"Oh, crap." Nikolai reached out with his arms.

Tasia waved him off. Her eye socket stung but otherwise she felt okay.

"Look at you," she said. "Guess you can hit a woman after all."

"Are you okay? Did I ... did I hit you too hard?"

"Shut-up."

Nikolai sighed. "We're done here, right?"

"Not quite," Tasia said. "We need blood."

"Oh, no."

"Oh, yes."

"You want me to shoot you in some soft tissue, far away from the main arteries and major organs? If that's your plan, forget it. They tried that in Luhansk and it didn't work so well."

"Did someone really try that in Luhansk?" Tasia said.

Nikolai's blank stare confirmed he wasn't joking.

"No wonder this special military operation never ends."

She sat down on the high-low examination table.

"Blade to my left earlobe," Tasia said. "Has to be the left side. We're inflicting all injuries on the same side. Makes it look like a bomb dropped and stuff hit me from a consistent angle. The blade has to be serrated so it leaves a jagged edge – otherwise it'll look too clean, like we're doing what we're doing."

Nikolai sterilized his knife with alcohol and sawed into Tasia's earlobe. When blood streamed onto her uniform, Tasia rubbed some on her neck and cheek.

"See if there's any cloth in the garbage bin," she said. "Remnants from clothes being removed – something we might have access to in the field. No gauze or bandages or even paper towels."

Nikolai found a piece of flannel. Tasia pressed it to her wound and studied herself in the mirror. She stood unevenly on her injured ankle, dirt and blood on her uniform and face, a red circle around her left eye.

She grunted with approval. "Now we're ready."

They took a sedan that had been impounded from a Ukrainian couple. A pair of FSB agents had rammed it from behind with their SUV to create an altercation. When the driver stopped and got out to take a look at the damage, one of the agents had shot him dead. The driver was not known to them or wanted for any alleged crime. His murder was merely a means to promote fear and chaos. His wife subsequently had been resettled in a remote part of Russia where she was likely planting potatoes in hopes of surviving her first winter in her newfound home.

As Nikolai drove, Tasia advised him on how to approach the attending nurse to extract intelligence regarding the medical center's treatment of Ukrainian prisoners. Nikolai asked questions and appeared to listen to her answers intently. Meanwhile, Tasia navigated, leading them to a condemned elementary school.

He parked in a discreet nook in the rear. Someone had painted a mural on the loading dock door. It featured the Ukrainian president in his trademark olive t-shirt, peering through a window splattered with blood.

"No more hospital parking lots," Tasia said. "Not after last time. We don't want anyone to see us coming. As far as they know, we're Territorial Defense, got separated from our unit and hitched a ride from some fine Ukrainian citizens."

"We'll be visible as soon as we're out in the clear," Nikolai said. "We should walk like we're hurt. Like you're hurt. Like we did last time once we were within range of the emergency room."

"Good thinking," Tasia said. "We should leave our mobile phones in the car, too."

"You think?"

"If it turns out hostile, right?"

"Right."

They stored their phones in the glove box.

They climbed out of the vehicle. Nikolai locked the car and circled around to Tasia's right side.

"Left side," Tasia side.

"Your injuries are on your left side."

"The ankle's the thing."

"Oh, right," Nikolai said.

He moved to Tasia's left side and leaned in. Tasia wrapped her left arm around his shoulder to use him as support. They took a few steps, the injured soldier hanging on to her mate as they limped to the clinic.

"Hold up," Tasia said. "I need to get my arm away from your neck. I have to find a comfortable spot a little lower on your shoulder."

They stopped. Tasia made the adjustment.

"Okay, thanks," she said. "Much better."

They resumed walking in tandem. With her left arm removed from harm's way, Tasia pulled the box cutter out of her right pocket, reached under Nikolai's chin, and slit his throat.

Nikolai's hands shot up to his neck. Tasia stepped back. Wave after wave of blood overflowed his fingers. Horror registered in his eyes. He dropped to his knees.

"It's over," Tasia said. "No more pain. There was just that little bit. Lie down. Get comfortable."

Tasia eased his back and head to the asphalt. The sound of the box cutter ripping through his tissue echoed in her ears. She could barely stomach looking at him. He was just an ambitious kid trying to advance in a dirty, rotten system that belonged to a dirty, rotten country.

Blood drained from Nikolai's face. He appeared disoriented until he looked her in the eyes.

"Traitor," he said.

"That's what they said about von Stauffenberg," Tasia said.

"Who?" Nikolai said.

"Claus von Stauffenberg. The German officer who tried to kill Hitler."

"I'm not Hitler."

"No," Tasia said. "You just worship the Russian version."

After he stopped breathing, Tasia retrieved his mobile phone and removed some tape from their first aid kit in the boot. She taped his eyes open, tapped the phone to start the face identification process, and held it in front of his face. The phone unlocked. She held her breath as she scrolled through his pictures, texts and e-mails. Her search confirmed her suspicions - he hadn't shared the photos with anyone.

She deleted the pictures, smashed the phone with a cinderblock and tossed it into a nearby drain. Afterwards, Tasia searched his remains for any evidence he was Russian. His wallet contained forged papers that identified him as a member of the Ukrainian Territorial Defense. She removed the picture of his Russian girlfriend, returned the wallet to his pocket, and pulled a black body bag out of the trunk of the car. After removing the tape from his eyes and sealing his corpse inside it, she hoisted it into the boot.

She admitted herself into the medical clinic but didn't engage the attending nurse in any conversation. Once her wounds and injury had been treated, Tasia drove to a transfer station where the Russian Army was burying the bodies of murdered Ukrainians in mass graves. She left the body bag containing Nikolai's corpse near the entrance. If someone checked the body in the bag, he'd find a military uniform and papers that identified the deceased as a Ukrainian soldier.

Once she was finished, Tasia dropped the car back at FSB headquarters. She walked home to her apartment and contemplated her next move. She could have initiated the procedure with Roman to request emergency exfiltration out of Kherson. Nikolai might not have shared his photos with anyone, but she couldn't be certain the case against her didn't already exist for some other reason.

But if she did that, she'd be compromising her chance to supply the Ukrainians with information about the Wagner assassins. Tasia adored the Ukrainian president. He was the first leader she'd ever admired in her life. The thought of him or his family being hurt horrified her.

If there were a way for her to minimize the risk to their lives, she was going to find it.

THIRTY-EIGHT

ADAM AND MIKEY drove through three additional road blocks manned by the Ukrainian Territorial Defense. The third was the least robust, consisting of a single saw-horse and two young men in Adidas warm-up suits. They were built for speed, as was the Mustang pointed in the direction from which Adam and Mikey were arriving. The guards informed them that this was the last known stop manned by Ukrainians. If they continued along their northeastern path, the next roadblock they encountered might be less hospitable.

Along the way they acquired a bowl, some water, and roasted chicken for Domino from the men and women at the checkpoints.

"I might be able to get some more current information," Mikey said, "about who controls what's up ahead. But it would help me a lot if I knew exactly where we're going."

"I told you where we're going," Adam said.

"A remote location, where previously extinct species won't drink the water. Which means it's a place where animals that stopped existing are back again. We going to Jurassic Park?"

"How exactly are you going to get more current information?" Adam said. "You know somebody who knows somebody, like you did when you got this car?"

"I know my uncle. He's connected. Maybe he can help."

"I get it. He's connected with the Ukrainian military, but you're not."

"Why is that so hard to believe?" Mikey said.

"Well, your excellent shooting, for one thing. Thank you for that."

"My uncle is who he is. That doesn't mean I'm into what he's into, but he's still my uncle. What if your uncle was a captain in organized crime? If you needed some help with a problem and you reached out to him, would he help you? And if he did, would that mean you're a criminal, too?"

Adam's phone sounded the arrival of a video-enhanced call. The number calling him belonged to Victor. Adam answered immediately, only to find the oligarch's man, Nazarov, staring at him with a grim expression.

"Hello, Mister Ziegler," Nazarov said. "Mister Werner Ziegler from Munich, Germany. Son of a civil engineer and a realtor. Master mountain climber who saved those two climbers I watched in New York, along with six other passengers, when their plane crashed in Siberia. Which is how you met your so-called uncle, Victor Bodnar."

Adam remained mute. Victor had concocted a fictional background for Werner Ziegler and Nazarov had bought it. No one could spray black mist like Victor. No one.

"How is my favorite courier?" Nazarov said. "Have you pushed any wheelchairs today, or saved any passengers from a burning plane?"

"Where's Victor?" Adam said.

"Right here. Just a stone's throw away. A big stone. The kind that leaves permanent damage. Where is my package?"

"I want to talk to him. Let me see him. Put him on."

"I don't like your tone of voice, Mister Ziegler. You work for me. You don't make demands of me. I paid you. You haven't delivered. I am the one with the right to make demands of you."

"You can make all the demands you want. You're not getting anything until I speak with Victor."

"I was hoping you'd say that."

Nazarov disappeared from view. A series of images filled the screen – burgundy upholstery, crown molding, an Art Deco ashtray, nicked-up hardwood flooring. Adam recognized every single detail. He was looking at the study in Victor's apartment, where his uncle smoked cigars and watched westerns.

Adam heard Nazarov's voice in the distance, away from the phone.

"He wants to talk to someone clever. Someone like that used to live here, but he's not so clever any more, is he?"

Adam took a deep breath. Nazarov had inflicted sufficient pain on Victor to force him to reveal Adam's alias and phone number. He hadn't truly tortured him, Adam thought. If that were the case, Victor might have revealed his real name.

The camera bounced around again. Three beats later, a vaguely familiar face appeared on Adam's screen, battered, bruised, and bleeding.

Adam tried not to flinch, then wondered if his attempt had betrayed him.

"Don't be upset, Werner," Victor said, the words coming out garbled past his swollen lip. "I enjoyed a long and rewarding life. And during that life, I was called many things. *Handsome* was not one of them."

"I'm not upset," Adam said. "Someone else is going to be upset. That I promise."

"Please don't promise me that you're going to break your promise to me. Vengeance is not ours. It doesn't boost your profit margin or lower your blood pressure."

"Are you on schedule with your pills?"

"I ran out today," Victor said. "I sent a text to the pharmacy that I would come by."

Victor had more than a twenty-day supply of all his medications when Adam departed for Zermatt. He hadn't run out of any pills. And he hadn't sent a text to the pharmacy. He'd somehow sent one to his daughter, Nina, not to come by today to keep her out of danger.

"I'll straighten all this out as soon as I get home," Adam said.

"You think that's going to happen soon, do you?"

"I think I'm needed there."

"Don't give him the package," Victor said.

Nazarov shouted something in the background.

"Don't give it to anyone – anyone at all," Victor said. "It's safe if you and you alone control it. It must never leave your possession"

The screen turned black. Adam heard more shouting and a thud.

A moment later Nazarov reappeared.

"Victor tells me you lost the package to a rival," he said. "A woman, no less. That it's something personal, not business. How could the Courier let such a thing happen?"

Adam didn't answer. For Victor to reveal Eva's involvement, Nazarov must have hurt him even more than the wounds on his face implied.

"Such a thing happened," Adam said. "Because life happens. You know what Victor taught me? There are only two certainties in life. One is death. The second is that you can't change the first one."

"You have forty-eight hours to deliver the package to me, unopened and in pristine condition. Otherwise, you'll be collecting your uncle's body parts from post offices in all the countries where you're fluent in the local language."

"I'll trade you the package for Victor but only if Victor is alive and well, physically and mentally. If any harm has come to him that can't be repaired, the deal is off."

Nazarov paused. "Mr. Ziegler," he said, with a thoughtful lilt, "are you fully aware of the implications to your uncle and his daughter – Nina – if you don't retrieve this package?"

Adam took a moment to conjure a heartfelt response. "Mr. Nazarov, are you fully aware of the implications to all your business interests if any harm comes to them?"

Adam ended the call. Only then did he remember where he was, who was driving, and where they were going.

"Trouble at home?" Mikey said.

"Something like that," Adam said.

"You said sixteen kilometers until the next turn. We've gone eleven and change."

"Then we're almost there. Just look for the sign."

"The sign for where?" Mikey said.

"The most magical place in the world."

"This place has a name?"

"Yeah. It's called Chornobyl."

THIRTY-NINE

TASIA RETURNED to the office as though nothing remarkable had happened. Strelkov wasn't there to debrief her on the hospital op but the Farmer had arrived with his daughter. She was completing her search of his phone when two of her colleagues brought him into the conference room.

"I understand you lost some valuable equipment," she said.

"Lost?" the Farmer said. "Yeah, that's it. My heavy machinery got lost. When the Russian Army invades, a lot of things get lost."

"I'm sorry that happened," Tasia said.

"I bet you are."

"You're going to learn something about me, sooner or later."

"What's that?"

"I don't lie."

"Oh, really? You're the one?"

"Honesty is the most powerful weapon in the world when you want someone to share some information with you."

"Then I'll be honest with you," the Farmer said. "I'm not telling you anything. My daughter isn't telling you anything.

That's how I raised her. We're Ukrainians now. Go ahead. Kill us both and be done with it."

"I can't get you your equipment back," Tasia said. "The only people who can do that are the people who took it from you in the first place, and I'm not that powerful. Not even close. If I was, I would. But I'm not."

The Farmer didn't say anything, but his eyes narrowed just enough to reveal that her honesty had surprised him.

"What I can offer you is two and only two things. The first thing I can offer you is life as you've known it so far – you and your daughter go home untouched and unharmed. I mean, I appreciate your bravery under the circumstances, but let's be real. No one wants to die – and no father wants his only child to suffer, that's for sure."

"What's the second thing?" the Farmer said.

"Your integrity."

His eyes narrowed some more.

"I'm not interested in anything related to the Ukrainian Army or the Territorial Defense," Tasia said. "I'm not interested in the Azov battalion, Nazis, or the treatment of Russian nationals. In fact, I'm not going to ask you any questions about any Ukrainians or anything related to the country of Ukraine."

"What are you going to ask me about?"

"A German tourist by the name of Werner Ziegler," she said.

Relief sprang to the Farmer's face, but was quickly replaced with suspicion.

"What do you want with him?" he said.

"We want to ask him a few questions."

"What kind of questions?"

"That I can't tell you. It's privileged. Someone else might make up a story – or beat you or your daughter with a lead pipe and get the information out of you that way. Me, I have my own way of doing things. I'm strange that way around here. What I can tell you with one hundred percent certainty is that we have zero interest in harming him in any way."

"He's a good man," the Farmer said. "He helped my daughter. I don't want to cause him any trouble."

"You won't be causing him any trouble, and we have no intention of hurting him. But words are cheap, aren't they? I can say that all day but you probably still won't believe me. I get it. Of course, I do. But look at this way. Is he a member of the Ukrainian International Legion?"

The Farmer didn't answer.

"No, he's not," Tasia said. "He's a non-combatant, a German citizen – a European. Have you heard any stories – any stories whatsoever – of Russia taking random tourists from other countries hostage in Ukraine?"

The Farmer didn't argue.

"Like we need those kinds of headlines?" Tasia said. "Like we need to deal with those kinds of problems, too?"

The Farmer took a moment to consider everything he'd heard. "You're saying that if I tell you what I know about the healer, you'll let me go home with my daughter, and you won't harm him in any way?"

"No," Tasia said. "I'm not just saying it. I'm making you a promise – wait, why do you call him the healer?"

"Doesn't everyone? I assumed he's a doctor of some sorts – psychiatry, psychology, or something like that."

"How did you find him?"

"I didn't," the Farmer said. "I told a friend of mine I needed some help for my daughter. And the healer came."

Tasia didn't pursue his friend's identity. The Farmer wouldn't have been eager to expose him to questioning by the

FSB. What the Farmer didn't know was that the questioning had already taken place, and he would never see Luca again.

"How did he help your daughter?" she said. "What exactly did he do?"

"He restored her confidence. I don't know how. All I know is she wouldn't come out of her room for days, and after half an hour with him, she was back to her old self."

"Just like that?"

"Just like that."

Tasia followed-up with some more questions about the NLO's visit. She asked about his companion, Mykhailo, but the Farmer told her he didn't interact with him at all.

"When they left, where did they go?" she said.

"I don't know," the Farmer said. "He got an e-mail from some woman. I got the feeling she was the reason he was in Ukraine."

"Did you see the e-mail?"

"I did. It came to me."

"I didn't see it on your phone."

"I deleted it from my mail but I took a picture of it. Give me my phone and I'll show it to you."

Tasia found the photo herself and read the note.

"Who's the Mystic?" she said.

"I don't know," the Farmer said. "But the location could only be one place."

"Where's that?" Tasia said.

"Chornobyl."

"You're kidding me."

"When I was student at university," the Farmer said, "I used to work at a meat restaurant in Kyiv. A poacher used to bring us wild boar from the Exclusion Zone. He said all sorts of birds had returned there, the kind that had ceased to exist on this planet. And all the animals knew where not to drink the water."

Tasia had the guards bring in the daughter while the Farmer was still in the room. They'd been separated for only an hour, but she wanted to reassure the girl that her father hadn't been harmed. The Farmer told Teresa to relax and answer all of Tasia's questions about the healer, but to say nothing about anyone else.

After the guards escorted the Farmer out of the room, Tasia asked Teresa to describe the healer. She responded in amazing detail, including approximations of the length of his nose, arms, and legs. Tasia also queried her about her conversation with him. Teresa's voice cracked whenever she spoke, never more so than when she described her harrowing experience with the Russian soldier named Blu.

"Do you happen to know this Russian soldier's real name?" Tasia said.

"No."

"That's too bad." Tasia was certain she could figure out which battalion had been stationed in her town, discover his identity, and find a reason to have him jailed. "So, you're saying that you didn't actually tell the healer what happened to you?"

"No. Not a word of it. He touched my hand, and just knew."

"What do you mean, he touched your hand and knew?"

"I mean exactly that. It was like he got me. He understood me. He knew my past, all my problems, and what I needed to feel better."

"Just by touching you?" Tasia said.

Teresa's face glowed. "Yes."

"And the treatment for what ailed you was cutting off your hair?"

"To make myself look less attractive to Russian soldiers," Teresa said.

"Just to be clear – because this is a little strange, you know –

he figured out what was bothering you with a touch of his hand."

"He did. He was .... he was not like anyone I've ever known before. He was like ... you know ... he was on a different level."

"In what way?"

"In every way."

After concluding her interview, Tasia escorted the Farmer and his daughter to the exit in the rear of the complex.

"You'll have to find your way back to your home in Pyrohovtsi," Tasia said.

"There are worse fates," the Farmer said.

Tasia opened the door. They stepped outside.

Strelkov greeted them with eight armed men. Four of them overpowered the Farmer and led him to one bus. The other four escorted Teresa to a different bus.

"Papa," the girl said, hysterical.

"*Tereska*," the Farmer cried, before turning to Tasia. "You promised. You lied."

Tasia stood helpless and horrified.

"Rot in hell, bitch," the Farmer said.

After the buses left, Strelkov cast a curious look at Tasia. "You were incredibly convincing when you promised them freedom," he said.

"It was easy," Tasia said, careful to make sure her tone of voice didn't betray her rage. "Ukrainians – not exactly the sharpest minds in their or any country."

Strelkov chuckled. "But the women are excellent at child bearing. That one is three or four years away from the proper age. She'll make a fine wife for a laborer in some remote part of Siberia. Not hard to picture her with a brood of three or more."

"That's an exponential gain in population," Tasia said.

"Indeed. How did it go at the medical clinic?"

"Nothing came of it. I ended up going in alone. Nikolai left to take care of a personal matter right before the op and never returned."

Strelkov looked incredulous. "A personal matter?"

"I warned him there would be consequences, but he ignored me. Haven't seen him since."

"Have you checked his living quarters?"

"Haven't had time," Tasia said. "Triage – I thought this was more important."

"And so it was," Strelkov said. "The only thing even more important was the identity of the traitor among us. But that's all resolved now, and neither of us has to worry about it anymore."

"You've identified the informant?" Tasia said.

"No," Strelkov said. "Young Nikolai did."

"That's incredible," Tasia said. "Who was it?"

"It was you, Lieutenant," Strelkov said. "You are the traitor among us."

Two men grabbed Tasia from behind. She didn't struggle. Resisting would have given them an excuse to deliver her an immediate beating. There would be plenty of those soon. There was no reason to accelerate their arrival.

"You vacationed in Dubrovnik, Split and Zagreb in 2013," Strelkov said. "Your fiancé was with you. As was another couple. All four of you stayed in the exact same hotels on the exact same days. The other woman who stayed with you was your half-sister. Your only remaining relative, Lena Privalova, now a member of the Alpha Group of the Ukrainian SBU."

"You've been misinformed," Tasia said. "I've never heard of such a person."

"Yes, yes." Strelkov smiled. "Deny, deny, deny. I would do the same thing."

"I look forward to seeing the evidence against me."

"And I look forward to discussing your trip to Croatia. You spent twelve days there. That practically makes you a local. The bars, the restaurants, the laundry and dry cleaning. I can't wait to learn all the secret handshakes from you."

Strelkov motioned to the guards. As they escorted her to a jail cell, Tasia recalled the fate the Deputy Mayor and Luca had shared. Hers would be different, that she vowed.

She wouldn't scream, no matter how bad the pain.

She wouldn't give the deluded bastard the satisfaction.

FORTY

ADAM GAVE Mikey precise driving directions around Chornobyl without the help of a map.

"The Exclusion Zone has a radius of thirty kilometers from the power plant," Adam said. "It's more than sixteen-hundred square kilometers in size."

"Bigger than I thought," Mikey said.

"The size of Luxembourg or Rhode Island. There's a main entrance with a gate - two metal doors that swing open. On either side of those doors is a fence about six feet high. That fence never ends. It goes all the way around the Zone."

"If the Russians control Chornobyl they'll be at the gate. The question is whether they'll have roadblocks before we get anywhere near it."

"We're not going anywhere near the front gate," Adam said.

"We're not?"

"No, we are not. Once the fence is out of sight of the main entrance, it becomes kind of a joke. At least it used to be a joke – the odds are zero the government invested money to fix it, so it should be an even bigger joke. Some rusty poles and barbed wire, maybe three feet high. I can give you a boost, no problem, then jump it."

"You seem really well-informed," Mikey said.

"I like to read about strange places. There used to be some spots off the beaten path that scavengers used as entry and exit points."

"Scavengers?"

"After the accident, the government buried everything that was exposed to radioactive fallout," Adam said. "Cars, ambulances, tractors. Plus, there was an entire city – Pripyat – that was built for the workers at the power plant. Anything valuable in the graveyards and the buildings – car parts, radiators, scrap metal – everything made its way back into Ukraine through the black market."

"You read a lot," Mikey said.

"There used to be bicycles on the other side of the fence along those spots. The scavengers kept them there. I doubt they're still there. But the spot I'm thinking about – that's closest to the Mystic's house – if there's no bikes it's going to leave us with about a six-mile hike."

"I'm not sure I'll be able to keep up."

"Think of it as building up an appetite for that hot meal," Adam said.

"You're still sticking to that?"

"A man needs something to look forward to."

They negotiated the drive to the spot that Adam remembered with only two miscues in navigation. A boulder in the shape of a parallelogram marked the spot that was familiar to Adam. The vegetation surrounding it informed him no one had used it for years – shrubs and wild grasses covered an area that had been matted down all the time. The barbed wire between the two metal fence posts, however, still drooped almost to the ground. No one had bothered to repair it since it had been raised in 1986 – concerns about Chornobyl and the Exclusion Zone were a thing of the past.

Mikey managed to wedge the Jeep between two trees by the side of the road, leaving a clear path if an unexpected motorist – or tank – wandered by. Adam poured some water into a thermos cup for Domino inside the Jeep, who promptly slurped it up. Then he removed his compass from his knapsack, stuffed Domino inside, and zipped it up so that only the cat's head was visible. Victor, a cat lover, had once told him that the average feline had the mental capacity of a two-year old child. Apparently Ukrainian cats were even smarter. It didn't protest one bit.

Once outside the vehicle, Adam spied Mikey removing a here-to-for unseen semi-automatic rifle from a long black bag he'd stored in the spare tire compartment in the back of the Jeep, and three magazines loaded with bullets. He glanced at Adam as though waiting for him to object.

Adam recalled the shot that had saved his life. He chose not to comment.

"No bikes, huh?" Mikey said.

"Sorry," Adam said.

"Do I need to be worried about radiation?"

"If we spend twelve hours in the Zone, you'll probably take in as much as you would during a four-hour flight at thirty-thousand feet."

"I've never been on airplane," Mikey said.

"Then you've accumulated a lot less radiation than most people," Adam said. "Try not to touch any vegetation with your bare hands, and stay away from water – streams, puddles, anything wet."

They had arrived late in the afternoon. The sun cast shadows among the trees. They hiked at a seven kilometer per hour clip, speeding up and slowing down as the terrain allowed. Initially,

Adam glanced at his compass to make sure they maintained a north-eastern heading. But everything was as he remembered it to be, and as his confidence grew, he referred to the compass less frequently.

Man had surrendered this land to nature over thirty-five years ago. Birds sang. Wolves howled. Lush greenery sprang from the earth in every direction. The Zone remained as calm and beautiful as Adam remembered. It was the most wonderful place he'd ever been. There were no tyrants or bullies. Even a godforsaken boy could fit in.

They arrived at their destination an hour before dusk. Mikey looked sweaty and exhausted, the weight of his weapon no doubt a drag on his stamina. They crouched behind some bushes, fifty meters away from the Mystic's house. It appeared long and narrow, with a lavender front door at one end, and purple shutters surrounding two windows on the right. The door was elevated two feet off the ground but no steps preceded it. Apparently, residents and visitors alike had to make a leap of faith – literally – to enter the premises.

"I didn't know people were still living here," Mikey said.

"Last I knew," Adam said, "there were a hundred eighty-seven residents. Probably fewer now, right? They got special permission to move back. No kids allowed. Just older folks who couldn't bear to be away from the only home they'd ever known, no matter what the risks."

A narrow street ran directly in front of the house.

"It's an active road," Adam said, quietly. "The asphalt is cracked but there's only low-level stuff growing in those cracks. No saplings or trees. Just grasses and things. And it all looks pretty matted down."

They bounded toward the house. Up close, Adam spied the electrical wires that ran just below the roof of the house. He'd never wondered before if the homes had electricity. Now he had to hope that the Russians hadn't caused an outage if he were to make good on his promise of a hot meal.

Adam knocked on the front door three times. When no one answered, he knocked again. As he waited, Mikey peeked into the house through one of the windows and shook his head.

Adam turned the front door handle but it wouldn't budge.

"Locked?" Mikey said.

"Just like life," Adam said. "Whenever I don't think about a worst-case scenario, it always seems to come true. I was worried about finding our way. I was worried about the Russians. But it never dawned on me that once we got here – with no problems – she wouldn't be here. And the house would be locked."

"There's got to be an emergency key around here somewhere," Mikey said. "I mean, really. If there was a fire or whatever and emergency services needed to get in here ..."

"Emergency services?" Adam said. "In the Zone?"

"The government let these people come back. Someone's responsible for them, right?"

"I doubt it."

"I don't care," Mikey said. "There's got to be a key."

There was no doormat beneath the front door. Adam and Mikey wound their way around the house and found a second door in the back. Unfortunately, that one was also locked. They also found a shed behind the house. Its door was painted the color of the sky, the walls a darker shade of blue. A padlock hung open atop hasps and staple.

"Gotta be a key in here," Mikey said. "Money says so."

Adam lifted the padlock from the latch and pulled the door open.

A woman thrust a shotgun into his stomach and sent him two steps backwards.

"Hands up. You, too," she said in Russian, alternately

pointing the gun at Mikey and Adam. "You're not soldiers. Who are you? What are you doing here?"

The Mystic would have been in her seventies by now, Adam imagined, her lithe frame still wrapped in black scarves and sweaters. This woman looked closer to Adam's age and didn't resemble a former ballerina. She looked more like the fighter and the ring, an overfed army of one that might have pinned Adam and Mikey at the same time in a wrestling match. He'd never seen a woman so thick, Adam thought, and yet the plump cheeks, beady eyes and the anvil chin looked strangely familiar.

"I'm from Lviv," Mikey said. "He's from Germany. We're sorry we trespassed. We don't mean any harm. We're looking for the Mystic, right Werner?"

The woman appeared transfixed by Adam. "Don't I know you?"

"Renata?" Adam said.

Her eyes narrowed further, and then shock sprang to her face. "Adam?"

"I can't believe it's you," Adam said.

"I didn't recognize you. You look different. Oh my God. Your ears ..."

"I had them fixed."

"What are you doing here?" Renata said.

"I'm looking for the Mystic."

"The Russians took her hostage. To the Power Plant." She looked them over again. "You better come inside. Your cat must be hungry."

Adam and Mikey followed Renata into the Mystic's home. She was literally the last person on Earth he ever wanted to see again.

She was the bully who'd terrorized him in school.

FORTY-ONE

ADAM RELEASED Domino from his backpack onto the tile floor in the spartan kitchen. Renata poured some water into a dish and searched the cabinets for food.

"Adam?" Mikey whispered

"Long story," Adam said.

"You lived here?" Mikey said.

"No one lives here. I lived nearby."

Renata found a can of tuna and emptied it onto a small plate. Domino promptly began gobbling it up.

"Should I call you Werner or Adam?" she said.

"Doesn't really matter, does it?" Adam said. "Why are you here? What's your connection to the Mystic?"

"She's my aunt," Renata said.

"I never knew that," Adam said. "All those years I was having trouble at school and coming to the Mystic for guidance, and she was related to you."

"I didn't know you talked to her. She and I weren't close back then, when my mother was still alive. I didn't know you knew her."

"Well, you didn't know much about me at all, and you didn't

want to know anything about me, did you?"

Renata blushed. "I'm sorry about all that."

"Doesn't matter. It was a long time ago. Who can even remember? Did your aunt tell you she was expecting me?"

"She didn't tell me anything. I haven't seen her in months. I came looking for her when I found out the Russians were on their way here. To get her out. But by the time I got here they'd taken her. One of the guards who used to work the front gate told me. What's your business with her? Why are you here?"

"I'm looking for a girl," Adam said. "I thought she might be able to help me find her."

Renata frowned. "Here?"

Adam shrugged.

Renata glanced at Mikey.

"Don't look at me," Mikey said. "I'm the driver. I don't know any more than you do."

"How did you guys get here?" she said.

"Same way everyone gets here," Adam said.

"That's a long hike. I'll get you water. I can make you eggs. They're fresh. And there's black bread and butter, too."

"A hot meal," Mikey said, glancing at Adam. "That would be greatly appreciated."

"Thank you," Adam said. "Please take care of my driver and my cat. Her name is Domino. She's experienced some trauma. The worst kind."

"What about you?" Renata said.

"I'll have a glass of water, please," he said. "And a handful of nuts of some kind, if you have them."

"And then what?"

"And then I'm going to go find your aunt," Adam said.

"I'm going with," Mikey said.

"No," Adam said. "I can't be worried about you, too."

"Don't insult me," Mikey said. "Please. I deserve better."

"I don't mean to insult you," Adam said. "It's a matter of speed. You know what I mean. If I have to work slower, it'll put me at risk. It's not an insult. It's the truth."

Renata found a bag of walnuts. Adam devoured two handfuls, washed them down with water, and retrieved his knapsack. As he slung it on his back, Domino straddled his foot and wrapped her tail around his leg to prevent him from leaving. Adam checked his cell phone.

"Four bars," Adam said. "In Chornobyl, no less. This feels like hope. Like a break, like my first big break since all this started." He glanced at Mikey. "I'll send you an update when I need to. You do the same."

Mikey acknowledged him with a blank stare.

Adam glanced at Renata. "You have a phone?"

She gave him the number. Adam sent her a text. Her phone pinged. He started toward the door.

"Take my flashlight," Mikey said. "It's going to be dark in less than an hour."

"My eyes will adjust," Adam said. "Light will only attract attention, or gunfire. And I've worked in the dark here, you know, once or twice before."

"How are you going to get into the power plant?" Renata said.

"I won't know until I get the lay of the land. You're a good person, Renata."

Renata froze.

"For coming here to help your aunt like this, in the middle of a war," Adam said. "The past is the past. Who we are today isn't defined by who we were yesterday. You're a really good person, Renata. Don't let anyone ever tell you otherwise."

She looked as though she might cry.

"You promise to take care of my cat?"

"I promise, Adam."

FORTY-TWO

ADAM HEADED EAST along the paved road that flanked the Mystic's house. His concern about Victor and Eva propelled him forward. Memories of his days scavenging in the Zone informed him of his surroundings.

Reactor number four at the Chornobyl Nuclear Power Plant exploded on April 26, 1986. It was the worst nuclear disaster in history. The other three reactors continued producing power until the turn of the century. After suffering serious incidents including more radiation leakage, they were also shut down. All four reactors entered the decommissioning phase in 2015. That process was expected to be completed in 2065.

In the meantime, the Zone remained the Zone, a forbidden place to all but the workers at the Power Plant, the tourists who paid hundreds of dollars to visit for a few hours, and the hundred and seventy or so people who'd been allowed to return.

Adam's route was straightforward. Once he got to within five kilometers of the Plant, he heard industrial-sounding noises. A white glow shone above the tree line in the distance. At first glance, the light appeared to be coming from the Red Forest, which was impossible. No one in his right mind would go near it. The noise grew louder and the lights brighter as he got closer. When he heard men shouting in Russian, Adam approached cautiously. He took shelter behind a healthy green pine tree and peered around it.

Portable generators powered manhole-sized lights mounted on twelve-foot tripods. They illuminated a field of armor – tanks, howitzers, rocket launchers, and other vehicles Adam couldn't identify. A separate part of the area consisted of what could have been best described as loot. Delivery trucks, firefighting equipment, spare tires, and stacks upon stacks of portable and mainframe computers filled the field. The latter had to have been removed from the Power Plant. What was the impact of their removal on the safety of the reactors and all the spent fuel still on site?

The most disturbing image, however, appeared further east, adjacent to all the machinery. Trenches lined the forest. Hundreds of Russian soldiers were digging like prisoners at a labor camp, tossing shovels of dirt out of ground that had remained untouched for thirty-five years.

It had remained untouched for a good reason.

Adam studied the design of the camp from afar. He found a square tent at its center with two sentries stationed near the front flap. Marking the tent as his destination, he plotted the course that would allow him the greatest probability of arriving without premature capture. When he was finished, he took a moment and challenged himself to find a better route. He failed and took off.

He used the generators as his initial shields – not a single soldier was wasting his time watching fueled and functioning machines. After negotiating a quarter of his route, he weaved his way through the armored vehicles. He crouched low and peered beneath the vehicle undercarriages, on the lookout for soldiers. He snuck past six of them.

Another dozen or so stood guarding the loot. One of them might have seen Adam as he raced by, but the sighting would have appeared more like a momentary apparition. Once he'd gotten beyond the loot, Adam blazed his way to within three steps of the sentries. From their perspective, Adam suspected he'd appeared to have flown in out of nowhere. Their shock and awe gave Adam sufficient time to pull out his passport, toss his knapsack to the ground and raise his hands in the air.

"I'm Werner Ziegler," he said in Russian. "I'm German. This is my German passport. I'm an expert on Chornobyl. I need to speak to your commanding officer immediately, please."

At first, the two guards didn't know what to do with him. They shouted for help. Four more soldiers came over. One of the guards searched him. The other bent down to look into his knapsack and was promptly warned that it might be a bomb.

"There's nothing in the knapsack except for my compass and binoculars," Adam said. "I mostly use it to carry my cat."

An officer with two red stripes and a gold star on the shoulder of his uniform stepped out of the tent. Initially he appeared to be blond, but then Adam realized his brown hair was actually covered with dust. The bags under the eyes suggested he hadn't slept since he'd climbed into the vehicle that had brought him here from Belarus or Russia.

"What's the commotion?" He frowned at Adam. "Who is this man?"

"He's a German, Major Stasi," the guard said.

Stasi studied Adam with curiosity. "A German? Here?"

One of the guards handed him Adam's passport.

Adam introduced himself, repeating what he'd said to the guards.

"What are you doing here ... "The Major looked down and studied the passport. "Werner Ziegler?"

"I'm here to save your lives," Adam said.

Stasi laughed. His men did the same.

"You care about our lives, do you?" Stasi said.

"No one else does," Adam said. "That's obvious."

"What do you mean by that?" Stasi said. "How dare you come to my camp and speak to me that way? Do you want to be shot where you stand?"

"No," Adam said. "But ask yourself, Major – why would I risk walking up to your headquarters like this, unarmed, if I didn't have something important to tell you? And I mean, life and death important."

Stasi studied Adam, confirmed the guards had searched him, and invited him into his tent. The Major took a seat on a collapsible chair beside a folding table with a map and documents atop it. The words *United Soviet Socialist Republic* were printed above the body of land featured on the map. Adam stood before him in front of a rumpled canvas bed.

"What is it you want to tell me?" Stasi said. "Whose life, whose death?"

"Yours and your men's," Adam said. "You all need to pick up and get out of here, and get to a radiation treatment center as quickly as possible. Belarus has a good clinic. It was hit hard by the Chornobyl disaster. They know a lot about radiation. A lot of radioactive debris crossed the border. It's only one hundred kilometers away"

"Radiation?" Stasi frowned. "What radiation?"

"Strontium, cesium, and the like. From the Chornobyl nuclear disaster of 1986."

"Rings a bell somewhere ..."

"It rings a bell?" Adam said.

Stasi nodded.

Adam waited.

Stasi didn't blink. He was dead serious.

"Oh my God," Adam said. "You don't know where you are."

Stasi frowned.

"That map," Adam said, pointing to his side table. "Did you use that map – that set of maps – for navigation purposes?"

"What does it matter?"

Adam shook his head. "It matters only if you want to go on living, Major. Do you know where you are right now?"

"Don't ask me stupid questions. Of course I know where I am."

"Your map is from the Soviet days. What year was it made?"

"Why does that matter?"

Adam pointed to the side table. "May I?"

Stasi didn't say no.

Adam glanced at the map's legend.

"This map is from 1970," Adam said.

"So?"

Adam stared at him, incredulous.

Stasi raised his chin. "It's a great map. It's from the days of the Soviet Union. We're going to recreate it, the way it was supposed to be. Just wait. Just you wait."

"Major, neither you nor your men are going to be around to see it unless you get medical attention immediately."

Stasi laughed, but the smile on his face quickly faded. "Why do you say that?"

"Your map doesn't show you're in Chornobyl because Chornobyl wasn't relevant at the time. The Power Plant didn't exist until 1978. The disaster happened ten years later."

"And this is a problem for me because ..."

"Because you've built your camp on radioactive soil. You're literally sitting on a giant hot spot. No one's lived here for thirty-six years. Your soldiers – the ones who are digging the trenches?

They're literally scooping up radioactive waste. The tanks and trucks you brought here? They stirred up radioactive dust. It's in the wind now, we're breathing it as we speak. Your hair is covered with it."

Stasi blanched. He raised his hand to his head but pulled it back before making contact.

"Did you see these pine trees in the daytime?" Adam said. "They're sort of ginger and brown in color, almost red in some places. That's why this area – the six square kilometers around the Power Plant – it's called the Red Forest. The trees absorbed so much radiation after the reactor exploded they died."

Stasi appeared mortified.

"The Soviet government bulldozed the area and buried everything they could underground. And now your boys are digging it up. And bringing radioactive waste back to the top – into the open air."

Stasi stood up. "What ... "He raised his hand to his head and pulled it back again. "What should I do?"

"This is your moment in life, Major," Adam said. "This is what you were born to do. You have to get all your men out of here. You have to get clean. You have to get to a radiation clinic immediately. Have you ever seen a man die from acute radiation sickness?"

Stasi didn't answer. Adam didn't expect him to answer.

"It's not the way anyone wants to go," Adam said. "Ukrainian, Russian, doesn't matter. It's the not the way any human being should go. All the people at the Power Plant have to leave, too. They have to leave immediately. The dust has gotten inside by now. All those people are at risk. All of them."

"I don't think I can make that happen," Stasi said.

"The Power Plant is useless," Adam said. "It doesn't produce power. You're not hurting the Ukrainians by occupying it. All you're doing is risking your own lives. If you blow it up for whatever reason, with all the spent fuel rods and all the radioactive material in the old reactor, you'll cause just as much a crisis in Russia and Belarus as in Ukraine. And the Russian Army is going to suffer. It's going to suffer big time."

"I'm not even sure I can make my end happen."

"Of course you can," Adam said. "If a man wills himself to do something, he can do it. Once your superiors in Moscow see what they ordered you to do, I think you'll be surprised how quickly they follow your lead. The world won't be impressed if Russia causes a second disaster here. And I'll help you. I'll help you any way I can."

The Russians had liberated a case of dosimeters from the Power Plant. Stasi put them to use. The trenches contained readings as high as 6.5 millisieverts. According to someone in Moscow, fifty percent of those exposed to such a level of radiation would receive a fatal dose.

Adam stayed with Stasi the entire night. By mid-morning the next day, the soldiers were breaking camp and preparing to return to Russia, the Power Plant had been handed back to the Ukrainians, and all hostages had been released.

After the orders had been given, Adam exchanged texts with Mikey and confirmed all was well on both ends. He waited for the Mystic at the monument to the first responders at Chornobyl, a sculpture of outstretched arms holding a nuclear power plant in their hands. When the hostages emerged from inside the Power Plant, the Mystic separated herself from the pack and marched straight towards Adam without ever looking in his direction, as though she'd somehow known where he would be waiting. It was flat-out scary, Adam thought.

Contrary to his expectations, she wore no scarves or sweaters, just a bathroom robe over her nightgown. Adam realized his miscalculation – she'd been ripped from her bed by the Russians, not even given a chance to put on some decent clothes. From the neck up, she looked as elegant as he remembered, with short silver hair and a diamond-shaped face which almost rendered all her wrinkles irrelevant.

"I have information for you," the Mystic said, with nary a *hello* or a *nice to see you*.

"What information?" Adam said.

"Your prize will meet you shortly at a familiar nearby location."

"What prize?"

"I believe it's a package. To be delivered by a girl. To be delivered by a girl named Eva."

FORTY-THREE

THE MYSTIC SET A SURPRISINGLY fast pace as they marched along the road back to her house.

"You bear little resemblance to your former self," she said.

"A surgeon fixed my ears," Adam said.

"Except for your eyes. You can't change the eyes. The eyes are a portal."

"He may have tweaked a few other parts of my face."

"Easy to change their color—"

"So I bear little resemblance—"

"Not so easy to change what lies behind them."

"To my former self."

"If you shine a flashlight into a person's eyes at midnight," the Mystic said, "you can see inside their soul. I don't need the flashlight. I know what's in your soul. The question is, do you?"

"Right now my primary interest is in that package."

"Perhaps they're related."

"My soul and the package?" Adam said.

"If you've come this far in its pursuit, if you've come back to the country you swore never to return to again, is it not inevitable they're related?"

"Nothing is inevitable."

"It's good to hear you say that. There are forty million people in this country right now who share that sentiment. How is your health?"

"I'm dehydrated. How's yours?"

"Better for your presence. The experimental treatments you received from Doctor Arkady?"

"What about them?" Adam said.

"When you were in your teens, I remember you discovering you had the gift of speed after they took hold."

"Yes."

"On ice."

"Yes."

"You played hockey."

"That was a prior life."

"Has that gift continued to evolve?" the Mystic said.

"I seem to have gotten ... a bit faster. A doctor in New York told me I have an enlarged heart. It happens to elite athletes sometimes. But my gift seems to have morphed into a second dimension – a metaphorical dimension."

"What do you mean?"

Adam explained.

"Before I came back here," he said, "I thought I understood this gift. I thought it was wonderful. But since I've been here, I see it in a new light. It's wonderful and horrible, both at the same time. It's scaring me, Godmother. It's scaring me so much."

"Why?"

"Imagine you're one person but living with the worst memories of three others. And then three becomes six, and six becomes twelve and so on. And these memories, they persecute you when you least want them to, when you're alone with your own thoughts trying to relax."

"May I offer you some advice?" the Mystic said.

"Please."

"You must tell yourself these memories don't belong to you. That you may learn from them the way you learn from a book or a film but they are not your responsibility. They are not yours. You must repeat this mantra five times a day – no less – when you wake up and go to sleep, and you must do so every day for the rest of your life."

"That's the thing?" Adam said.

"That's one thing," the Mystic said.

"There's another?"

"You must be realistic. You're still young. Your gift, so to speak, may not be fully developed yet. There may be a third dimension. You may yet to have discovered the full extent of your capabilities."

They walked in silence for the next minute.

"In the sixteenth century," the Mystic said, "there was a fortress in the south of Ukraine called the Zaporizhian Sich. The soldiers there called themselves Cossacks – it was the Turkish word for *free people*. According to the myth, there were sorcerers among them, men who could catch bullets, ride magic carpets over the sea, transport themselves from one side of a mountain to another, and even change the weather."

"Are you suggesting I'm the living manifestation of these Cossack-Sorcerers?"

"Of course not. Such human beings cannot exist. Such human beings do not exist. But a human being such as you also cannot exit. And yet, you exist."

"I'm not sure I want to exist this way," Adam said.

"And what type of life would you lead if you were not your true self?"

"A healthier and longer one?" Adam said.

"Perhaps in Russia?" the Mystic said. "Denial is a way of life there."

They walked in silence a bit further.

"You said Eva will bring me the package," Adam said. "Have you seen her?"

"Not for years. Not since I saw you last. She sent me some text messages a few days ago. At first, I thought it was a hoax. But then I knew it was really her. She was very well informed. She knew things about your childhood only the two of you would know."

"Can I read them?"

"The Russians took my phone."

"Ah. What did she say?"

"She asked me for my help. She said she was playing a game with you. She said she was trying to reconnect and this was the only way."

"She said that? She said she was trying to reconnect with me?"

"She said she was trying to reconnect. I assumed it was with you? Who else could it be?"

They continued walking and talking. Less than a mile from the Mystic's house, Adam received a text message from an unknown number. The message consisted of a picture of a long-legged woman in jeans and a short black leather jacket. She was also wearing a black motorcycle helmet with fluorescent green trim. Its tinted shield concealed her face. Her long black hair fell below its rim. Her motorcycle, which matched the color scheme of her helmet, rested beside the Jeep in the place where Adam had parked it. The woman's arms hung by her sides. In her right hand, she held the package.

When Adam was finally able to take his eyes off the picture, he realized he'd sped up and left the Mystic behind. He waited for her to catch up and apologized.

"Eva texted you?" the Mystic said.

"Hopefully."

"I don't understand."

"I'll be leaving as soon as we get back," Adam said.

"Go on ahead of me, if you like."

"No, thank you. She can wait."

"I retract my original statement," the Mystic said. "You do bear a resemblance to your former self. You still have your manners."

"I hope so. That's what it means to be European."

They arrived at the Mystic's house. Mikey gathered their possessions. Adam retrieved Domino from Renata's care and spoke to the cat about the coming journey. After some rubs and pets, he placed the cat in his knapsack. As he was saying his good-byes to the Mystic and Renata, the sound of tires rolling over asphalt echoed in the house.

The Mystic stepped over to the window to peak through the blinds with Renata on her heels. They glanced outside just as Mikey shouted from the interior of the house.

"Get away from the window. Down, down, everyone get down—"

A hailstorm of bullets ripped through the house. They shredded the Mystic and Renata. Adam dropped to the floor on his side. He covered the cat's head and pressed it to his chest. The bullets continued flying until someone outside shouted stop in Russian.

Mikey scrambled over to Adam, rifle in one hand, bag in the other.

"I'm going to cover you," Mikey said, as he removed clips from the bag and wedged them under his belt. "You take off through the back door, do your thing to get to the Jeep. Don't look back."

"I'm not leaving you," Adam said.

"If you get killed, all my work will have been for nothing."

"Work? What work? What are you talking about?"

"I told you," Mikey said, as he loaded his rifle. "I'm your protector. Don't you see yet, don't you see? It was all planned, it was all planned. On three – two – one – go, go, go."

Mikey rose to his feet, smashed the window with his rifle and fired at will.

Adam snuck out the back door, raced toward the Power Plant, crossed the road and circled back behind the vehicles that had arrived. He slowed down just enough to see three black SUVs with Russian license plates. The shooting had stopped, he realized, and heavily armed men in plainclothes were rushing into the house.

Mikey had been hit, Adam thought. That was the only reason he would have stopped shooting. That realization slowed Adam further, enough for him to spy the lone remaining Russian near the vehicles. He looked too neat and clean to be standing in the wilderness. He wore a look of astonishment on his face, similar to the one Mikey had flashed when he'd seen Adam racing across the bridge with bodies slung over his shoulder. This man, however, channeled an entirely different energy. His carriage projected a palpable sense of superiority.

As Adam accelerated, he heard three quick shots behind him – rat, tat, tat – and he knew.

Mikey was gone.

FORTY-FOUR

STRELKOV HAD NEVER SEEN anything like it.

Ivanova had nailed it when she'd described the image they'd seen from the Russian campsite. The man was a blur, until he slowed down. Then he became a man again. Until he sped up and became a blur again.

But he'd run from a gunfight which meant he could be killed just like any mortal. And it was just a matter of time until Russia caught him, for as the bishop himself had said, reuniting Ukraine with Russia and Belarus was inevitable. No bullet-fearing NLO was going to prevent the will of God.

Strelkov wondered if Ivanova knew more about this man than she'd let on. He was an expert at extracting information from prisoners, especially women.

Given she was also a traitor to Russia, he looked forward to that opportunity.

FORTY-FIVE

ADAM FOLLOWED the motorcycle along the narrow road to the outskirts of Chornobyl. Domino slept in the passenger seat beside him, stressed out from their six-mile run. When Adam sped up in hopes of pulling up to the driver, she surged ahead of him effortlessly. After two attempts, he resigned himself to reality. Eva, or Almost Eva, as he called the woman when he imagined she might be an imposter, was in control. He was going wherever she led, more so now than ever before.

He'd gotten his priorities straight once he got back on the road. Victor's life was in jeopardy. He needed to reacquire the package to save Victor. Unlike all the horrific memories he'd absorbed, the murders he'd personally witnessed, and now the senseless killing of his godmother and her niece, that was the one tragedy he had a chance to prevent. Amidst all his confusion regarding his journey since he'd last left New York City, this was the one certainty he could hang onto.

His uncle was in trouble. It was up to him to save him.

Mikey's final words rang in his ears. *It was all planned. It was all planned.* That suggested Eva was with the Ukrainians, and Mikey was with them, too. A group of people including them had created an elaborate plan to give him a tour of Ukraine's plight for reasons beyond his comprehension.

It had worked. He was informed now, too much so for his own liking. Russia wasn't conducting a special military operation or a war. It was trying to subjugate what it perceived to be a lesser form of life. Russia didn't contemplate the cruelty of its motive or methods. It didn't believe all men were created equal. Hell, it didn't consider Ukrainians to be human beings at all.

But why was this group of people so keen on Adam getting a first-hand look at the war in Ukraine? And how did this plan, as Mikey described it, tie in with Victor and the package?

Adam's southbound pursuit of the motorcycle soon offered clarity on where he might find the answers to his questions. The country road led to an access ramp that put them on a highway. The signs left no doubt in Adam's mind about their destination.

They were headed to the capital. They were headed to Kyiv.

A roadblock presented itself thirty kilometers south. Until that point, Adam hadn't seen a single vehicle other than the one he was following. Eva raced past the checkpoint, weaving around the barricades made of welded metal rods, her body leaning at a 45-degree angle to make the necessary turns. The guards didn't stop her.

Adam wasn't as lucky.

Two soldiers motioned from afar for him to pull over. Adam saw the blue and yellow patches on their uniforms. They left no doubt who was in control of the road from there to Kyiv. One of them compared Adam's passport photo to his face, returned the document to him, and waved him through. It was the first time no one had inquired about his reason for being in Ukraine, or his destination.

Eva waited by the side of the road a hundred meters ahead until he resumed driving. The roadblocks that followed made the first one seem like a veritable inquisition. No one stopped either of them. Open lanes awaited him. The soldiers at the checkpoints clearly knew they were coming. Adam sailed through, slowing down the first time out of caution, not bothering to reduce his speed thereafter.

Sporadic traffic appeared as they got closer to the city. Bombed-out craters revealed themselves in the tarmac. Other stretches of highway contained lanes that had been ripped from the ground, leaving piles of asphalt scattered in their midst. Adam followed the bike to avoid the rubble.

The trip from Chornobyl covered one hundred kilometers. Once they got off the highway, Eva took a dizzying set of turns that left them somewhere in the city center. Adam didn't know Kyiv at all. He'd never been there before in his life.

When she turned into an alley and disappeared, Adam pulled up and saw it was half the width of the Jeep. He watched through the side window as Eva came to a stop a hundred feet away and turned off the engine. She climbed off her bike and leaned it gently against a brick wall. After removing the helmet from her head, she stored it atop the motorcycle and disappeared out of sight down a perpendicular alley.

She didn't bother glancing Adam's way.

She knew he was there. She knew he would follow.

Adam parked the car, gathered Domino into his knapsack, slipped his arms through the straps. and bounded down the alley. He took a right onto the perpendicular alley where Eva had disappeared but there was no sign of her. He marched onward for a hundred feet until the alley deposited him onto a fancy promenade made of blue stone.

Stately concrete buildings surrounded the walkway from all sides. To the left stood an empty white guardhouse. To the right, two Ukrainian soldiers in full gear, including helmets. Beside them stood a bear of a man in military fatigues. He wore no sidearm or helmet.

"*Pane Adam*," he said, bowing his head a bit.

Mister Adam. Casual and friendly yet entirely respectful, this was the most disarming way of addressing another person in Ukrainian. Simply hearing the phrase slowed Adam's pulse.

"This way," the man said, extending his arm to the right.

Adam marched onward, cat peering from the knapsack attached to his chest. The irregular shaped stones, the ultra-wide walkway ... he'd never been to Kyiv before and yet the place felt entirely familiar. Four more men awaited him at the far end of the promenade. They were casually dressed in pants and sweaters. All of them appeared to be in their forties. They, too, smiled and bowed their heads slightly as Adam walked up to them. The bow was a European thing, Adam thought, and yet it seemed like a bit more in this case.

"Mister Adam," they said, and pointed to the right.

Adam turned.

A man stood at the end of an adjacent walkway. He wore an olive-green t-shirt, khaki pants and brown boots. To his left stood a woman with long dark hair.

Adam was too far away to make out her face.

He started toward her, oblivious to everything else. All he wanted was for the woman to be Eva. If this was the last time he saw her, he'd be content to know she was alive and living the life she deserved. He longed for more, of course. He longed to be with her every second of every day, to go to bed thinking of her, and awaken to the sweet realization that she was his, and that nothing else on this Earth mattered.

Adam picked up his pace. Her face came into proper view.

Teresa, the farmer's daughter, had been right. This woman shared the same height and coloring as Eva but up close, the structure of her face was a bit different.

She was not Eva.

She was Almost Eva.

When their eyes met, she didn't speak. Instead, she looked at him with a blank stare, as though she was there, but not entirely present.

The man to her right stepped forward, grasped Adam by the shoulders, kissed him on both cheeks, and gave Domino a scratch on the head. Adam realized why the promenade seemed so familiar. He'd seen it on television when the leaders of the free world showed up unexpectedly in Kyiv to lend support to Ukraine.

"Mister Adam," the President of Ukraine said. "Welcome home."

A third person emerged from behind a stand that held the Ukrainian flag. He looked exactly as Adam remembered prior to leaving New York for Switzerland, not a blemish on his face. The only difference was he'd ditched the wheelchair. He was leaning on a cane instead.

"Hello, Uncle," Adam said.

"Hello, Adam," Victor Bodnar said.

"Shall we?" the President said to Adam, motioning towards the building behind him. "We have a package for you. It's waiting inside."

FORTY-SIX

THEY GATHERED in a simple office with basic wooden furniture. A Presidential aide took the cat to get it some food and exercise. The President sat behind his desk, the Ukrainian flag on his left. The bear of a man who'd first welcomed Adam stood on his right. He was a general in the Ukrainian Army. Victor and Almost Eva sat further on either side of the President in upholstered side chairs. They all faced Adam, who'd been relegated to a wooden desk and chair, the kind one would find in an elementary school. The potential symbolism of the chair he'd been assigned wasn't lost on him.

The package rested on the tablet arm attached to his desk. Besides the package was a folding knife.

They all stared at Adam as though waiting for him to do the obvious. Adam, however, wasn't in the mood to suffer fools or make assumptions. In fact, he was almost too livid to sit still. If someone didn't say something soon, he might leave the country straightaway, and no outdated Sukhoi fighter jet was going to catch him.

As soon as Victor had revealed himself, hale and hearty,

almost all had become clear to Adam. The only mystery left was the contents of the package and how it tied into his being here.

"Please," the President said, motioning toward the writing surface attached to Adam's desk. "If you'd be so kind."

"You want me to open this?"

The President smiled.

Adam turned to Victor. "*Needless to say, under no circumstances are you to open it.* Isn't that what you said to me about the package, Victor?"

Victor smiled. "And *given it was I who said that, you thought it suggested I actually wanted you to open the package.* I just didn't say when you should open it, did I?"

Adam unfolded the knife and eyed the resin-covered pouch.

"*The package contains a technology that will give one country an advantage over the other,*" Adam said. "You said that, too, right Victor?"

"A great leader sits before you and you choose to quote a common thief," Victor said.

"This technology," the President said, "it works only if it's in your hands, Adam. And only if you hold it shoulder-high."

Adam continued glaring at Victor.

"Please," the President said, without a hint of irritation.

Adam inserted the tip of the blade into one of the corners, turned the sharp end to the outside and slipped the rest of the shaft into the package. He sliced through one end and set the knife aside. He remained cool on the outside but butterflies swirled in his belly. How could they not, he thought? He'd been through hell for the damn thing, whatever it was.

Adam took a deep breath, slipped his fingers inside, and removed a thin black box from inside. It fit in the palm of his hand. It contained a narrow aperture between the top and bottom. Adam placed his thumb into the gap and pulled.

A compact vanity mirror popped open.

Adam raised it shoulder-high. His reflection appeared in the mirror.

"What do you see?" the President said.

"I look like shit," Adam said.

"No, really," the President said. "Tell me truthfully, what do you see?"

"I'm the thing?" Adam said, glancing at each person in front of him in rapid succession. "You all think I'm the advantage?" Then he bore into Victor. "You're insane."

"I believe I've been told that a few times over the past few years," the President said.

"You've been misinformed, Mr. President," Adam said. "I'm not a soldier. I'm not even a courier. I'm a common thief who works for another common thief and does jobs for other criminals. That's all I am, Mr. President. I don't even deserve to be sitting in front of you."

"Perhaps you're being a bit modest, Adam?" the President said. "From what I've heard, there may be a few people in Ukraine – and in Switzerland – who disagree."

Adam glanced at Victor again. "Nazarov?"

"Is who he says he is," Victor said. "His boss is privately sympathetic to the Ukrainian cause. He's not the only Russian oligarch who is."

"I thought Nazarov was hiding something," Adam said. "That's why he seemed so uncomfortable in his own clothes. The Amber Lady, the professor in Lviv – Boyko, Luca and the Farmer ..."

"All sympathizers," Victor said. "They knew as much as they needed to know, which is to say, as little as possible."

"You shared my most intimate childhood memories with her," Adam said, glancing at Almost Eva. "Right down to the shampoo Eva used to use. That's the only way she could have succeeded in making me think Eva was still alive."

"The ends justified the means," Victor said.

"You betrayed me," Adam said.

"It was the only way to get you here," Victor said. "The only way you would have ever come back to Ukraine was in pursuit of your long-lost love."

"And what about Eva?" Adam said. "There are no new developments, right?"

Victor held his gaze.

"Of course not," Adam whispered, more to himself than anyone else. "*Reconnect*. My Godmother said that word was in the note she got from her." Adam nodded at Almost Eva. "But it wasn't about reconnecting me with my girlfriend. It was about what, reconnecting me with Ukraine? You thought what, Victor, that I'd see the horrors of the war, and enlist in the Foreign Legion? Are you kidding me? You don't know me better that?"

"No one would ever suggest such a thing," the President said. "It is as you said it is. You're not a soldier. We would never put you or the brave men in our International Legion at risk by asking you to do something that you're not trained to do, that you have no experience in doing."

"What then?" Adam said. "Why am I here?"

"First, you must understand that this war cannot last forever," the President said. "All wars end, and so will this one."

"Russia can't sustain the types of losses it's taking forever," the General said. "Losses in manpower, weapons, machinery. Their domestic economy is deteriorating."

"And the support we're getting from the West," the President said. "The weapons systems, the training, the financial assistance. That can't last forever, either. Ukraine will never cede its territory to Russia. That won't happen. But we have to be realistic. Without the West's support, the theater would change dramatically."

"There's a plan being developed," the General said. "By the Americans, with input from our European allies, as well."

"The plan is to negotiate a peace based on the principles used to end the Korean War," the President said.

"Russia will be like the North," the General said, "We will be like the South."

"Ukraine will cede a contiguous strip of land along its entire Russian border," the President said. "We will cede this land but not to Russia. No one will own it - the world will own it. It will become a demilitarized zone with a dedicated international peacekeeping force. In exchange for giving up its territory, Ukraine will get security by becoming a member of NATO. Simultaneously, the Russian President will proclaim victory - as a result of his actions, Russians will never have to worry about a Westernized Ukraine touching its borders. It will be spun as a win-win."

"Ceding the land will be excruciating," the General said. "Grown men and women will cry in the streets. But such is reality if we want peace. Finland ceded ten percent of its land to Russia after the Winter War in 1940. And look at Finland now."

A moment of silence passed.

"I don't understand what any of this has to do with me," Adam said.

"The only alternative solution is for Ukraine to win the war outright," the President said. "And for that to happen, given its advantages in weapons and manpower, Russia would have to lose the war."

"I still don't understand," Adam said.

"Even if Russia didn't lose the war," the General said, "if their effort faltered, if we regained some territory before the pressure to negotiate came to bear, the terms of the treaty might be a bit more in our favor."

"Where exactly do I come in?" Adam said.

"Have you heard of the Russian *siloviki?*" the President said.

"No," Adam said.

"They're the Ministers of Force," the General said. "They control all branches of the Russian government. They're the police chiefs, military leaders, prosecutors, the ministers of justice. They use coercion and violence on behalf of the Russian state. Maybe six or seven of them are the most powerful men in Russia. The Russian Boss takes his counsel from them, and they keep him in power."

"These men," the President said, "they're so wealthy, they travel freely. Sanctions do nothing to stop them. We were thinking, after a little training with the General, perhaps you would go say hello to a few of them, or some of their friends."

"Say hello?" Adam said.

"Have a conversation with them," the President said. "The way you did with the Farmer's daughter."

"You mean, literally talk to them?" Adam said.

"As only you can, of course," the President said. "If you think it through, what could possibly be better?"

Adam considered the President's logic.

"Even if I had an up-close and personal conversation with one of these men," Adam said, "that doesn't mean I'm going to be able to find the good in him. Some people are evil. Some people need to die."

"You'll never know unless you try," the President said. "And we desperately need you to try. You're the only human being who can help us this way."

Adam glanced at Almost Eva. She was looking right at him but there was no spark in her eyes. And why would there be? She wasn't Eva. What was he thinking?

The President's plan was not for him. And to hell with the

luxury apartment in Florence. He longed for his three-room junior four in Manhattan, the remote to his sixty-five-inch TV with every streaming service known to man, and his favorite food delivery app at the ready. Once he got back, he'd never leave the comfy confines of New York City again.

"My Godmother," Adam said, "the Mystic in Chornobyl. She's dead. So is her niece. That happened because those men came looking for me."

"And we are very sorry for your loss," the General said. "Such tragedies occur daily here. If you hadn't secured her release from the Power Plant, she might have gone a different way at a different time. There's no logic or solace during war."

"You're the only known person to have been born in the Zone of Exclusion since the nuclear disaster of 1986," the President said. "The life you had here ... the childhood you experienced ... it can't have been easy."

"Not easy?" Adam said. "That's one way to put it, Mr. President. Every single person in this country – with maybe four or five exceptions – hated me from the moment I was born. My mother – she never had a chance. My father, my hockey coach, my Godmother, and Eva. That's about it. Those are the only human beings who didn't wish me dead every time they looked at me for the first sixteen years of my life."

"I'm truly sorry," the President said.

"I was born with certain disabilities because of the effects of radiation poisoning. My thyroid, my ears – they didn't used to look this way. I wore a hat twenty-four seven to try to look normal. It didn't matter. People could smell it off me. Everywhere I went, anyone I met, no one wanted to be near me. At school, it wasn't just the other kids. Teachers, cooks, the principals – everyone who worked there. I went on a train once, and the entire cabin emptied once I sat down. A couple came in, took one look at me and left as though I was poison."

"Your uncle told me you do not work east of Poland," the President said. "Now I understand why."

"I was a living symbol of Ukraine's shame. No one wanted to talk about Chornobyl. No one wanted to acknowledge there were survivors. People were scared we were contagious. But it was more than that. They thought they were better than me. They thought I was less than a human being. I could see it in people's eyes every day of my life. And now, what, Ukraine wants something from me?

"You know who's good to the Children of Chornobyl? The Irish are good to us. There's a couple of women in Ireland, they built a hospital in Kharkiv for our kind. Want to know who paid for it? They did. Charity did. I did. If it wasn't for those women, there wouldn't be such a place. No one else gives a damn."

The room turned silent. Adam's heart pounded in his ears. He'd never spoken the words, not to Eva, Victor, or anyone. He hadn't expected to say them. But now that he'd spoken his truth, he felt momentarily relieved until a sense of guilt and embarrassment set in. The leader of a nation at war was sitting before him, and he'd just prattled on about his childhood misfortunes.

Adam felt his face redden. He looked at the floor with newfound shame.

The President rose to his feet and circled around his desk. Almost Eva immediately stood up. Victor followed, and Adam did the same.

The President placed his hands by his side, thrust his shoulders back and looked directly into Adam's eyes.

"On behalf of a grateful nation," the President said, "grateful for your bravery and skills that allowed us to trade the bodies of dead Russian soldiers for Ukrainian POWs, grateful for the help you provided young girls trying to protect their virtue during a time of war, grateful for your ingenuity in the rescue of hostages at a nuclear power plant and the evacuation of the enemy before it created a second disaster, I apologize to you and to all the generations of survivors of the Chornobyl nuclear accident. We will not forsake you. We will do a better job."

The President bowed his head slightly before Adam.

Adam didn't know what to do.

"It may seem convenient for me to say this now," the President said, "but history shows that it's at times like these that a nation takes stock of itself and acknowledges the changes it needs to make. This ... this is but one of ours."

The President returned to his desk and everyone sat down.

"I appreciate those words, Mr. President," Adam said. "But I don't think what you propose is for me. I've seen the horror firsthand now. Like I said to someone when this whole thing started, if I could end the war in your favor, I would do it today. But I can't. I have nothing but admiration for your people."

"Your people?" the President said, twinkle in his eye. "My people are also your people, aren't they?"

"I'm an American now," Adam said. "America takes everyone. Everyone has a chance in America. Once you experience that kind of freedom, that kind of opportunity, you realize how lucky you are to be American. My American passport, the thing that proves I'm an American citizen? Say what you want about me. Take all my things. But you can't have that."

"Understood," the President said. "But a man can be a citizen of two countries, can't he? No one has taken your Ukrainian citizenship away."

"I don't mean to be disrespectful or unsympathetic," Adam said. "But the worst thing I could do is pretend to go along with this when my heart's not in it. It's just not for me."

"I'd tell you about our mutual friend," the President said, "if I thought it would help."

"What mutual friend?" Adam said.

"Mykhailo Dobrohovich," the President said. "The man you called Mikey."

"What about him?" Adam said.

The President turned to the General.

"He volunteered for the mission," the General said.

"Volunteered?" Adam said. "He said his father was in the army but he was an actor."

"His father was a fireman," the General said. "Mykhailo himself is one of our finest soldiers. He volunteered for the job as soon as it was presented to him. No hesitation even though he fully understood the risks involved."

"Why?" Adam said. "Why would he do that?"

"Because he's also a child of Chornobyl," the President said.

"What?" Adam said.

"His father was a liquidator at reactor four," the General said. "He was a local fireman assigned to the Power Plant. He lived in Pripyat with his wife, Mykhailo's mother. His father was one of the first to go in. He carried cinderblocks covered in radiation with his bare hands. He died within twenty-four hours."

"Mykhailo was born without sexual function," the President said. "Those sensations we experience that bring us closest to God? He cannot have them. He has never enjoyed them. He will never know them. For him there is only food and drink and his beloved films. For him, there is only duty and honor."

Adam took a moment to digest the President's words. The three shots he'd heard in the Mystic's house echoed in his mind in excruciating detail.

"Maybe you guys don't realize this yet," Adam said, "but Mikey's gone."

Adam described seeing the Russians burst into the house in Chornobyl and the shots that ensued.

"We're not so sure he was killed," the General said.

"You're not?" Adam said. "Why?"

"Because there's a radio transmitter sewn into the hem of his pants," the General said, "and it shows that he's on the move as we speak."

Adam sat up. "Really?"

"If the Russians had shot him," the President said. "They would have left him where he fell."

"But if he was alive and they could interrogate him ..." the General said.

"Where's he headed now?" Adam said.

"South by southeast," the General said.

"Kherson," the President said. "We think they're taking him to Kherson."

"There's an FSB officer there named Strelkov," the General said. "He's running a filtration camp. The place and the man – they're both known to us."

"We have an important asset there right now," the President said. "A plan to extract her is in the works. If he's also there ..."

"I'd like to go along," Adam said.

"That's not realistic," the General said. "You're untrained. Your mere presence would put the team at risk. Worrying about you would put them in danger."

"No one needs to worry about me," Adam said. "I'll be hanging back. I won't get in anyone's way."

"No," the General said. "A prisoner rescue operation is based on violence and speed."

"Are you saying I'm not fast enough?" Adam said.

The General started to laugh but checked himself. "You know what I'm saying, Mister Adam."

"And you know what I'm saying, General," Adam said. "If I was to go along, I might be open to further conversations about your ideas on how I can help you."

The President and the General exchanged a glance.

They discussed the risks of the operation for another five minutes. Adam listened, but didn't retract his demand. In fact, he didn't say another word. When the meeting was over, Adam went in search of Domino but stopped to speak with Victor privately first.

"What's in this for you?" Adam said. "There must be money. You don't leave your chair, let alone the country, unless there's money."

Victor appraised Adam. "Did I ever tell you about my time in a Soviet prison?"

"No," Adam said.

"The reason I never told you about it is the reason I'm here. Very few things matter more than money. This is one of them. There can never be a Soviet Union again. Ever."

"You expect me to believe that?" Adam said.

"I expect you to be your true self," Victor said, "whoever that is."

"All this time," Adam said, "from the minute I got to Zermatt and everything started to go south, I said to myself, on countless occasions, there will come a moment when I'll be able to tilt the field in my favor. That kind of moment, it always comes, if you just stay patient. Now I know why it never came."

"Don't be hard on yourself," Victor said. "Most of the time, there's law and order in the stadium, and the players don't even know you're in the game. In this case, the stadium was under attack, and you were the game."

"Oh, thank you, coach. That makes me feel so much better. And what if I'd been killed, Victor? There were a dozen or more moments where I could have died. What then? I could have been killed so easily."

Victor studied him thoughtfully. "But you weren't, were you?"

He pulled a cigar out of his jacket pocket and walked away.

FORTY-SEVEN

TASIA SAT in a wooden chair with a disturbing feature – a hole had been drilled in its middle such that she was sitting directly atop it.

Hand-held trouble lights illuminated the room. They hung from hooks attached to the plywood ceiling. The three walls that surrounded her were also made of wood. Tasia wondered if the room had been sound-proofed – great care appeared to have been taken to seal every nook and cranny.

Metal restraints bound her wrists and ankles. Glancing over her shoulder, she saw that the lower portion of the wall behind her was made of concrete. A black pipe fell from the ceiling, connected to a joint, and disappeared through the wood outside the building.

Strelkov sat before her in his custom-made basement office. He looked freshly showered and shaved. His hair shone from sort of gel, and he reeked of a pine-based after-shave. Tasia's cooler rested on the table between them.

She wondered what was inside the cooler, which exactly what Strelkov wanted her to be doing. By bringing the cooler he'd activated her imagination. Now it was running wild conjuring the possibilities. She didn't fear death. Everyone died. The key was not to waste a second thinking about it. But Tasia feared pain. She feared unbearable and unrelenting pain.

One thing was certain. The cooler didn't contain beer and doughnuts.

"What was your handler's name?" Strelkov said.

"Maurice," Tasia said.

Strelkov frowned. "Maurice?"

"Barry was the best-looking. Robin had the best voice. But Maurice was the glue that kept them together."

"Oh, I see." Strelkov chuckled. "You're making a joke of some kind? We'll see how that works for you. What do the Ukrainians know about Wagner?"

"That I'm not sure of," Tasia said.

Strelkov's eyes flickered as though he'd finally broken through to her and she was being genuinely forthcoming.

"Tell me more," Strelkov said. "Why not?"

"I haven't spent much time in this country," Tasia said. "This assignment – it's my first trip here. So, I just don't know. I'm sure the *intelligentsia* knows all about him, but I don't know if the overall population is into opera."

Fury flashed on his face. A patronizing smile replaced it just as quickly.

"Tell me about your sister," he said.

"What would you like to know about her?" Tasia said.

"Her name is Lena, yes? Do you speak often?"

"Not as often as I'd like."

"Is she in-country now?" Strelkov said.

"Where else would she be?"

"Perhaps I can arrange a reunion."

"Be careful what you wish for," Tasia said.

Strelkov asked her more questions about her family, her

recruitment and the information she provided the enemy. Tasia gave him nothing.

"You're not the future of Russia," she said.

Strelkov smiled. "Oh, no? Says the traitor to her country?"

"After World War II, a psychologist did a study on the Nazis," Tasia said. "He found two types of men. Those who hated Hitler and did as little as necessary just to stay alive, and those who loved him and his fascist state. The true fascists all shared the same background – they had brutal fathers whom they could never please, and mothers they idolized, so much so that any woman who made the slightest mistake was an immediate disappointment."

"You are the greatest disappointment of all," Strelkov said.

"The post World War II leaders of Germany?" Tasia said. "They came from the first group. Aren't we fighting World War III right now? I think we are. The future leaders of Russia? You're not one of them."

Strelkov managed a smile. "You're wasting your time worrying about the wrong things. What you should be worried about is what's in your cooler."

Tasia tried not to look at the cooler but glanced at it anyways.

"Care to guess?" Strelkov said. "I'll give you a hint. I used to play with the plastic equivalents when I was a child. Oh, how I enjoyed playing with them, but not nearly as much as I love working with the real things now. Think about it. You're a clever girl. I'm sure you can figure it out."

Tasia ignored him. She thought of her father, instead. He once told her that when a person approached the end of her life and looked back at it, if she'd done one good thing – one noble act – she could die knowing her life had meant something.

Strelkov removed the contents of the cooler – pliers, a hammer, a saw and some wire cutters.

Her life had meant something.

FORTY-EIGHT

ADAM SAT NEXT to Almost Eva in the armored personnel carrier during the drive from Kyiv to Kherson.

He still didn't know her proper name. No one had introduced her to him, she hadn't volunteered her name, and he hadn't asked. Everyone shared an unspoken understanding that Adam needed to cure himself from any notion that Almost Eva was a substitute for his deceased girlfriend. The more he viewed her as a Ukrainian soldier and ignored her gender, the better off he'd be. Almost Eva's body language left no doubt that she was a professional with no interest in casual conversations. But there was something else about her, too. She seemed possessed by a melancholy bordering on controlled fury. If she were to blow, Adam thought, a prudent person might be well-served to be on a different continent when it happened.

Two hours into the drive, she fell asleep. Adam had never used his gift to indulge his curiosity about a person's past. To-date he'd only tapped into people while on the job, as he'd done in Zermatt, by accident on the train platform in Lviv, or to help the Farmer's daughter. He had a moral code in that regard, and it was important to him. Violating that code struck him as an abuse of personal power, a breach of the rules that kept him sane and whole, a serious mistake.

But in this case, Adam simply couldn't resist. He glanced at the soldier to his right and saw his head bobbing – he was sleeping, too. Adam took a deep breath and wrapped his thumb and index finger around Almost Eva's wrist, so gently he barely made contact with her skin.

He closed his eyes. The images came rapid-fire and faded just as quickly

Villagers fall to their knees after tossing fresh flower bouquets onto a street ahead of a funeral procession ...

A decorated female officer in the Ukrainian Army stands in front of a coffin surrounded by grieving civilians ...

A Ukrainian flag covers the coffin ...

A sixteen-piece military band plays ...

Six soldiers fire three volleys each into the air ...

Two soldiers fold the flag and hand it to the priest, who hands it to the female officer ...

Her eyes well, creating the illusion they're twice their size, but not a single tear flows ...

Adam gently removed his fingers from around the widow's wrist.

Then he closed his eyes and said a prayer for her departed husband.

FORTY-NINE

ADAM SPENT an hour in a briefing with the General and a commander of the Alpha special forces team of the Security Service of Ukraine. He learned many things relevant to the operation being planned for Kherson.

A successful prisoner rescue was entirely dependent on the intelligence gathered before the operation commenced. The Alpha team had every possible advantage where the FSB headquarters in Kherson was concerned. They had the original blueprint for the building, and an informant within the FSB had provided details regarding its current layout, security systems, and personnel.

The operation was supposed to consist of three phases – sealing off the area, snatching the package, and speeding to safety. Speed was security, the commander told Adam, but the intelligence was everything.

In this case, the intelligence came up short.

After the trucks arrived, a team of twelve had sealed off the area and stormed inside. Shots had been fired. A search ensued. Civilians began hurrying out the building, guided by two Alphas at the rear. They came out in groups of ten or twelve and dispersed into the night. Mikey and the woman they'd come to rescue, however, were nowhere to be found inside the building.

"No prisoners," the Alpha said, after receiving a message via his headset.

Adam crouched low beside him, across the street from the building, twenty meters away.

"How can that be?" Adam said.

"Civilians only," the Alpha said. "No POWs."

Helicopters whirred overhead in the distance.

"Crocodiles approaching," the Alpha said into the microphone. He waited for a response. "Roger that." He turned his head slightly toward Adam, keeping his eyes on the building. "They're going to do one more sweep. But after that, we're gone."

The moon had cooperated for the evening, as had the stars – they were absent from the sky, leaving darkness in their place. Adam's eyes, however, had adjusted to the night. He studied the faces of the people rushing past him, fantasizing he might see Mikey's among them.

He didn't.

Instead, he saw a collection of eager men and women who were being given a second chance at life as they'd known it. Among them, however, was an outlier. He held his head down but Adam spied its shadow of dismay. It stood in contrast to the echo of hope the footsteps of the others left in their wake.

The man raised his eyes momentarily to check his bearings.

Adam suffered a jolt to the heart.

He was the man Adam had seen outside the Mystic's house after she and Renata had been murdered, and Mikey's rifle had gone silent.

Adam took off after him.

The Alpha scolded him in hushed but urgent tones, asked

him what the hell he was doing, and demanded he come back right away.

Adam ignored him.

The man knew where Mikey was, Adam thought, and if Mikey was dead, this was the bastard who'd killed him.

Adam took aim for the Russian and shifted into top gear.

FIFTY

STRELKOV MARCHED AT A MEASURED PACE. In this case that meant moving with a certain urgency, as though he were one of the so-called Ukrainians escaping to freedom to resume the life of a sub-human serf born to farm and wash his dirty underwear. It also meant not running like a fine Russian colonel trying to evade capture. Such a challenge wasn't easy. Anything that required him to think like a sub-human was excruciating.

They'd freed the civilians. Congratulations, Strelkov thought. There were forty million more where they came from, and every one of them would eventually be reminded that their country appeared under Russia on a map for a very good reason. More importantly, they'd never get Ivanova or the impertinent little bastard that had killed three of his best men. They'd never find them because Strelkov's methods of interrogation were so extreme he had to conduct them in private lest he demoralized his own staff – especially the women.

Once he was thirty meters beyond the building, Strelkov contemplated his choice of opera and beverages for the evening. The man was upon him so quickly he barely heard a footstep.

Strelkov rolled as soon as he hit the ground with the man on his back. He executed a perfect reversal, ending his roll atop his assailant. To say his Spetsnaz training kicked in was to suggest it ever strayed far from his consciousness. He pinned the man's left shoulder with his left hand, rendering his right arm useless with the weight of his elbow. Strelkov whipped the knife out of his back pocket and opened it with a single flick of the wrist. He held it high, prepared to strike.

Only then did he focus on his attacker's face.

"You," Strelkov said. He could hear the amazement in his own voice. "The NLO ... Mr. Werner Ziegler ... from Munich."

The man may have boasted superhuman speed, Strelkov thought, but he was neither muscular nor trained in combat. What a gift for him to appear like this, Strelkov thought, practically begging to be assassinated.

"Tell me about the restaurants in Munich, Mr. Ziegler. The drinking establishments and the laundry and the like. You locals, you always know the best places, all the secret handshakes."

Strelkov brought the knife down with all his might.

One of the NLO's arms slipped out of his grasp. Strelkov wasn't sure which one. He could feel his chest fall, the weight beneath it lighter as the NLO's limb found daylight. The ease with which he freed it surprised Strelkov.

Their arms collided. Strelkov's knife came within three inches of the NLO's heart and stopped. Strelkov swore and tried to yank the knife back to try to stab him again, but the NLO had grasped his wrist—

Strelkov tried to break free but couldn't move his right arm. He tried to wrestle his left arm away but he couldn't move that one either. His legs, his mouth, his voice – he tried them all. Nothing moved. Nothing worked. He could see, understand, and think as always, but he was otherwise paralyzed.

Panic set in. He tried everything again to no avail. He

couldn't comprehend what was happening to him and wondered if these were the sensations one experienced before death.

A seizure gripped the NLO. His eyes closed and his body convulsed for ten seconds, and then an eerie calm enveloped him.

In the ensuing minute, Strelkov had the strange sensation that all his thoughts and actions were laid bare for the world to see. He felt emotionally violated. It was the most loathsome, sickening experience of his life. Shame and humiliation overcame him for no apparent reason. He wasn't contemplating any person, place or thing. He wasn't dwelling on his past.

As the seconds ticked by, Strelkov realized that he was having an increasingly difficult time breathing.

And there was nothing he could do about it.

FIFTY-ONE

AS SOON AS Adam closed his eyes, the images came rapid-fire and faded just as quickly until only a few remained—

A boy snuggles in his mother's bosom surrounded by chickens and other farm animals.

The boy's father wallops his naked backside with a belt, all the while berating him, a school report card on the table over which he's bent over.

The father hangs a sign around the boy's neck and instructs him to walk back and forth along a street.

Passersby stop to read the sign.

The sign says "I am an idiot."

Blood spurts onto a man's forehead as he snips the ear off a woman's head with wire cutters. He wipes the blood with his shirt sleeve, a concrete wall in front of him.

Adam opened his eyes.

The last memory didn't make any sense. Only the very best

and worst memories remained at the end of the tap. This man had executed the Mystic and Renata, and wounded or killed Mikey. He'd also probably done far worse things, too. Why would a man like that regret torturing another human being?

He wouldn't, Adam thought. That memory wasn't one of the man's worst ones – it was one of his favorites. Evidently, he hated the woman so much – she'd done something to offend him to such a degree – that torturing her exceeded any joy his family had ever given him. It was also more memorable than any other atrocity he'd ever committed.

This man was true evil.

Adam was so deep in thought he didn't realize he'd failed to let go of the man's wrist. He'd never done that before. He automatically let go of the person once he'd absorbed his memories. What reason was there to hang on? In this instance, however, Adam had become lost in his own thoughts. As a result, he'd maintained his grasp of the man's flesh. And now the man was hyperventilating. Adam wondered what he should do. When he looked around, he saw the Alpha running his way. Good, he thought. The Alpha would know what to do.

Adam glanced at the man's face again. When his eyes fell to his wrist, Adam noticed the red stain on the man's sleeve. It was the same stain Adam had seen in his memory, a product of the blood he'd wiped from his forehead after removing the woman's ear. That suggested he'd tortured her tonight, before the raid interrupted him.

The wall in the room where the man was torturing the woman, Adam thought. There was information there. He knew there was. What was it he'd seen? Ah, yes, he thought. He remembered now. Part of the wall was made of concrete. There was something else, too, wasn't there? Adam focused harder. As the memory flashed before him, he ignored the woman being tortured and focused on the background.

There it was, arriving in the room via a joint in the concrete wall, and disappearing via another joint through the floor above – black PVC piping.

The Alpha arrived and glanced at Adam's captive.

"Strelkov," he said, voice etched in disbelief.

"There's a dungeon," Adam said.

"What?" the Alpha said.

"A cellar," Adam said. "The prisoners are in a cellar. Tell them to find where the gas comes into the building."

"The gas?"

"The natural gas. It comes in along an exterior wall via a black PVC pipe. There's a room in that cellar. The pipe is in the room. If the prisoners aren't in that room, they'll be in cells thereabouts. Why would anyone take them anywhere else once the torture started?"

"Torture? What torture?" the Alpha said.

"The torture this man committed."

"How do you know all that?" the Alpha said.

"Tell them to check the plans. Tell them now. There's a cellar. You'll find the prisoners in the cellar."

FIFTY-TWO

STRELKOV HAD BEEN CHOKED unconscious as a young man during self-defense training. The difference was his instructor was choking his neck at the time. In this case, some skinny so-called Ukrainian NLO was choking him out by holding his wrist. How was that remotely possible?

The sensations Strelkov had suffered when the NLO had grabbed his wrist were even more problematic. The only way Strelkov could describe them was to say the man seemed to have tapped into Strelkov's soul. To those who thought a human being didn't possess a soul, they needed to exchange a pleasant handshake with Mr. Werner Ziegler, and then they'd learn what was what. Strelkov remembered telling the traitor, Ivanova, that the NLO's speed alone would be a concern to Russia if he was loyal to the Ukrainian Army. But this, what Strelkov had just experienced, amounted to an entirely different level of concern.

Kosachev and Yarovaya, the two members of the Russian parliament, were recently quoted in Kommersant, the Russian daily. The duo revealed bombshell findings from their investigation that proved the Americans had turned Ukrainian soldiers into super-human killing machines through secret experiments in their biolabs. It was nonsense, of course. The Boss needed to explain his failure to win the war to the average Russian. He certainly couldn't tell them his army was overrated and his commanders were incompetent.

The NLO rendered those fictional killing machines the equivalent of truculent teenagers. It was one thing to kill a human being, and another to kill an ideology. In the long run, the fictional killing machines would have served only to unify Russia against Ukraine. The NLO, however, might be able to do the opposite. He could read a man's mind. And if he could read a man's mind, perhaps he could change it, too. Perhaps he could unify Russia with the West.

Beware the enemy with a weapon like that, Strelkov thought, just before he drifted into unconsciousness.

FIFTY-THREE

HER LIFE HAD MEANT SOMETHING, Tasia thought. Her life had meant something.

She shivered, naked in the corner of her cell, a blacked-out crawlspace carved out of the dungeon from hell. There was a canteen near her somewhere, but to find it she would have needed to move and she was afraid to do so. Every inch of her felt like a raw wound. She was missing body parts. The latest was her ear. Which one? She couldn't remember. What else had she lost? She couldn't remember that either.

She focused on her mantra, repeating it over and over again. It slowed her pulse, took her mind off the pain. More importantly, it took her mind off the pain yet to come. Maybe it was good that she couldn't reach the water. The sooner she died, the less pain she'd suffer.

Death, sweet death. How she longed for death.

Her life had meant something ... Her life had meant something

Footsteps sounded. At first the mere sound of them made her contemplate swallowing her tongue – couldn't she choke on it if she tried? But then she realized there was something different about them. They were heavier – they belonged to boots, not rubber-soled shoes, and more than one pair was making them. They were moving with a sense of urgency, too, not the swagger of a psychopath delaying his gratification.

Lights flashed through her cell door. She shielded her eyes. She heard voices, male voices. She could have sworn they were speaking in Ukrainian, but how could that be?

A gun fired. An object smashed against a wall. Her ears rang. Tasia raised her hands to cover them and remembered she was short at least one ear ... and all her nails ... and some fingers maybe, too ... and God only knew what else ...

The cell door creaked open and Tasia heard a familiar sound. It was a sound so lovely not even the singing yellowhammer of the Carpathian Mountains could have competed. It consisted of one and only one word, and it came from the lips of a woman, a moment after her flashlight shone in Tasia's eyes.

"Sister!"

Her life had meant something, Tasia thought.

And it wasn't over yet.

FIFTY-FOUR

ADAM KNELT BEFORE THE BUILDING. The Alpha assigned to him was busy loading Strelkov into one of the Mi-24 Crocodile attack helicopters. Meanwhile, Adam had dug his back foot into the gravel road and effectively created a starting block. All he needed to do was push off and he'd be gone.

The General and the squad commander had given him strict orders – he was to stick to the man who'd been assigned to watch over him. Under no circumstances was he to enter the building. Adam had already violated his first commandment when he'd gone after Strelkov, and once a man committed his first sin, the second one was so much easier.

He galvanized his senses to summon all of his skills. As soon as he began running toward the building, his brain would sense danger and he'd be able to fly. He'd burst into the building and negotiate the labyrinth of hallways like a cheetah that smelled pray in an English garden maze. He wouldn't slow down until he found the entrance to the cellar, until he was lifting Mikey from his cot, returning the favor that Mikey had bestowed upon him when he'd shot the sniper on the roof, and in the process Adam would—

Promptly get himself killed, he thought. Even worse, he might get one of the team killed.

He was not a soldier. No one would benefit come from his self-indulgence. These men were warriors. Mikey was one of them. They were going in to save one of their own. Adam had done what he could to help them, and he needed to remember his proper place. It was the one that minimized the risk to the men and women who'd brought him here. That was the difference between a child and a man – the latter could summon restraint when he needed it the most, but wanted it the least.

Hence, Adam did what did not come naturally – he remained in place, and waited. Seconds seemed like minutes. Finally, his Alpha returned to his side, and two of the man's teammates came rushing out of the building. They looked in each direction and shouted to someone still inside. Almost Eva promptly emerged carrying a naked woman across her shoulders. The injured woman was covered in blood and appeared to be missing toes on both feet. The other soldiers wrapped her in a blanket and lifted her into one of the helicopters.

The rest of the team came running out of the building in pairs. Adam tried to keep count, and when he got to twelve despair set in. They had all returned and Mikey wasn't among them. Adam considered his options. He could stay behind. It was a matter of honor to do so. With the Alphas out of the way, he could only harm himself.

The door flew open one last time and the last Alpha emerged from inside the objective. A wave of euphoria washed over Adam – he had miscounted. Mikey followed. He was limping badly, barely able to move despite his escort's assistance.

Adam ran over and propped-up Mikey from the other side. Mikey's face was a bloody mess, his eyes so swollen they appeared as slits. He did a double take when he recognized Adam.

"You think we can get home without you being taken prisoner again?" Adam said.

"What can I say." Mikey tried to laugh but made a croaking sound instead. "I'm a popular guy."

"I can't imagine why," Adam said.

Mikey fired a disapproving glance at him. "You should have stayed in Kyiv." He shook his head. "Too dangerous."

"That was not an option, Little Brother."

They boarded one of the Crocodiles. Each chopper had room for eight people tightly packed on two benches. Strelkov was not among the seated. He laid on a sleeping bag in the middle of the cargo area, conscious and cuffed, headed for interrogation and trial.

As they flew back to Kyiv, Adam reflected on his discussion with the President. An obvious thought occurred to him, but as with many such realizations, it had taken a while for it to dawn on him.

When he was a child, his fellow Ukrainians had looked down upon him as an inferior human being. Now the Russians had invaded their country because they considered them inferior human beings, too, unworthy of being a nation. As Adam studied the faces of the Ukrainian men and women whom he'd accompanied this evening, he no longer felt alienated from them. They shared a common bond now – they were all godforsaken in someone's eyes. And as a result, for the first time in his life, Adam saw himself among people who considered him an equal, and whom he viewed the same way. He was, to his great satisfaction, finally among his own kind.

Truth be told, he was in awe of the men and women on the helicopter. Everyone had underestimated them. They'd been outnumbered at the start of the war by a factor of more than 4:1

– Russia had a total of 900,000 active soldiers while Ukraine had fewer than 200,000. Russia's Boss had gone on national television and asked the Ukrainians to lay down their arms and go home after launching a special military operation that was supposed to last three days. The experts in the United States had expected Kyiv to fall to the world's second-best army after the first weekend of fighting. In response to such expectations, these soldiers had gone and proven everyone wrong. They'd showed the world that the vaunted Russian army was, indeed, second best – the second-best fighting force in Ukraine.

The attack helicopters powered their way home through the night. One of the Alphas doubled as a medic. He tended to the injured woman. Once she was stabilized, Almost Eva came over and sat opposite Adam. Gone were the melancholy and the anger. For reasons beyond Adam's comprehension, the mission seemed to have lit a spark inside her. She exuded a different energy. It carried the promise of hope and joy.

"Lean on," she shouted, in passable English.

"Excuse me?" Adam said. The noise inside the cabin made it very difficult to understand anyone. He looked to each side and behind him for something to lean on but found nothing. "Lean where?"

"No," she said, managing a half-smile.

Upon closer inspection, she really didn't look like Eva at all.

"Lena," she said. "My name is Lena."

"Oh."

"Nice to meet you," she said.

Adam nodded. "Nice to meet you, Lena."

They arrived in Kyiv early morning to the sound of air raid sirens.

The package had arrived at its intended destination.

That job was done.

The war continued.

ALSO BY OREST STELMACH